Hope and Other Punch Lines

JULIE BUXBAUM

DELACORTE PRESS

Copyright © 2019 by Julie R. Buxbaum Inc.

All rights reserved. Published in the United States by Delacorte Press, an imprint of Random House Children's Books, a division of Penguin Random House LLC, New York.

Delacorte Press is a registered trademark and the colophon is a trademark of Penguin Random House LLC.

Visit us on the Web! GetUnderlined.com

Educators and librarians, for a variety of teaching tools, visit us at RHTeachersLibrarians.com

Library of Congress Cataloging-in-Publication Data
Names: Buxbaum, Julie, author.
Title: Hope and other punchlines / Julie Buxbaum.
Description: First edition. | New York : Delacorte Press, [2019] |
Summary: "The tragic 9/11 event in NYC that changed the world altered the life of Abbi Hope Goldstein as well as that of Noah Stern. They did not know each other back then, but they know each other now, and while Abbi is trying to move forward with her life, Noah still has unanswered questions that he believes Abbi can help answer"—Provided by publisher.
Identifiers: LCCN 2018050353 (print) | LCCN 2018055358 (ebook) |
ISBN 978-1-5247-6679-5 (ebook) | ISBN 978-1-5247-6677-1 (hardback) |
ISBN 978-1-5247-6678-8 (library binding) |
ISBN 978-0-525-64444-6 (international pbk edition)
Subjects: LCSH: September 11 Terrorist Attacks, 2001—Juvenile fiction. |
CYAC: September 11 Terrorist Attacks, 2001—Fiction. | Fame—Fiction.
| Loss (Psychology)—Fiction. | Camps—Fiction. | New York (N.Y.)—
Fiction.
Classification: LCC PZ7.1.B897 (ebook) | LCC PZ7.1.B897 Hop 2019
(print) | DDC [Fic]—dc23

The text of this book is set in 11.5-point Dante MT.
Interior design by Betty Lew
Jacket art: iStock / enjoynz
Jacket design by Connie Gabbert

Printed in the United States of America
10 9 8 7 6 5 4 3 2
First Edition

For my grandmother Charlotte,
who would have freakin' loved
to see this

In its desertion of every basis for comparison, the event asserts its singularity. There is something empty in the sky. The writer tries to give memory, tenderness and meaning to all that howling space.

—Don DeLillo, *Harper's,* December 2001

. . .

All photographs are accurate. None of them is the truth.

—Richard Avedon

. . .

Now, Andy, did you hear about this one?

—R.E.M., "Man on the Moon"

BEFORE

Tuesday, the least descriptive day of the week. Neither beginning nor end, not even the sad, saggy middle.

A nothing day.

No. A *before*.

Picture a blue sky.

A beat, to breathe it in. All that blue.

When you let out your last clean breath, you look up.

And the world splits itself in two.

(FIFTEEN YEARS
AND
TEN MONTHS . . .)

AFTER

CHAPTER ONE

Abbi

Even back in my fairy-tale days, I never liked those inevitable opening words—*once upon a time*. Their bookend—*happily ever after*—at least made sense to me. The main character ended up happy forever. That was a no-brainer and nonnegotiable, the absolute bare minimum we could expect from a good story.

The *once upon a time,* though? Let's just say I had questions. What "time" were they talking about—Today? Yesterday? Tomorrow?—and what did it mean to be *upon* it? I was uncomfortable with its free-floating slipperiness. It felt like a cheap literary dodge.

I've long outgrown fairy tales, but I still have trouble with the concept of time. Maybe it's because my own life has always been an exception to the rule: I lived once when I was supposed to die. And so this story, the one I'm telling you now, has two distinct beginnings.

There's the one that starts with, and feel free to groan, a *once upon a time*. Or at least, it feels that way to me because I don't remember it happening, and yet, *once upon a time,* a click of the camera changed the entire trajectory of my life. I know exactly the when: Tuesday, September 11, 2001, approximately 9:59 a.m. The morning of my first birthday. In the photograph, the one that turned me from Abbi Hope Goldstein into *The Baby Hope,* I'm being whisked away to safety by Connie Kramer, one of the women who worked at the day-care center in the World Trade Center complex. I'm wearing a paper crown and holding a red balloon, and behind me the first tower is collapsing. An AP photographer managed to capture the dust-filled moment, though I have no idea how.

You've probably seen the picture. It's everywhere. You can find it hanging on living room walls and in dorms and nursing homes and museums and even printed on T-shirts and tote bags. I kid you not, I once saw baby me on a hat at Six Flags.

Like in an actual fairy tale, there are some sad parts to this story, which are an unfortunate narrative necessity. Let's get those out of the way as quickly as possible.

Connie died seventy-five days ago. Her diagnosis was ovarian cancer. Stage IV. Which for reasons I don't know—maybe because it's serious—is written with Roman numerals.

She was only forty-six.

XLVI.

Connie was thirty on September 11, 2001.

In my house we all knew that Connie really died of 9/11 syndrome, the catchall diagnosis for the group of health problems caused by the exposure to toxic chemicals in the air at Ground Zero. For some survivors, it starts with inflammation of the lungs. For others, like Connie, it's mutations and tumors, the assault of that day being retold on the cellular level.

On September 11, 2001, twenty-four thousand gallons of jet fuel blew up. Those of us there breathed in a chemical bouquet that included crystalline silica (which = bad), asbestos, carbon monoxide, hydrogen sulfide (or "sewer gas"), and God only knows what else.

No. We do know what else: human ash and human bone. Hair and teeth and nails and dreams.

Before things get any more morbid, let me share an important bit of happily-ever-after. Not only did I survive on 9/11 (and get almost sixteen bonus years so far), but somehow, defying all statistical odds, so did my parents. My mom and dad both worked in One World Trade (the North Tower), on floors 101 and 105, respectively, when no one survived above the 91st floor. Ninety-five percent of the people in the company they worked for got wiped out. Had they been at their desks like they were supposed to be, I would be an orphan. Instead, when the planes hit, my parents were sipping Frappuccinos three blocks away at a ground-floor Starbucks, which is the best advertisement for dessert disguised as coffee I've ever heard.

In 2001, my parents went to fifty-three funerals in one month. They bought condolence cards in bulk from Costco. And then they went back for more.

We live in Oakdale, New Jersey, which is the town outside New York City that had the highest number of 9/11 casualties, so the loss was everywhere: colleagues, neighbors, friends. Five kids from my class alone lost a parent on the same day, including my former best friend, Cat. Sixteen years later, Oakdale High is this weird hybrid of those who don't really care about September 11 and those whose whole lives were shaped by it. For the former, the event is just another chapter in our history books, like Pearl Harbor or the Vietnam War or landlines. For the latter, it's forever part of our peripheral vision. We may not remember, but we can never forget.

That's the first beginning, which I tell you only because otherwise the rest won't make any sense. To meet Abbi Hope Goldstein is to meet Baby Hope, and to understand that in my town, at least, I get pointed at—people know my name even though we've never met—and occasionally, someone will corner me in a supermarket line while my hands are full of deodorant and hummus and tell me where they were that morning, like it's something I want to know about them.

The absolute worst is when I make strangers cry.

But as promised, there's a second beginning. Right here, right now, in a moment of rare triumph, the first days of summer vacation. Sunday night, nine p.m.: me, age sixteen, rocking out alone in my bedroom. I belt a girl-power ballad into a make-shift microphone, aka a dry shampoo bottle, because I can't find my brush.

Shimmy. Shimmy. Hair flip. Shimmy.

Tomorrow I start as a counselor for four-year-olds at Knight's Day Camp, two towns away. When I visited for the interview, there were lush green lawns and an old-fashioned red barn and something they called the "plake," which is a hybrid pool/lake. We'll have pajama day and a bouncy castle water slide and a Color War. Also arts and crafts and potato-sack races and even a Dance Dance Revolution activity block. Knight's is a happy place, by far the happiest place I could find in the tri-state area, and believe me, I looked. Even went as far as to Google "happy places in New Jersey." Now I get to go there eight hours a day five days a week, and for two months, not a single person will look at me and see Baby Hope.

Time is still confusing and slippery. Based on some unexpected medical developments, there's a good chance I'm running out of it. But for the next blissful eight weeks, I am going to be just Abbi Goldstein.

I'll get to make little kids laugh and not a single stranger cry.

CHAPTER TWO

Noah

It's not like I'm going to burst into tears or drop my coffee or make a big scene or anything. I saw that happen at the Blue Cow Cafe last spring, and it was bananas. Abbi Goldstein, aka Baby Hope, walked in, and this middle-aged dude knocked over a full mug and started weeping right there in front of everyone.

We all have our wounds, especially in a town like Oakdale. Mine are pretty gruesome. But I wanted to tell that guy to get it together. Find a coping mechanism. I abuse comedy the way other people abuse drugs, and that seems to work pretty well for me. He should try a Chris Rock special.

She's a teenage girl, after all. Not the freaking Messiah. It's not fair for him to put his shit on her.

At least, that's what I used to think. Because when I see Abbi Goldstein across the field at Knight's Day Camp, of all places, I'm not going to lie: I hear an actual click in my brain. As if all the pieces of a plan I've been working on for years but haven't yet figured out how to implement suddenly fall into place. Yes,

I fully recognize my own hypocrisy, and I have surprisingly little trouble ignoring it. Not even a twinge of guilt.

This feels like fate, which to be clear is not a word I'd ordinarily use. That's the domain of bad poetry and greeting cards and also, idiots.

But she—well, Baby Hope—is *exactly* what I need.

CHAPTER THREE

Abbi

I can tell when someone recognizes me. There's this double look, a one-two sweep, that I feel as much as see: a tiny tingle at the base of my neck.

Today, I feel it two hours into camp orientation. A boy across the lawn. Crap.

"Just so you know, you'll be in charge of all accidents," Julia, my new senior counselor and essentially my boss this summer, says to me, and I use this as an excuse to turn around to face her. Now his view is only of my back. Better.

"No problem. My parents made me take a first-aid class," I say cheerfully. We're standing on a grassy field in the blazing sun, and I try to imagine what this place will look like tomorrow when the kids get here. Until my grandfather died a few years ago, I spent my summers at my grandparents' house in Maine, and after that, Cat, my then–best friend, and I worked at Torn Pages, Oakdale's used-book store, so this is my first time taking part in camp life.

I can handle accidents. Some Neosporin and a Band-Aid, preferably adorned with a cartoon character, and the cute little monsters will be good to go.

I have no idea how to handle that boy, though.

"I'm not talking about skinned knees. Our campers are four," Julia reminds me. "Their control over their sphincter muscles is limited at best."

"Oh, so there's a poop element to this job. Gotcha," I say, thinking it's funny that people still have to shit even in happy places.

Julia's black, probably twentyish, and the kind of beautiful that feels like a trick. It's a slow build, but once you notice, you can't stop staring. A small star-shaped stud dots her right nostril, quiet confirmation that she's also effortlessly cool. She's short, like me, though built more like a gymnast than a prepubescent boy. I wonder if we were both assigned to the youngest kids so that people wouldn't mix us up with our campers.

"Also, my future boyfriend is the four-year-old boys' counselor, so we'll be paired up with them a lot. That's Zach."

Julia points across the expanse of grass to a giant with blond hair and a crooked, goofy, *I'm game for anything* smile. He's wearing a tie-dyed Knight's Day Camp T-shirt, slouchy sweatpants cut off into shorts, and a wide-brimmed hat with a Velcroed chin strap. Of course, he's standing right next to the boy I'm trying to avoid, who is, presumably, his junior counselor.

"I mean, swoon, am I right?" she asks. I choose to treat this question as rhetorical, because I'm not swooning. Sweating, yes. Pondering how this guy's outfit came about—the hours he chose to spend chopping his pants and tie-dyeing his shirt with the help of YouTube tutorials. But I'm not even feeling something second-cousins-twice-removed from the swoon. Instead,

I'm thinking how sad it is that my plan for a summer of anonymity lasted only two hours. "Let's go say hi."

I have no choice but to follow Julia. The boy, despite his wearing normal, mass-produced and store-bought clothes, somehow looks even goofier than Zach. He has on big plastic black glasses and beat-up black Converse and his hair is ruffled and messy.

As we move closer, I realize he's from the class below me at Oakdale. I tell myself not to panic. I tell myself it's possible my Spidey sense was off this one time, that I recognized him and not the other way around. Maybe he doesn't know my name. Maybe he has his own reasons for taking a job two counties away and is as psyched as I am about pajama day and will have absolutely no interest in bringing up the fact that an earlier iteration of my face can be found on walls the world over.

"I like your vibe. Total norm-core, hipster-geek," Julia says to the boy once we've crossed the field. Then she looks at me, up and down and then back up again, a slow, steady, calculating evaluation. "Like her, I guess. But you pull it off."

This comment is totally fair. Generally speaking, in both appearance and dress, I'm the human equivalent of a fern—not particularly offensive, but no one is going to be like, "Wow, that's such a beautiful fern! What amazing combination of plant food and light produced such spectacular results?" This is somewhat intentional, at least on the fashion side. I'm usually better off when I blend.

"Thanks," the boy says, a little thrown by Julia. I would bet good money that he's never heard the term *norm-core* in his life. "I'm Noah. We go to school together, actually."

He looks at me again, and the neck tingles are back. No doubt he's about to blow everything for me in T-minus three . . . two . . . one . . .

"You're Ba—"

I shake my head, once, hard, the only way I know how—other than tackling him—to signal that he shouldn't say the words *Baby Hope* out loud.

"You're Abbi, right?" he course-corrects, and my body floods with relief. If it weren't weird, I'd hug him in gratitude. I decide I like his face. It's friendly: big brown curious eyes, and ears as enthusiastic about being noticed as mine. Something about his hair and glasses adds a slight wackiness to his appearance, like he's Clark Kent's weirdo younger brother who's super into anime.

"Hi," I say, and hold up my hand and give him a dorky wave.

"I realize it's summer, but it turns out I'm rising editor in chief of the *Oakdale High Free Press*. Number one way to pad your college application, if you want to join in the fall," he says, with purposefully cheesy ironic jazz hands. He then smiles at me, a big splash of a smile, and I smile back.

"Cool, thanks," I say. He seems nice. No way he's going to out me as Baby Hope.

" 'Cool, thanks'? I could pinch your little cheeks. Zach, aren't you so glad to be done with high school?" Julia asks.

"Dude," Zach says, like that's an answer.

"Let's have coffee," Noah says, all casual, ignoring both Zach and Julia, and his eyes steadily wash over me, as if he is trying to do complex calculations in his head.

Wait, is he asking me on a date? No. Not possible. Things like that don't happen to me. To Cat, my former best friend, yes—she once picked up a guy at a funeral—but never me.

"How's tomorrow after camp?" he asks.

"Um."

"Did he just ask her out?" Zach asks Julia. "In front of us?"

"I think he did," she says, and my face blazes hot and red.

"Wait, no! I didn't mean it like that. I'm not asking you *out* out. Just thought we should have coffee together," Noah says, still looking only at me. "I'm not creepy or anything."

"That was a little creepy," Julia interjects.

"I didn't think you had it in you," Zach says, and hits Noah on the back with condescending pride. Noah's smile gets wiped clean, and if it's possible, his face turns even redder than mine.

"Not-asking-out-just-coffee sounds great," I say, because I'm hardwired to try to make other people feel comfortable in uncomfortable situations—which is both my favorite and least favorite thing about myself—and I don't think I can survive another second of this awkwardness. "Tomorrow, then."

"Cool, you won't regret this, *Abbi*," Noah says, again using my name with entirely unnecessary emphasis, like he's proud of not slipping and calling me Baby Hope.

"I have a feeling these two will be even cuter than our campers," Julia says to Zach.

"Dude," Zach says.

CHAPTER FOUR

Noah

Operation Get Answers is on like *Donkey Kong.* Could I have been suaver—*Let's have coffee? Seriously?*—sure. But cut me some slack. I was unprepared. If you had told me this morning that there would be another person from Oakdale working at Knight's Day Camp and that person would be Baby freaking Hope, I wouldn't have believed you. God, Yahweh, Allah, the incredible flying spaghetti monster, whatever the hell you want to call him/her/it works in mysterious ways.

Baby. Freaking. Hope.

This might actually work.

As soon as Uncle Maurice, which is what we are supposed to call the camp director—this silver-haired dude with a killer seventies stache—and Zach, my new senior counselor, aren't looking, I pull out my phone to text Jack. He's not just my best friend, he's also the only person in the world who will understand what this means to me.

Me: BABY HOPE IS AT CAMP. WE ARE HAVING COFFEE
TOMORROW. IT'S A SIGN

Jack: What's up with the all caps? Who are you?

Me: You are right. Caps were uncalled for

Jack: Glad we cleared that up. Also, NOT A SIGN

Me: I really think she might be able to help

Jack: She was a baby at the time

Me: I have a plan

Jack: You really need to let this go. You sound insane

Me: You've seen the pictures

Jack: People have doppelgängers. It's a documented
phenomenon

"Hey, put that away," Zach says to me, and swats at my phone. "That's how a kid drowns."

My new senior counselor epically sucks. So far today, and I've only know him approximately six hours, he has whispered "dibs" in my ear three times when we were introduced to a new girl, and he keeps talking about his "boys back at school," always in reference to some dumb prank they pulled, like replacing someone's shampoo with Nair. Apparently *It was sick, dude, so sick.*

Just as I was wondering how it's possible to bro that hard without a keg nearby, he started talking about his meditation practice and his deeply held commitment to veganism. Which is to say: his existence is confusing.

"Last time I checked, you can't drown in grass," I say. Jack would hate Zach, because Jack hates anyone who is easily classifiable, and though this guy falls into two contradictory categories—Zen stoner and frat boy—I have no doubt the hating would still apply. "Uncle Maurice gave us a ten-minute break."

"Don't talk back to your elders," Zach says, and then laughs his bro laugh, a hard *heh*, and walks away.

I give him the finger in my mind.

Me: My senior counselor is the worst, so don't crap all over the one thing that has made this day bearable

Jack: This Baby Hope thing is . . . unhealthy, and when I say unhealthy I don't mean calorific

Me: What are you talking about?

Jack: I realized today calorific is a word we don't use nearly enough. Calorific. It's funny, no? I feel like there may be a bit there

Me: Not really. Anyhow, Abbi seems cool

Jack: She's a little short for my taste

Me: She's a little too much of an actual girl for your taste

Jack: True. Now are you ready?

Me: For what?

Jack: I'm going to be serious with you for a minute and it might get awkward because we're never serious with each other, but then we can get right back to our regularly scheduled shit talking

Me: Ok

Jack: You need to let this 9/11 stuff go. For real. Enough is enough. Consider this an intervention

Me: I'm not crazy. It's him

Jack: Break's up. Must go do God's work ringing up tampons and eggplant. Good talk, man

CHAPTER FIVE

Abbi

The first time I realized that I'm going to die, that we are *all* going to die eventually, I was in the third grade. Of course, by then I had already learned that no one gets to live forever, and that doesn't mean just the old, just the sick, but babies and mothers and teenagers and real estate agents. Also pilots. And orthodontists. I understood that death was cruel and didn't play fair. I was, had been for as long as I could remember, the girl who *survived*, and so for whatever reason—I'm sure Dr. Schwartz, our family therapist, has a working theory—I didn't think the normal rules of mortality applied to me.

I was fashionably late to the existential panic party.

Then one day in third grade, I found myself peeing on my goldfish, Orange, who somehow simultaneously had flat-lined in the toilet bowl and was swimming happily in her small aquarium on the kitchen counter.

"Mom!" I screamed, thinking at first that I had relieved myself on some other poor fish that had swum its way up our pipes. When my mother realized what had happened—she'd forgotten the crucial step of flushing when secretly replacing my dead fish—she smiled right into my horrified face.

"Well, now you know."

She said this like it was good news, in the same tone she'd used to show me the house she had bought two doors down from my father after the divorce, and then again the first time I got my period. Matter-of-fact optimism in the face of something grim. "That was Orange number nine, may he rest in peace. Number ten seems to be adjusting well to his new bowl."

Once I caught up, my previous innocence astounded and embarrassed me. Of course there was no magic tooth fairy who traded cash for slimy canines. And of course I was going to die. It was hard to remember ever being so stupid as to believe anything else.

I guess it's easier to give up all our myths at once.

When the cough came a month ago, tight and jagged and without warning, it wasn't a total surprise. I've known my whole life that there had to be consequences to being *The Girl Who Survived*. I have been lying in wait.

I had read about the "World Trade Center cough," common enough among survivors to have a name. I'd seen the obituaries in the newspaper from 9/11 syndrome, which seemed to increase exponentially in number around the fifteenth anniversary. And I knew what had happened to Connie.

Standing there in the bathroom with my wad of bloody tissues, like I had stumbled into a crime scene, it became clear: I was next. In a single moment, my expected life span shortened from decades to, if I was lucky, years.

You would think I'd have screamed for my mother, like I did when I peed on Orange. That I would have handed the responsibility over to someone more qualified to deal with it. That I would have, at the very least, freaked out.

I didn't.

Instead, I flushed the tissues and cleaned the red stain on the bath mat. I washed my face and hands. I deleted my Google history from my phone, in case somehow it showed up on my mom's computer. In short, I covered my tracks.

In the days that followed, whenever I felt my lungs start to close and the cough claw at the back of my throat, I'd make an excuse to leave the room. And in that paralyzing calm, I came to a decision. I knew I couldn't keep this a secret forever; eventually, I'd need medical intervention. But I could give myself one small gift in the meantime: eight weeks.

One last summer. One last summer before the mobilization of troops and the cavalry of doctors' appointments and the paper hospital gowns. One last summer of ignorance is bliss, when the cough could be nothing more than a cough. One last summer when no one talks about Baby Hope. (If I need to have coffee with a strange boy to make that happen, so be it.)

I want one last summer packed full of pure joy: of learning how to box-stitch a lanyard, of singing camp songs, of dancing on fluorescent squares.

When you think about it, in the context of everything to come, that really doesn't seem like too big an ask.

CHAPTER SIX

Noah

Here are the cold, hard facts: All the people identified in the Baby Hope photo—Chuck Rigalotti, Constance Kramer, Abbi Hope Goldstein, Jamal Eggers, Sheila Brashard, and Raj Singh—survived the attacks of September 11. They were later profiled for the newspaper in the November 1, 2001, issue, where they discussed running to the Brooklyn Bridge. To this day, three people in the background of the photo remain unidentified, and no information is publicly available about any of them:

> A woman in a ruffled blouse and a tight skirt with a big
>   pair of glasses covering most of her face.
> A bald man in a suit and a striped tie, looking over his
>   shoulder, so he's only caught in profile.
> A man in a blue University of Michigan hat, jeans, and

an untucked flannel shirt with two days of stubble;
he's staring straight at the camera.

No one has ever come forward and identified themselves,
though all are believed to have survived.

It's number 3 who keeps me up at night.

CHAPTER SEVEN

Abbi

"Why don't you want people to know you're Baby Hope?" Noah asks as we turn out of the camp gates. We are walking to Starbucks, which, according to his app, should take us no more than eight minutes.

Did he have to start with the photograph? I could use a little warm-up before jumping into such complicated waters. We could talk about camp. How Zach and Julia like to do yoga together on the south lawn in the morning and it's weird for everyone. We have a lot of conversational options.

I shrug and stare straight ahead at the road unfolding before us. There are fewer trees here than in our neighborhood, and the summer afternoon sun gleams hot and bright and unobstructed. I watch my shadow, notice how my arms seem too long relative to my short body. Like a chimpanzee's.

"It seems a weird thing to want to hide," he says again, clearly not understanding that my shrug was supposed to say, in not so many words, *Let's not talk about this. Definitely not now, and maybe not ever.* "You're a national hero."

"I am not a hero," I say.

"Fine, a national treasure, then."

I snort, and then wish I could time travel and stop the sound before it happens.

"I wanted to leave some of that stuff behind this summer, that's all," I say.

"What do you mean?"

"I wonder if it will rain later," I say, apropos of nothing—there isn't a cloud in sight—but I need a subject change. I decide to fold my arms across my chest instead of letting them dangle by my sides. I wonder: When did I forget how to walk?

"Abbi, I need to confess something to you right now and get it over with," Noah says, with excessive seriousness, and I feel my stomach drop. He must have some terrible ulterior motive for going for coffee. "I'm the worst at small talk. Like I am biologically unable to chat about things like the weather. I'm sorry."

"Okay," I say, loosening up. "Tell me, what *are* you biologically able to chat about?"

"How about big life plans? That's sufficiently not-small-talky. What do you want to do post-Oakdale?" he asks.

"Like for a job?"

"Yeah, and please don't say weather forecaster. Because then I'll feel like a jerk for belittling your life's passion."

"Nope. No big plans as of yet. How about you?" I decide to play it vague. No need to step into the land mine of my future.

"I want to go to college, in an ideal world, in the Ivy League. Then move to New York. Work in politics. Do stand-up at night. And ultimately have my own political comedy show. Online, I think, because the networks will be totally obsolete by then." He ticks his fingers with each step, as if this is often repeated or written down somewhere. "Just so you know, I realize how that sounds. Disgustingly ambitious. Also obnoxious. Probably pompous. Supercilious, though I don't even know what that means, but I like the sound of it. Crap, I'm out of *-ous* words. I thought I had a few more."

"Wow. Those are some e-nor-mous plans," I say, and he smiles at me, an explosion of delight on his face. These days, I only allow myself one limited daydream about the future: college. In my mind's eye, it's glorious: hooded sweatshirts and food trucks and library carrels. Coed dorms and lectures on feminist theory and parties full of people from anywhere and everywhere but Oakdale. I imagine myself happily eating my way toward the freshman fifteen, which might be the answer to the problem of my cavernous chest, and laughing late into the night with the perfect roommate and then sleeping until noon without thinking of the hours wasted. I want to go to school on an urban campus, I think, but in a smaller, nonthreatening city. No New York. No DC. Maybe Philly?

The one way I can accept this whole getting-sick/limited-time-left-on-this-planet thing is if there are—and I truly believe there will be, *there have to be*—at least a few good years for me to get used to the idea.

Connie was ill for half a decade. I tell myself there's no reason I shouldn't have a similar trajectory. Five years seems manageable. Five years makes my plan of putting off dealing with the cough for one summer seem totally reasonable.

"A comedian, huh? Are you funny?" I ask.

"Hilarious," he says, just flatly enough that I surprise myself with a laugh.

* * *

We sit down across from each other in the lounge-ier section of Starbucks, where the chairs are upholstered and the tables are low, and all of sudden, our conversation, which has been flowing nicely after that bad start so far, begins to taper off.

"You're probably wondering why I asked you to have coffee with me." Noah clears his throat, as if about to commence the official portion of our meeting. He's simultaneously dorky and earnest and also sarcastic, the sum total of which is a kind of sneaky charm. I've found that sarcasm usually brings with it a certain amount of unpleasant defensiveness when it comes to the boy species. Here it seems unencumbered. Joking purely for the pleasure of it.

"I figured you wanted to talk about the weather," I say, and brace myself, though for what, I have no idea. It's not like someone is going to jump out from behind the glass muffin case. We're far enough away from Oakdale.

"I have a proposition for you. It sort of involves, well, Baby Hope."

The disappointment twists my gut. Before he even starts his spiel, I already know the word I'm going to say back, in the nicest way possible—*no*.

"I want the first issue of the *Oakdale High Free Press* to be dedicated to hunting down all the other nine-eleven survivors in the Baby Hope picture, and I need your help to do it," he says, and then, once it's out in a quick rush, he looks me straight in the eyes and spreads his hands as if writing a triumphant headline in the air. He smiles, like I'm supposed to think this is a brilliant idea. Something fun and exciting, like skipping work and spending the day at the beach.

"I don't think so," I say.

"Why not?" he asks, and I don't answer. "If you do this with me, I really think we could get the newspaper national exposure." He grins again, though this time it's slightly slower to take off. He uses that weird enthusiastic tone, like I might actually care about the "national exposure" of the *Oakdale High Free Press,* when the last thing I can ever imagine wanting is publicity.

"No, but thanks anyway. This was fun." I stand up to leave, unsure why I reflexively thanked him. I should be able to say a polite no and leave it at that. These are exactly the sort of life skills I need to learn in my hypothetical college feminism lectures.

"Abbi, please. Wait," Noah says, and signals for me to sit down. I do, but only because my phone is dead and I left my backup charger in my car and I have no idea how to get back to camp.

"Was it something I said?" he jokes. I laugh despite myself.

I meet his eyes again, and inexplicably, embarrassingly, mine begin to water.

"Seriously, why don't you want to do this? Aren't you curious? Who are they? Where are they now?" His voice sounds urgent. Like he still thinks there's a chance he can convince me. He doesn't notice my wet eyes, or if he does, he ignores them. "Do you know?"

"Nope," I say, a blanket nonanswer. I don't mention Connie. That I know that at least one person in the photo, the most important person, is already dead. That I suspect the rest of us have more in common than that terrible moment. "No one cares anymore, anyway. It was a long, long time ago."

"Look," Noah pleads, changing tactics. "I feel like the world should really hear your side of the story."

"There is no my side of the story. I was a baby. It's ancient history." I think about all the *Where Is Baby Hope Now?* pieces that tend to pop up around the anniversary. Last year, the fifteenth, after I refused to participate in an interview, *People* magazine ran a sidebar with my yearbook photo anyway. Of course, that led to even more teary confessions and me hugging strangers in line at Home Depot and the Smoothie King and, once, in the ladies' room at Bloomingdale's. I have no idea what would happen if the world found out about the cough.

"Please." His voice is hopeful, as if there is a lot more riding on this than the school newspaper.

"Sorry," I say, even though it's a straight-up lie. I'm not even a little bit sorry.

CHAPTER EIGHT

Noah

I help Jack collect shopping carts during the last fifteen minutes of his shift. Assembling the long metal caterpillars turns out to be relaxing and hypnotic. Also, it beats my house, where I'd have endured yet another lecture from my stepdad, Phil, about how I should have interned in his law office this summer instead of spending my time wiping butts at a summer camp. Later, Jack and I have big plans to eat at the diner and play some Xbox in his basement and watch stand-up on our phones. There may or may not be Cheetos involved.

Don't let anyone tell you I'm not living my best life.

"I probably shouldn't have led with the Baby Hope Project. That was dumb," I say as I weave a six-carter into the rack and almost get sideswiped by a smart car in the process. Jack stands nearby, picks at his chipped neon-blue fingernails, and watches me do his job.

"You think?" he says.

"I assume that was sarcasm," I say.

"How could you tell?" Jack asks.

"Time for plan B," I say.

"Wow. You move fast. You can buy it right at the pharmacy here. Over the counter," he says, grinning, which he always does when he has a decent comeback.

"You're not going to help me with this, are you?"

"Putting away the carts or enabling you as you go down a terrifying rabbit hole of conspiracy theories and misplaced magical thinking?" Jack asks. He actually talks that way. The way teenagers talk on television—with an inflated vocabulary and in complete sentences.

"Both."

"This Abbi thing might be the worst idea you've ever had, and I say that fully remembering that time when you learned a bunch of magic tricks to get girls to pay attention to you in middle school. So nah and nope and also no. But I'll take a cart or two. That's the least I can do," he says, but makes no effort to actually move. Instead, his eyes are following a tatted-up dude in a white T-shirt and a ShopRite name tag who's walking into the store. That must be the famous "Clean-Up on Aisle 5" guy Jack has mentioned a few times since starting work. I decide not to call him out on the staring.

"I'm working on a bit about how the words *testicles* and *tentacles* sound alike," I say.

"Meh. How's the nine-eleven joke coming?" he asks, turning back to face me, and a middle-aged woman with a shopping cart full of soda stops to glare at us.

One of my life goals is to craft the perfect September 11 joke. But, yeah, better not to announce that in an Oakdale parking lot.

I get it. There's nothing funny about that day. Hands off. It will forever be too soon. It's wrong to even try to spin it into comedy. To that glaring lady, 9/11 is no joke, and it's not to me either.

Which is exactly the whole point.

I can't think of anything more cathartic than staring all that ugliness straight in its pus-filled face and slaying that dragon with a slash right in its oozing belly. I want to give it one big mother-effing ninja kick-ass hilarious *hi-yah*.

I've studied what's out there. Pete Davidson talking about his firefighter dad. Kumail Nanjiani working the Islamaphobia angle. Only two semi-successful 9/11 jokes in the entire history of comedy. *Two*. I submit there's room for more.

"I've got nothing," I say, because everything I've come up with is gross. My jokes land too hard, like a knee to the nuts.

"Have you tried 'Nineteen jihadis walk into a bar'?" Jack asks, and even though it's only slightly funny, or maybe not even funny at all, we both crack up. If we ever get the chance to do real stand-up, we'll both have to learn to stop laughing at our own terrible jokes.

CHAPTER NINE

Abbi

Later, I find myself on my second stroll through a New Jersey suburb in one day. This time, I'm with my mom in Oakdale on the way to get ice cream, so there are no worries about where my arms go or whether we will have anything to talk about. The humidity has lifted, and the summer sun breaks through the trees and rests warm on our shoulders. Our flip-flops snap in rhythm, and I let myself bask for a minute in the perfect evening.

We don't say anything until we pass the town's 9/11 memorial garden, which is a beautiful patch of green right next to the train station. Cat's father's name is engraved on the big slab of stone in the center of the courtyard, one of many, though when Cat talks about her dad now, she means Stewart, her stepfather.

Every year, on the anniversary of 9/11, my parents and I visit the monument and say the names of the lost out loud. We make two offerings to the Gods of Survivor's Guilt. One, a beautiful floral bouquet so heavy that we have to drive the half mile from our house to deliver it. And two, I don't have—and have never had—a birthday party. Not when I was little and dreamed of having Spider-Man paint my face in our backyard, like Cat did. Not for the celebration of my bat mitzvah.

These are tiny sacrifices. Actually, they're not sacrifices at all. These are the minor material things we are lucky to be able to offer up in thanks for being alive. Don't play even your tiniest violin for us. We don't deserve it.

Because here is our shameful truth: The rest of the year? On almost-perfect nights like this? We stare straight ahead so we don't have to look at the monument. We do not take even a moment to stop and read the names in the quiet of our own minds.

We go on like it never happened.

"We need to talk, Abbi," my mother says once we're in line at the Churnery. We look up at the menu with our heads tilted back and our mouths open in awe at its offerings. In recent years, Oakdale has seen an influx of rich families from Manhattan in search of square footage and good public schools, and perhaps because those people prefer their ice cream not to taste like ice cream but instead a weird smorgasbord of the most random of flavors—fennel or parsnip or even Peking duck—we no longer have access to straight-up chocolate or vanilla. Everything is *artisanal,* which is a word that means fancy-pants and over-priced and borderline disgusting. I was about to suggest that my mom and I play a quick round of the game where we think up the grossest flavors the store could realistically serve for which people would still pay six bucks a scoop—I won handily last time with fish roe bacon vanilla.

"Okay," I say, feeling only slightly nervous. If she knew about the cough, she would not be bringing it up here. In public. That would trigger DEFCON 9. My guess is she wants to talk college applications.

"Grandma was found wandering around without pants today," she says, which is of course the opposite of what I expected her to say. Or not exactly the opposite, because that would mean I expected her to say Grandma was found walking around *with* pants, and obviously I didn't expect that either.

"Thank God it's summer," I say. I realize this is not an appropriate time to be making jokes, but funny is easier than sad.

"She was a block from her house," my mom says. "The police were called." She's smiling, but it's not a happy smile. It's the smile that she uses when she has to deliver bad news. A smile that is not a smile but a frown masquerading as a smile, because frowns are frowned upon in my house. When I was nine my parents sat me down with such big grins I thought they were finally buying me a puppy. Turned out they were splitting up.

My parents generally swear by the worldview that no matter what, the Goldstein family is A-OK, which is why my mother would think it totally normal to drop such big news on me in an ice cream shop. (Despite the divorce, we still consider ourselves a single family, because my parents are best friends who live two doors down from each other, and no, I don't understand it either.) Anything that conflicts with this ethos of perfection and solidarity is met with ridiculous false cheer and feigned enthusiasm for the challenges ahead, usually accompanied by some athletic company tagline (*Just do it!*) or political slogan (*Yes, we can!*).

"I know we've talked about this before, but it's getting worse. Grandma's getting worse," my mom says.

I should point out here that I have two grandmothers. My

father's parents live in Florida in one of those condo developments with a pool and a tennis court and a "clubhouse" that advertises a certain brand of growing old involving a chumminess I can get behind. That grandmother has deep brown leathery skin that resembles a dog's chew toy because she spends her days lying in the sun, and a throaty smoker's voice that I believe was earned not so much from cigarettes but from a lifelong affinity for gin. She always smells like Chanel and always hugs me with her hands stretched out, as if she's worried I'm going to smudge her nails. I call her GiGi, because the word *grandma* makes her feel old. My mom's mom, on the other hand, lives alone in Maine in a house that's too big for her and with a diagnosis that's too scary for all of us. So when my mom says my grandma was found without pants, it's very clear which one she's talking about.

As much as I love my GiGi, my mom's mom has always been my favorite. My best memories involve those childhood summers in Maine; they smell like salty bathing suit and grass and roasted corn. I'd spend whole days with my grandmother, both of us barefoot, running around with matching silver colanders on our head pretending to be aliens visiting planet Earth for the first time. "Ooh, what's this strange contraption?" my grandma would ask, and then point to random items around her house and reinvent their uses. A toilet was for washing hair. The stapler for decorating walls. Tweezers were to pinch naughty children.

She is one of the few people who have always understood me, who see the world through a similar distorted lens. She was the one who'd read me fairy tales, and she'd make up more exciting endings when I complained that my happily-ever-after needed more than being stuck in the drafty castle with the pasty prince. If I were going to confide in anyone about the cough and the dying thing—how I both know and don't want to know, how I'm choosing ignorant bliss temporarily, how I'm choosing *joy*, which is way better than *happily ever after*—it would have been my grandma. But not now. Not anymore.

"I think it's time we moved her in with us, whether she likes it or not," my mom says. My grandmother has early-onset dementia, which, not unlike 9/11 syndrome, only gets worse with time. She no longer gets to wear confusion like it's a game for laughs. This is another ball that only rolls downhill.

"I know she wants her independence, but I need her safe. The aides we hired aren't enough," my mom says, and again her voice is cheerful, like this is good news. She's spinning this to herself (as she soon will to her friends and then to everyone else) as her mother coming home to us, when we both know that my grandmother, who has always said she'll never leave that house in Maine unless it's on a stretcher, is not the person who will be coming home at all. "Dad has already offered to take her a couple of days a week."

"Did he get joint custody of her too?" I ask.

"Funny," my mom says, but she doesn't laugh.

"I can help," I say, serious, because my mom's eyes are beginning to well, and I'm not sure I can handle seeing her cry, especially here in line with only one other customer before we have to order. At least when strangers unload on me in town, I know the encounters will eventually end, that after I've hugged them and they've dried their tears, they will go one way and I will go another. I have no obligation to take their grief with me. But with my mother, whose cheery martyrdom doesn't usually allow for tears, I can't separate our feelings so easily.

I have no idea who my parents were pre-9/11, but sometimes I think that the fact that they were two of the lucky ones, that they were among the random survivors, explains everything about who they are now. Like they hope to retroactively earn their ridiculous good fortune by being good sports about whatever else life throws their way.

"We'll figure it out," I say.

"Of course we will. We'll be fine," my mom says after a moment, again smiling, her mask slipping right into place, where it fits best, just in time to order. "We're always fine."

"Chocolate hemp with a ribbon of bone marrow, please," she says, turning toward the ice cream guy.

When it's my turn to order, I order the closest thing to a flavor I recognize—Madagascar vanilla with roasted turmeric and sea salt—and ask for rainbow sprinkles and two cherries to add a little cheer.

I consciously relax my furrowed brow.

I am, after all, my mother's child.

I too am a lucky one.

And so I smile back. Because she's right.

We are always fine. We will always be fine.

CHAPTER TEN

Noah

I should make clear this is not the first time I've tried to get information on the Baby Hope photo. I've attempted other, less direct routes. The Internet, of course, which has led me nowhere. There are only so many times you can Google "University of Michigan," "Baby Hope," and "Blue Hat Guy" in various combinations.

A few years ago, I dragged Jack on a research mission to the 9/11 Memorial and Museum, which turned out to be, at least for me, the weirdest freaking place on earth. It's free for family members of the victims. Not that anyone should have to pay. Obviously they shouldn't. But why would anyone want to go?

Maybe one day when I'm older and possibly wiser, I'll find the museum cathartic or beautiful or respectfully commemorative, and maybe I'll even be grateful for its existence. But at the moment, it pisses me off. I can't understand why anyone would want to see the place where the most horrific thing you can imagine happening actually happened. Worse, why would you want that turned into a tourist attraction?

Do some people think, *While we're here, let's make sure to buy a commemorative hat from the gift shop. I've always wanted to turn a mass tragedy into a material possession!*

I'm pretty sure that's not what we mean by *Never forget*.

There's this whole special area reserved for VIPs, where you stand in the Reflection Room and view the remains repository. Those are literally the words they use, *Reflection Room* and *remains repository*, as if its patrons are kindergarteners or Kardashians and take comfort in alliteration. This is an underground lookout point—a window onto a cavernous room filled with mood-lit drawers. A gold star to anyone who can guess what's in those nifty cabinets. Yup, those lucky people who were so incinerated there aren't even DNA traces left.

That's what you're supposed to reflect on. In your free time. By choice. They provide complimentary tissues.

Unidentified remains.

Here's the strangest part of all: the museum has its own Twitter feed. *A fucking Twitter feed.* Of course it's about the most depressing shit imaginable. They don't even try to be funny.

Which is a long way of saying the 9/11 museum turned out to be a dead end. No pun intended.

I'm really hoping Abbi isn't.

CHAPTER ELEVEN

Abbi

The girls swim with two instructors while a lifeguard named Charles—who is hot in exactly the way lifeguards are supposed to be, all tanned abs and disinterested glare—watches from his perch on the side of the plake with a flotation ring in his lap.

"You look sort of familiar to me," Julia says, and these are the first words she's said to me all day that haven't been some sort of command. "Where do I know you from?"

"I get that a lot. I have resting *I know you from somewhere* face," I say. I cup my hands over my eyes and pretend to be fascinated by the girls' swimming progress. I've come too far to be outed now. "So how are things with you and Zach?"

"I used to think he was cool—did you know he meditates every day?—but last night we went out and he seemed over me already. It's only been a couple of days, which I realize is like a month in camp time. Still . . ." She trails off, and we both turn our attention to Charles the Lifeguard, because he has his whistle between his lips, and that's all he has to do, bring a whistle to his mouth, to get girls to look at him.

What's camp time? Is it like dog years? Perhaps there was some sixth sense at play when I picked this job—perhaps I somehow knew this summer would feel longer and bigger when it was all over.

"Maybe you should upgrade, then," I say, and subtly point at Charles, who has now dropped the ring and therefore provided us with a better view of his perfect torso.

"Nah, he's as dumb as he looks."

"Those abs, though," I say. Julia looks him up and down, slowly and without embarrassment or shame. Like it's her God-given right to look at whomever she wants.

I want to be her.

I want to be her looking at Lifeguard Charles.

I want to be her looking at Lifeguard Charles and understand what it feels like to have him look right back. To feel like you own even just a tiny corner of the world.

I've never had a boyfriend, barely even kissed anyone, unless you count a rowdy game of spin the bottle in ninth grade. I own no part of anything.

"You're totally right. I could forgive the stupid for a night."

"Be careful. That's like ten days in camp time," I say, and Julia laughs.

I mentally give myself a high five.

When I next see Noah, before pickup at afternoon meeting, I do that thing where you stare straight ahead at something intently so you can plausibly pretend you don't see the person you are avoiding. It doesn't work. Noah, who is apparently as shameless as Julia, gets right into my face.

"Hey," he says, planting himself in front of me. "Nice try ignoring me."

"I wasn't ignoring you," I say, and look at the stage, where Uncle Maurice is leading the kids in a round of rah-rah songs. This is my favorite time of the day. When all the campers sit tired and cross-legged on the floor and sing out the rest of their energy. I love the feeling of camaraderie, the pure light in their voices, like we are all part of some magical club full of wonder and delight. "I was lost in thought."

"What were you thinking about?" he asks, and for a second I think he actually wants to know. I could tell him how afternoon meeting makes me nostalgic for my own childhood, reminds me of dancing to the Beatles in my grandmother's farmhouse kitchen, reminds me of all my happiest befores. And then I remember yesterday, and his ulterior Baby Hope motive, and I want to kick him in the shins.

"So listen. About yesterday," he starts.

"Answer is still no. I'm sorry." Again with the reflexive apology. I should start an *I'm sorry* jar. Put in a buck every time the words slip out.

"But—"

"Seriously. I can't."

"There must be some way I can convince you. Or bribe you, even? I'm not above selling my body."

I smile, and then, when I realize I'm smiling, I attempt to rearrange my face.

"I really, really need your help on this," he says. "No one will talk to me without you. Believe me, I've tried." Noah looks

48

earnest now, almost sweet. He ruffles his hair in a charming way, a back-and-forth swoop, which leaves it standing straight up like uneven grass. In the background, I hear my girls' quavering, off-key kid voices singing "Knights Forever, One and All!" which will now be stuck on a loop in my head for the rest of the day. I won't mind.

"Find someone else."

"There is no one else. *You* are Baby Hope." He says it too loudly just as the music comes to a stop.

"I told you. Just Abbi. Please," I say under my breath, and look around to make sure no one over the age of four has heard.

"Exactly how badly do you want to keep this whole Baby Hope thing a secret?" Noah leans in to whisper, and I feel the tickle of his breath on my ear. I shiver.

Does he think I'm playing here? I am not playing. He has no idea what it's like having people assume they know you. Being treated like a symbol, not a person. People look at that photo and see patriotism, resiliency, sometimes, perversely, even a happily-ever-after. None of which has anything to do with me. There was a "think piece" in the *New York Times* that went viral after they ran it last year, blaming Baby Hope for the Iraq War. That writer looked at the photo and felt that I was a false idol, a bait and switch, but how ridiculous to accuse me of selling a war. Yet I'm not so sure he was totally wrong. Maybe the photograph did play its small part.

"What do you mean? I told you . . ." I hate how long it takes me to figure out his subtext. I take a step back. "Wait. Are you blackmailing me?"

"Define *blackmail*."

"Come on."

"If you won't help me on this article, I guess I won't be as motivated to keep your secret. I scratch your back, you scratch mine."

"I'm not touching your back. Even figuratively," I say.

"How about with one of those long backscratchers with the creepy plastic hands?"

"This is not funny."

"Or one with an equally terrifying shark mouth?"

"No."

"Other counselors are bound to ask me about you since we're the only ones here from Oakdale. I can't make any promises about what I'll tell them." He throws me an exaggerated shrug and looks around pointedly, like he may not be able to stop himself. Like he's going to scream it out: *Hey, you guys, guess what? Abbi is Baby Hope!*

"No one's going to ask about me," I say, reassuring myself that I've already covered my tracks as best I can. I left my middle name off the camp forms to make it harder to find me online. Uncle Maurice doesn't even know who I am.

"The lifeguard already did."

"Charles?" A hungry eagerness creeps into my voice. Which is silly for a variety of reasons, not least of which is that I have no real interest in Charles. I'm sort of interested in his superhuman abs, but even then only clinically. I'm curious how that happens. How many crunches does he do a day? How long can he hold a plank? Does that leave time for any other hobbies?

"I knew Captain America would get your attention."

"Stop it. He didn't ask about me."

"Maybe he did. And I'm sure Julia would find it interesting." The song has switched to "This Land Is Your Land" and Uncle Maurice has busted out a battered old acoustic guitar and all I want is to be sitting on the floor, indistinguishable from my girls, singing along. My voice, me, lost in the crowd. I want to sit there and feel pre-nostalgia, which probably isn't a real thing, but I want to feel it anyway: that potent mix of optimism and yearning and the tiniest bit of sadness that comes with the certainty that something will one day be over even if it's barely yet begun.

"Please, I really need your help," he says. His tone has switched from playful to serious, like this all really matters. I want to tell him it's futile. That the photograph is just a picture of a bunch of lucky people at a single moment in time.

I look over at Julia, who signals that she needs my help. Her hand motions seem friendlier than they did this morning. More *Come on over*, less *Do this NOW*. Livi, already my favorite camper because she's always lost in some imaginary world, squeezes her eyes shut when she belts out *to the New York Island*. I feel a swell of tenderness as I watch her wipe away a string of mucus with the back of her little hand.

My heart grows along with the music. Next Friday, I need to come to camp dressed in superhero gear. Our lunch was chicken nuggets in the shape of dinosaurs and Tater Tots. This afternoon, we created dream catchers out of paper plates and dyed feathers. I've given myself eight weeks. I won't let Noah take them away from me.

"Fine," I tell him. "I'll do it."

"Awesome," he says, and throws his arm around my shoulder. I shake it off. "I knew you'd come around."

CHAPTER TWELVE

Noah

I am on an intergalactic space mission to save my fellow Mars colonizers from alien predators. My character in this game looks nothing like me. He has a goatee, neon-green hair in an Elvis swoop, a badass tat on his cheek, and a scar that slices from lip to eye. Jack, currently busy consuming a taco, usually plays as a blue-haired girl with an anarchy sign on her forehead. She kicks my butt every single time.

"Duck!" Jack screams as a space dino roars in my face. I shoot instead, and the animal explodes, drenching me with its guts.

"I can't believe you resorted to blackmailing Baby Hope," Jack says, apropos of nothing, which is typically how conversations go for us. "Terrible idea."

"Thanks for your support, man. Means the world," I say as I drop and roll across a giant boulder and toss a grenade into the swarm of alien invaders. I suck at video games, but we've exhausted the Netflix comedy options and all the new stuff online, and I'm not feeling vintage YouTube today.

I want to blow some shit up.

"Just telling it like it is. Remember 'Clean-Up on Aisle 5' guy? Brendan?" he asks. His voice goes a little high. Nervous. I know what this means. New crush.

"The one with the tattoos?" I ask, trying to remember any other details he may have given me but coming up empty. Jack is a better talker than I am a listener.

"Yeah. He's not an actual high school dropout, but he has that look. I think of it as delinquent-sexy."

"That would make a great band name. The Delinquent Sexies. Or for my Netflix comedy special. Picture it: Me totally nerding out on the billboard. Big glasses, socks pulled up, maybe even suspenders, and then it would say *Noah Stern: Sexy Delinquent*." As I drop the controller to write the billboard with my hands, I take a bullet to my chest. Serves me right.

"Would also work for a porno title," Jack says.

"I'm pretty sure Abbi has a thing for the lifeguard at camp," I say. "He's super cut. Totally the type who should consider an alternative career in porn."

"You're the only straight boy I've ever met who doesn't care if you sometimes sound super gay," Jack says. "I think it might be one of my top three favorite things about you." I take this for the compliment it is. Worrying whether I seem gay—which, for what it's worth, I'm not—seems like a colossal waste of time, and I say this as someone who is in hour three of wasting my life pretending to kill alien dinosaurs. "And must everything come back to Abbi now?"

"Sorry. Tell me more." Jack's bursting to talk about the random guy he has cast as his love interest this summer, and as his best friend, I must do my duty and pretend to listen. I reload,

53

pick up a booster, and settle into a hiding spot behind a metal door on the space station.

"Well, I'm thinking something more plotted than your typical Internet porn. It would star this kid who's a delinquent, and spoiler alert: he's also been a very naughty boy."

"Stop. I meant about Brendan."

"Okay. So he's seventeen. Takes college classes part-time at NJCC. Has a tat on his left bicep that was ill-advised." Jack starts pacing behind the television, which he does whenever he's (a) practicing a bit or (b) discussing a guy. One time, when he used a stand-up routine at our school talent show to ask out Alfonso Simeon, it was (c) both.

"What's the tattoo?"

"Let's just say it's a fish. . . ."

"Like a Jesus fish?"

"No, a normal fish . . . but with mammary glands."

"A mermaid?" I ask.

"A sexy mermaid. I can't talk about it. Anyhow, he's a really good person. Sometimes when people use EBT cards to pay, he'll put stuff in their bags without charging them. He thinks no one notices, but I've seen it a bunch of times. He's a superhot grocery store Robin Hood. He keeps a book in his back pocket, which is the cutest thing ever. Careful! Top left. Use the power combo." I ignore Jack and get shot again. Of course.

"Crap," I say.

"You never listen. Anyhow, I know you think most of my crushes are unrealistic, but this one feels different. I really like him," Jack says, and because I am not a douche, I don't say what we are both thinking, which is that he says this every single time.

"That's great," I say. As much as I like to make fun of Jack— it's my favorite hobby—I try not to tease him about his wholly theoretical love life. It's not easy being one of only a handful of out kids in Oakdale, and any guy would be lucky to have him. I mean it. I may have sucker punched Jack in the face once in the third grade and he annoys the living shit out of me, but I love him. We're brothers, and I don't mean that in a bro-y way, like we're bonded because some asshole made us drink fifty beers together one night and now we *think* we're friends for life. We actually will be.

"Nah, I think he might be straight. Ugh. Why are we both so bad at this?" Jack asks.

"At what?" I ask, because the truth is there's a pretty long list of stuff we are bad at.

"Pretty much everything except hanging out together and coming up with terrible jokes."

"At least we know we're not peaking in high school," I say. I shoot a power rocket at nothing in particular. The sky explodes like the Fourth of July. It feels awesome, which perversely ends up making me feel even more pathetic.

"Thank God," Jack says. "Because peaking in high school would have been a real tragedy."

"The worst," I agree just as an alien dinosaur opens his giant jaws and swallows me whole.

CHAPTER THIRTEEN

Abbi

"Your mom is worried about you," my dad declares over dinner at his house. Well, technically, it is my house too, since I live at both 11 and 15 Lexington Road, my time divided exactly fifty-fifty, as mandated by the divorce decree. Not that it really matters where I sleep, since the houses are so close we tend to treat them like they're interchangeable. Sometimes, on Monday or Thursday mornings, when we're out of milk, my dad and I walk over and eat breakfast at my mom's. On Tuesdays and Fridays, Mom and I like to stop at Dad's to fill up our travel mugs because he splurges on the good coffee.

I don't answer my father right away. Take a bite of pizza to buy some time and gauge where this conversation might be heading.

Grandma again? I thought I took it like a champ when we went for ice cream.

College applications? I signed up online for a bunch of catalogs.

New friends? I'm working on it.

Since Cat and I had our own little divorce and she got custody of the rest of our crew, I've been decidedly less social. The thing is, I used to be part of a happy foursome—Me, Cat, Ramona, and Kylie. They all had hair colors not naturally found in nature and lots of piercings and an enviable fluency with pop culture. As a fern, I have standard-issue brown hair, unpunctured ears, and basic tastes, so we were never a perfect fit. When I hung out with my friends (now ex-friends), it was an irony not lost on me that my natural inclination to blend actually made me stand out.

Cat and I had done the best friends necklaces, the blood-sisters thing, the sleeping over at each other's houses every weekend for as long as I could remember. We had been so entwined in each other's lives that it seemed a foregone conclusion that we would always continue that way. I wish I could explain what happened, why we unraveled junior year, with a few dismissive words about me stealing her boyfriend or her stealing mine—I've never had a boyfriend, and Cat would rather die than commit to a guy she was hooking up with—or how one of us turned mean or some other girl-feuding cliché. Instead, when I look back, I think we outgrew each other. It's as simple and as sad as that.

Which was fine—these things happen—but the hard part is I still haven't quite found a new group to fill the void.

"Nothing to be worried about," I tell my dad. "I'm fine."

There is no part of me that thinks this could be about the cough. If it were, we'd already be in a waiting room at the pulmonologist. I used to go so often for my asthma that my entire family was invited to Dr. Cohn's son's bar mitzvah. I danced my very first slow dance under a cardboard Ferris wheel that said *Cohny Island*, and last year, we went to his daughter's sweet sixteen, where I ate delightful pigs in a blanket.

I have no intention of outright lying about the cough. I'm just not going to bring it up first. If my parents sat me down and said, *Hey, Abbi, have you been coughing up blood and wheezing and do you think maybe you have 9/11 syndrome?* I would say, *Yes, as a matter of fact I have and I do. Sorry about that.*

"Mom says you seem preoccupied," he says, all faux casual, like my parents did not plan this pizza-plus-fishing expedition. My mother has always liked to outsource our difficult conversations. It was my dad, not her, who sat me down last spring and asked if I'd be interested in going on the pill. *I appreciate your liberal open-mindedness, but do you see any guys around here?* I asked. *I'm pretty sure I can't get pregnant watching movies with Cat.*

Yes, I'm fully aware my parents are different from most teenagers' parents and also that they are wasted on virgin me. On the other hand, it's entirely possible that they know that it will be wasted on me, that they are well aware I'll be lucky if I lose my virginity before my senior year of college, which is why they're comfortable being so liberal in the first place.

"Nope, not preoccupied. I love camp so far," I say.

"You making some new friends?"

I take a deep breath. I can feel the tiniest whisper of a wheeze rev up in my lungs. So slight, it's almost like a lisp. The slightest of crackles. A match against the grainy side of a box.

A few months ago, when it became obvious that Cat and I were no longer friends, my father asked me outright: *Did you stop being her friend, or did she stop being yours?* It was a cruel question, though I'm sure he didn't mean it that way. He didn't realize that would be like me asking him *Did you leave Mom, or did Mom leave you?*

My dad still works for the same company he was working for on September 11. Back then, he was a bond trader, but through the years, he's moved steadily and swiftly up the ranks, his ascent no doubt helped by his being one of only a handful of survivors in his office. He commutes into the city each day and takes an elevator to the thirty-fourth floor of a shiny new building in Midtown and goes to meeting after meeting, and I don't know if he thinks about all the people he used to work with who are now gone. Each person has his or her own plaque in the lobby, like they do in Oakdale, though the installation is, by necessity, bigger.

My dad's company lost close to three hundred people. That's the size of my entire senior class.

I wonder if he ever stops to look at the plaques.

I imagine not.

"I really like my senior counselor." I hate when my parents worry about me. On my first birthday, it took forty-eight hours for them to confirm that I was safe and alive. Forty-eight hours for them to track me down in that broken city full of robot guts. I used up an entire life's quota of worry in two days.

"Why do I feel like you're not telling me something?" he asks.

"Dad, come on. Mom has enough on her plate with Grandma. Report back that I'm totally fine," I say, and trace my finger along one of the laminated placemats I made in preschool a million years ago, which my father still insists we use. On them, our prebreakup family is drawn in stick figures. All of us hold hands and stand within the confines of a single square house under a single triangle roof.

Childish geometric perfection.

"Also, you know you two chat way too much for divorced people, right? It's getting a little weird," I say.

*　*　*

59

A few hours later, when I'm back in my room and my lungs decide it would be a good time to put on a show, I don't overreact. It's not so scary anymore. I think of it as a small bodily betrayal, like a gluten allergy or a sprained ankle. No big deal, just something to be accommodated or worked around.

While I cough, I flick on some music so my dad can't hear me.

I receive my first text from Noah. I have no idea how he got my number, since I purposely didn't give it to him.

> **Noah:** Where should we start? Who do you know best? Connie Kramer?

I could tell Noah that Kramer is Connie's maiden name. That she got married a decade ago, and that if he Googles Connie Greene, he'll get her obituary from a small regional paper. At least there, finally, they focused on her, not me. The headline read *Local Hero Who Saved Baby Hope Dies at Forty-Six*. In it, I learned all sorts of things I hadn't known: she had two children (a boy and a girl, eight and four), she'd spent the last decade working as a first-grade teacher for kids with special needs, she was fluent in French.

Sometimes, for fun, I write my own obituary in my head: *Abbi spent the last few years of her life alternating between the houses of her dysfunctional but loving parents, was an awkward conversationalist, and had anonymous social media accounts since people are creepy and also anti-Semitic.*

> **Me:** It's not like there's a Baby Hope photo club. I don't really know any of them

Noah: Oh

Me: Did you think I was going to do all the hard work for
   you?

Noah: Let's start with Chuck Rigalotti, right behind you

Me: You don't need me for this

Noah: I do! You make me legit. If I contact them out of the
   blue, they'll ignore it. Listen, I realize I'm being a big
   jerk in this one small instance. I'm sorry

Me: You should be

Noah: I'll call Chuck. Set up an interview

Me: K

Noah: And, Abbi, I am really sorry

Before bed, I Google "Noah Stern." And there it is, the very first
result. Exactly what I didn't realize I was looking for. An article
from the *New Jersey Courier*, dated October 10, 2001.

. . . Mrs. Stern, an Oakdale resident, says she held out
hope her husband was still alive for an entire week after
the attacks, since she hadn't known he had plans to go
to Manhattan that day. Still, records tracing his Metro-
Card put him within a one-mile radius of the World
Trade Center early in the morning on September 11. At
the time, Mrs. Stern's infant son, Noah, born September 3, was in the neonatal intensive care unit of Garden State Community Hospital fighting his own battle
for survival. On September 13, he underwent emergency heart surgery to fix an abnormality. Today, after
looking at all available evidence, including credit card
records, a county court judge officially declared Jason

Stern dead in absentia. He will be added to the tally of victims of the September 11 attacks, taking that number to 2,604, though this figure continues to fluctuate and is expected to increase as similar claims are verified. Oakdale has sustained the highest number of deaths of any town outside of New York City. On a happier note, Noah came home from the hospital one week ago and is expected to make a full recovery.

Damn it, damn it, damn it. I should have known. The relatives have always been the most interested in the Baby Hope thing. Not the people who like to remember where they were that day, as if their exact location when they heard the news is somehow meaningful or telling even if they were fourteen hundred miles away eating a Moons Over My Hammy sandwich at Denny's. Or even other teenagers, the ones who think of 9/11 as something that happened in the distant past. Or something that belongs wholly to *their parents*, like New Kids on the Block and the Yellow Pages. Not the survivors themselves either, who like me, probably marvel at the desire to hold on to a single memento. We've Marie Kondo'd anything tangible, if not the feelings.

I understand that the photograph is a historic artifact, something for a museum, maybe, but not a bedroom wall or a tote bag. I understand that I'm the flip side of *Falling Man* and *Dust Lady*, two other famous photographs from that day. The first shows the one thing no one is ever supposed to discuss: a jumper. The second focuses on a black woman turned yellow with head-to-toe dust, looking understandably traumatized, the New York around her now a postapocalyptic hellscape. In contrast to these other images, Baby Hope is optimistic, maybe even happy. A glimpse of innocence within a tornado of pain. Triumph in the midst of destruction.

When I die, will people pull down their posters of me? Will they feel betrayed? Like I didn't deliver on what Baby Hope promised all those years ago?

It's those left behind who thirst for information, who weigh and hold each of these artifacts like talismans and want to know *more, more, more.* Cat used to ask my mom all sorts of questions about 9/11—What did it sound like? How did you get home? Did it smell?—as if she was trying to turn an abstraction, a hazy, evaporating dream, into something real. My mother always answered patiently, always told Cat she could ask her anything, but after she'd leave, I'd hear my mother on the phone with Cat's mom offering Dr. Schwartz's number.

She needs to talk to someone, Mel, she'd say. *Both of you do.*

This was all back when we were little kids. Mel is remarried now, to Stewart, and Cat has a half brother, and if you saw them all together on the street, you would never know that someone died to make that family possible.

Cat stopped asking questions long ago.

I do not understand what would make Noah want to start asking them now.

CHAPTER FOURTEEN

Noah

Another question that keeps me up at night: Is Andy Kaufman dead? Now, I get that most people don't even know who he is anymore, which is depressing—how could someone that funny be forgotten? When I asked Phil, my stepdad, he was like, "The guy that R.E.M. song 'Man on the Moon' is about? Of course he's dead!" which wasn't surprising. Phil isn't known for his imagination or his sense of humor.

Andy Kaufman might be the greatest comedian who ever lived. For real. And despite dying of cancer in 1984 at the young age of thirty-five, he *still* has a devoted cult following all these years later. But here's the cool part, and this is a fact, you can look it up: true Kaufman fans believe his sudden and shocking death was a hoax and an extended prank. "Kaufmanheads" are convinced that he will one day soon show up and return to public life and pick up his routine right where he left off.

If they're right, and I like to believe they are, Kaufman's rising from the dead will turn out to be the longest joke ever told.

CHAPTER FIFTEEN

Abbi

"What are you doing this weekend?" I ask Julia, who is sitting cross-legged on the grass next to me. I try to keep my voice casual, like I'm not begging her to invite me somewhere but I also happen to be quite open to the possibility if she does. No one ever tells you how awkward it is to make new friends when you are no longer four and can't bond over your mutual distaste for princess culture.

"The usual. Camp party," she says. We are almost two weeks into the summer, and every outfit she has worn so far has been perfectly calibrated. Today: a pretty floral summer romper with rope sandals. Casual and flirty and a touch bohemian. Her eyes are hidden behind a giant pair of plastic retro sunglasses, and a couple of leather studded wraplets dangle from her wrists. I wish she could dress me.

"Cool," I say.

"Yup," she says.

"Sounds like fun," I say, leaning a little too hard on the word *fun*. Damn it.

"Yup," she says again, not taking the bait.

"Another Friday night in the big bad burbs," I say, *out loud*, apparently, though I have no idea what I even mean. I would love to be one of those people who can shut up and wait out an awkward silence. If I could choose a superpower, that would be it: to be effortlessly comfortable without words.

So badass.

"Yup," Julia says for a third time, and pretends to be engrossed in the game, which means she watches intently as Livi, the smallest in our group and still my favorite, taps heads and lisps the word *duck*, so it sounds alarmingly like, well, you know.

"Whose party is it?" Apparently I have no dignity.

"Natasha's," Julia says, and shrugs her shoulder toward an aggressively healthy-looking girl with a cascade of wavy brown hair who is running an archery clinic nearby. Wonder Woman to Charles's Captain America. She's wearing a tank top with a complicated sports bra underneath—spiderweb straps, no actual support—and skintight three-quarter-length yoga pants, clothes hugging the sort of body that combines the perfect ratio of genetic lottery winnings with thrice-weekly stadium cycling. Her eyebrows too are a thing of beauty. Thick, arched, bold. "Her parents are away for the weekend."

"Cool," I say.

"I have an idea: If you'd like to come with me, you can just say, 'Hey, Julia, mind if I tag along to the party?' Would be much less awkward for both of us that way." Julia says this without looking at me, and at first I assume it's because I've annoyed her. Then I realize she's watching Zach, who is standing close to

Natasha, getting an intimate one-on-one lesson on how to hold a bow. Noah, meanwhile, is giving piggybacks to his boys, and he looks surprisingly dorky-cute with his socks pulled up and cargo shorts and a T-shirt that reads *This T-shirt is dry-clean only, which means it's dirty—Mitch Hedberg.*

"Hey, Julia, would you mind if I tagged along to the party tonight?" I ask, my voice still a touch too hopeful. I wonder if I'll die before I'm able to rid myself of all this terrible earnestness. That seems even more of a shame than the likelihood that I will die a virgin.

"Sure."

"I can be your designated driver," I say.

"That would be great."

"Also, I can bring snacks."

"Stop talking now, Abbi."

"Done," I say, and for once, I shut up. Just like a badass.

"Are you driving?" my dad asks. No hello, even. He calls as I'm pulling out of the camp parking lot to head home. I'm in my 2009 Toyota Prius, the car my father bought for my mom as a divorce present eight years ago and now belongs to me. He does weird stuff like that sometimes. Once, long after my parents split up, my mom came home from work to find a new washer and dryer on our front porch. A more cynical person would say these are easy ways for my dad to assuage his guilt for leaving our family, but the truth is, as I've told Dr. Schwartz for years, he didn't leave. He moved two doors down. I really think he just uses the money he works so hard to earn on the people he loves the most in the world, even if he's no longer married to one of them.

"Bluetooth."

"Still."

"Dad," I say, in the way daughters have been saying *Dad* for millennia: with a heavy hint of affection hidden behind a whine.

"Please just pull over," he says, and I do as he asks even though he can't see me. "I was calling to see if you want to watch a movie at home with your mom and me tonight. We were thinking that new *Pride and Prejudice* adaptation set on Mars after Earth has been destroyed in a nuclear apocalypse? We both missed it in the theater, and you know how I feel about Jane Austen remakes."

"You and Mom are watching a movie together tonight?"

"Well, we were both hoping we were watching a movie with *you* tonight," he says, and then I realize what's happening here. My parents are so worried about my dire social situation that they are uniting to fill in the void. I have reached a new low of patheticness, which I realize isn't a word but totally should be. In the dictionary, under its definition, all they'd have to write is *Abbi Hope Goldstein, right now.*

"Can't. Going to a camp party tonight," I say.

"Oh, great! That's so great, honey!" my dad says with entirely too much enthusiasm and relief.

"Most parents worry about their kids *going* to parties, not the other way around."

"Most parents aren't as cool as I am. So do you need me to pick up some snacks for you to bring?" he asks, and I rest my head on the steering wheel and close my eyes. I was always going to be exactly who I am and there is nothing I can do about it. "I can get those sour cream and onion potato chips you like? Or Doritos? Do kids still eat those? I haven't seen a Dorito in years, come to think of it. Why is that? What happened to Doritos? Also, is the singular of Doritos Dorito? Am I right about that?"

"Dad," I say again, same whine, less affection. No doubt, he is where all my awkward excessive verbiage comes from. My dad might be super liberal, but he's definitely not cool. "I'm *not* bringing snacks."

"Okay, beer, then?"

"Seriously? You'd buy me beer?" If my dad bought me alcohol, then I'd definitely start getting invited more places. This could be the answer to all my social problems. I can't believe I didn't think of it sooner.

"I was kidding. I would never buy you beer."

"Oh."

"But I can score you some pot."

"I'm going now."

"Oh, you know what? I can combine the pot and the snacks and get you edibles. How does that sound?" he asks, full-out laughing at me now.

"Goodbye," I say.

"I love you, sweetheart," he says.

"Yeah, yeah," I say, but I'm smiling when I hang up.

CHAPTER SIXTEEN

Noah

"We're going to a party tonight," I tell Jack. We are in his basement, because . . . we are always in his basement. I wonder if one day, when I am old, I'll regret the ridiculous number of hours I've clocked down here. I hope not. I hope future me will remember and understand how limited the options were in Oakdale.

"Were we invited to this party?" Jack asks. He hits a ball against the wall with a ping-pong paddle, since he does not own, nor has he ever owned, an actual ping-pong table. I still have no idea where these mysterious paddles came from.

"Has that ever stopped us before?" I ask.

"Yup. Every single time. Name a single high school party that we've been to," Jack challenges, and I don't say anything because the answer is zero. We have been to zero parties. "We didn't go to homecoming, which only works as an example if I allow you to broaden the category so as to include school-sponsored events, to which everyone is automatically invited. And even then, my friend, we did not go."

"Fine," I say.

"There was that party we went to a few years ago. . . . Oh, wait, that was your bar mitzvah." Once Jack gets started, it's impossible to get him to stop until his rant has run its course, so I don't even try. I pick up the second paddle, and we start playing an impromptu game against the wall. "I know! What about that time at school when Mr. Caruso brought soda and chips and there were girls there? Crap. That was a newspaper meeting. Or when we all stood out back of school during first period? Right. Fire drill. Not. A. Party."

"You've made your point," I say. I aim the ball for the far corner, make Jack run a little. "But this is a college party. And we were invited. Kind of."

"Kind of?"

"It was implied. Zach mentioned that a bunch of people were going."

"I thought you said that guy was an asshole." Jack hits the ball high, and it bounces off the ceiling. I return it with a swing behind my back that nails the wall low. Jack dives onto the carpet and sends it back across the room. A perfect shot that lands in the opposite far corner. I steeple my hands together and bow to him. This might be the best part of Jack's basement. We can nerd out all we want and no one can judge us.

"True. Imagine if the universe purposely, like, created the exact genetic code of the person you, in particular, would be most likely to hate and you'll get a close approximation of Zach," I say. "So he totally sucks."

"You're not really selling this thing," Jack says.

"Remember when I went with you in full cosplay to Comic Con, even though I hated every second of it? I wore *red leggings*, dude. Or when I camped outside the Apple store because you wanted to get the new iPhone? I watched the Super Bowl last year, even though football is dumb and inhumane. Come on. I beg you. Do this one small thing for me," I say, already knowing he will say yes.

"Will Baby Nope be there?" he asks.

"I don't know," I say.

"Liar."

"It's sweet that you're worried about me making a new friend and you being left behind," I say.

"I wish this were about you making a new friend. Anyhow, it'd be awesome if you found a girlfriend. Then everyone would stop thinking we were a couple," Jack says.

"People do not think we are a couple." I say this though I have no idea if it's true. We do spend a ton of time together.

"Come on, you know I'm prettier than Baby Nope," he says.

"Not even close."

"My boobs are totally better." I throw my paddle at his head. He ducks unnecessarily. I was three feet wide.

"Didn't realize we had a line, but you just crossed it. So you'll come?" I ask.

"That's what he said," Jack says.

"I hate you."

"No. You love me because I'm going to go to this party tonight and be the world's best wingman even though I'm a little lovesick and heartbroken that the boy I'm crushing on from work is likely to be arrested for his Robin Hooding ways and also probably isn't gay," he says.

"Thank you."

"You are very welcome."

"People don't really think we are a couple, right?" I ask.

"Nah. Well, except for my mom," Jack says.

CHAPTER SEVENTEEN

Abbi

No one is going to ruin this party for me. Not Noah, who is standing near the keg with another junior from Oakdale and who has twice tried to talk to me about setting up a schedule for our interviews. Not Julia, who it turns out lives in the exact opposite direction, which means there is no way I will make it home before my already generous curfew. Not even my parents, who stood at the door and waved goodbye with ridiculously proud grins, like I was headed off to do something amazing like win an Academy Award or attempt a solo flight over Antarctica. Certainly not my lungs, which started flaring up as soon as I entered this dusty room. Nope. This is a party, a *college party*, filled with all sorts of new and interesting people from an entire county away to whom I can hopefully introduce myself as simply *Abbi*.

So far, the only catch is I'm not quite sure how to join in. As soon as we got here, Julia beelined for the bar. She is now out back somewhere hanging with Zach, who, when he first saw her, said, "Well, hello, beautiful, shall we alight to the out-doors?" and flashed that cheesy smile just at her, his laser focus making it clear that he was not inviting me along. That the *beau-tiful* was singular.

Right now, I'm standing behind Charles, but his broad back is to me, and even if it weren't, what could I say? *Sure was a big poop in the plake today! So kind of Knight's Day Camp to provide me with latex gloves to clean it up.*

He's talking to Natasha, whom he calls Tash because of course girls who look like her get cool nicknames not horrible ones like "Baby Hope." They are discussing how they are both English majors and isn't it funny how they will be unemployed forever. I want to interrupt and remind them that everyone knows pretty people get hired first, so they should both be fine.

"Hey, Abbi," Noah says again, and now he's standing next to me and his friend is here too, and we make a semicircle of awkward high school–ness among grown-ups. I wish I weren't wearing my Wonder Woman T-shirt and my cutoff shorts and stupid flip-flops, which somehow only now, in retrospect, seem an immature choice. Why didn't my mom stop me? Of course, I should be wearing heels and a sundress or one of those cool rompers that Julia pulls off. So what if they make me look like a preschooler? Also, why am I wearing fox earrings, which are cute in exactly the wrong way? Foxes are cute, yes. Not girls wearing fox earrings. And yeah, yeah, I shouldn't be dressing for the male gaze, but I don't particularly enjoy feeling toddler-esque.

Cat would have told me to take them off. She would have been right.

"I'm Jack," Noah's friend says with a small wave. At first, they seem like a strange pair. Jack is tall and striking and rocks an artsy punk look; he'd fit in perfectly with my old friends. His brown hair is tufted into a casual mini-Mohawk, his nails are painted an electric blue, and though he's currently instrument-less, he's the type of guy who could get away with wearing a guitar strapped to his chest like a samurai sword. Still, somehow, like Noah, he exudes a certain goofiness.

"So, Abbi, I hear my friend here has been harassing you," Jack says.

"More like blackmailing," I say, and mirror his happy, slightly nervous grin. Though it hurts my neck to look up at him, I want to stand on my tippy-toes and touch his hair. "Any chance you can talk him out of it?"

"Sorry. He never listens to me. Noah's a good dude, though."

"I'm not so convinced," I say.

"You guys do realize I'm standing right here?" Noah asks.

"Yup," I say, and decide that after spending a solid half hour at this party not knowing how to insert myself into a conversation with one of the college kids, I'm happy to have people to talk to, even if one of them has taken on torturing me as an after-camp hobby.

"What do you think of camp counseloring?" Jack asks me.

"Better than school," I say.

"Anything beats school," Jack says.

"Syria. Syria doesn't beat school," Noah says. "Nor does the Sudan."

"Did he just bring up Syria at a party?" I ask, but I keep my tone jokey, not mean. I'm still looking at Jack, but I can see Noah out of the corner of my eye. He's grinning at me. All right, then. He can take a joke. Good. The back of his hair, I notice now, looks wet. I wonder if he took a quick shower and put the same clothes back on. Did he too stand in front of his closet for half an hour and then give up?

"And he said 'the Sudan,'" Jack says. "Not just 'Sudan.' Of course he *had* to add the *the*."

"He really is *the* worst," I say, and though it's a terrible joke, Jack laughs anyway.

"I like her," he says to Noah, and I feel like I've passed a secret test I didn't know I was taking.

I spend the rest of the night with Jack and Noah, and before long, I forget all about my Wonder Woman T-shirt and the fact that I'm the third-youngest person at this party. Jack even compliments my fox earrings. And though I may only be talking to Oakdale people, I am decidedly Abbi here.

When Jack heads off to the bathroom, Noah brings up our first interview, and just like that, I feel Baby Hope seep back into my bones, and with her, an asthmatic rush of insecurity and disorientation. I have no interest in meeting my fellow survivors, or in reliving that moment of me with that balloon like the star of a dystopian Gerber commercial.

"I called Chuck Rigalotti. We're all set for Tuesday after camp," he says, and for the first time, he sounds a little worried, maybe even a little sorry. "You won't have to say anything. I promise it won't be so bad."

"Ugh."

"He wasn't willing to talk to me until I brought you up. Seriously, I need you for this."

"You're lucky I'm in a good mood right now," I say, though I feel that good mood starting to wobble.

"I'll make it fun. I'll bring you a Slurpee."

"The giant one," I demand. "Cherry."

"Fair enough. Anything else for your tour rider?"

"Twizzlers, please."

"That's funny. Your friend Cat wanted our Twizzlers the other day too," Noah says, and my stomach craters. "You guys only eat red foods or something?"

"Wait, you know Cat?" I ask, and my tone shatters the rhythm of our banter, which is too bad. It was just taking shape.

"I don't, not really. I mean, we met her the other night outside ShopRite. She was pretty wasted, so Jack drove her home." Noah looks at me, like really looks at me, as if he doesn't trust my words and wants to see what my eyes have to say.

"Cat was drunk? On a weeknight?" I ask, and then lighten my voice. Noah's actually pretty cool, minus the whole blackmailing thing. It's not his fault that hearing about Cat, especially hearing about Cat drinking, makes me hurt. Not sure her favorite new recreational activity—getting stoned and drunk with Ramona and Kylie and this group of senior boys after school—was the exact reason for our friendship breakup; let's just say our interests diverged.

"You okay? You look a little . . . piqued, a word I have never before said out loud until now," he says. He doesn't know whether he's still allowed to joke with me. Whether by mentioning Cat, he's crossed some big boundary and in response I've revoked his new privileges.

I decide to change the subject. Cat isn't my responsibility anymore. She has Kylie and Ramona to watch her back now, though they were never much good at it.

"I've never said piqued either. Piqued. Piqued. Yeah, feels weird, like I'm a character in an eighteenth-century British novel or something. Like someone is about to swoon and then be revived by smelling salts."

"What do you think smelling salts actually smell like?" Noah asks. "I bet they smell like the boys' bathroom near the cafeteria."

"You're such a pessimist. Why can't smelling salts smell good? Maybe they smell like roses."

"Or chocolate."

"Or fresh-cut grass."

"Or your perfume," Noah says, and I blush, because though I sometimes have no idea how to be a girl in the way that Tash is a girl or Julia is a girl, I do dab a light sugar scent on my wrists every morning as a ritual. Subtle, not obvious in the way that putting on a dress tonight would have felt.

"It's just Cat and I aren't really friends anymore." This is a confession I am surprised to hear myself make out loud. A non sequitur too.

"Oh," he says. "I used to see you two together all the time, though I guess now that I think about it, maybe not so much lately? I mean, not that I've seen you a lot. You know what I mean. Sorry for bringing it up. I'm going to stop talking now."

"It's okay. The fact that we're no longer friends kind of sucks. People grow apart, I guess. But bringing her up is fine. Still, you know . . . it's . . . hard? Now it's my turn to stop talking," I say, and we both look down at our feet. He has on his beat-up black Chucks, the same ones he wears every day at camp, and he leans over and kicks the side of my flip-flop gently. Just once. A kind, *Cheer up, kid* gesture. I kick back. One small *Thank you*.

And then Jack reappears from the bathroom and Noah and I both take a step back, like we were caught doing something we shouldn't have been.

CHAPTER EIGHTEEN

Noah

"Slick first move," Jack says, when I tell him about the sneaker/ flip-flop tap. I'm about 95 percent sure he's being sarcastic. We're driving home from the party in his beat-up black Civic, which always smells like an old gym bag. Jack inherited it from his older brother, Kyle, who plays football on scholarship somewhere in Ohio and whose right arm is the size of an entire Abbi. No matter how many air fresheners Jack uses, he can't seem to erase years of team carpooling. Athlete funk sinks in deep.

I was the first person Jack came out to. Kyle was the second. Both times went as well as a coming-out can when everyone already knows you're gay. To be honest, I think Jack was disappointed. I fist-bumped him and said, "Cool." Kyle said, "No shit, Sherlock. Come back when you have something interesting to tell me." When Jack finally told his mom, which took an extra couple of months, she said, "Sweetie, you came out to me when you were three. This is not news." Jack's dad left when his mom was pregnant, and I've sometimes wondered if we became such good friends because we both grew up without fathers. Then I remember that we both laughed so hard we cried the first time we listened to a Mitch Hedberg set and realize that explanation is bullshit. We get each other.

"It wasn't a move. But she's cool, right?"

"Remember the kid who asked Kelly Bateman to prom by shaving the words into his bountiful chest hair?" he asks.

"Seared into my eyeballs. Especially that gash next to his nipple. Ouch."

"You and Baby Hope playing kid detective together? An even worse idea than that."

"Kelly Bateman said yes to prom, though," I remind him.

"Think of the price tag on that date: a nipple scar, and I bet he has uneven chest hair for the rest of his life. Every time he goes to the beach, he looks down, and he's like: *Damn you, Kelly Bateman!*"

"What do Eli Crouch's nipples have to do with Abbi, again?"

"It's a metaphor and a cautionary tale. Also a great band name: Eli Crouch's Nipples."

"Not following."

"You shave letters into your chest hair, you'll never be the same again. You go down this path with Abbi, and *bam!*" He slaps his hand hard on the horn to highlight the point. "You get figurative bloody nipples."

"You just want an excuse to say the word *nipples,*" I say.

"It's good word," Jack says, and shrugs.

CHAPTER NINETEEN

Abbi

In the morning, my dad sits at my mom's kitchen counter drinking coffee out of one of her mugs, which is weird because his machine is way better and has one of those fancy frothers. Also, my parents don't tend to linger in each other's homes. Instead, they quickly stop by and grab things, like shopping at a 7-Eleven. A random in-and-out plundering.

"I came to see how your night was," my dad says. He's way too cheerful for not-yet-nine a.m. Recently, since the cough started, I've morphed into a morning person. Well, not exactly. I still hate mornings, but now I make sure to experience them.

"Where's Mom?" I ask.

"Still sleeping, I guess," he says.

My parents divorced when I was too young to question much beyond the story they told me: they still loved each other, and of course me—that was repeated over and over again—but they thought it best if they started living in different houses. Through the years, I've cobbled together more information. Like everything else in my life, it seems their divorce circles back to 9/11. My mother wanted to reorient their lives to helping the families of the victims, to heed what she saw as a wake-up call and a chance to find meaning in tragedy. She quit her job and went back to school, turned from investment banking to psychology.

My father, on the other hand, decided to stay at work, taking the lead in helping set up a new, temporary office in Jersey City with the few employees the company had left. Both of my parents threw themselves into their new ventures—legit coping strategies—and I guess while they weren't paying attention, their marriage fell apart.

"So how was the party?" My dad's clearly elated that I may have stumbled into a new social life. Box checked off the worry list. I can't break it to him that high school friendships don't seem to work that way. You don't go to one party, have a surprisingly good conversation with the boy who usually looks at you and sees only Baby Hope, and then be set with friends for life. Still, surviving my first party post-Cat is a good thing. I should take it as a win.

"Fun."

"That's all I get?" he asks. "I hate when you go all teenagery on me."

I pour myself some coffee and wrap my hands around the warm cup. I take a sip and revel in its bitter promise. Wait for my personality to be caffeinated back.

"Abbi! Talk to me, please."

"It's the crack of dawn on a Saturday. You're lucky I'm even awake," I say. My dad sits across from me, leans forward on his elbows. There's a jitteriness to him that makes me think I need to drink at least two more cups of coffee to catch up. "I'm excited to see Grandma tomorrow."

"You know she's going to be . . . different, right?" he asks.

"Of course."

"She might not recognize you," he says. The shame makes its slow creep up my spine. Why haven't I thought about this before? Now that my dad has said the words out loud, I realize this is not so much a possibility as an inevitability. If not this week, then sometime soon. I try to feel the feelings before they happen—what that will be like, for my favorite person to not remember that I'm theirs too, for the love I feel for my grandmother to go unrequited—but I find I can't.

I have no trouble fantasizing about fun, unlikely things: First kisses. Someone holding my hand in a darkened movie theater. A boy tucking my hair behind my ear. But with the heartbreaking, likely things, the ones guaranteed to come with a piercing sadness, my mind goes blank with denial. I'm not naive—I know they will happen. It's just that my instinct is not to go there until I have to.

"I know," I lie with a breeziness that surprises even me.

My mom walks in wearing pajamas, a cute pink plaid pair, and she doesn't seem surprised to find my father here, in our kitchen, holding the Best Mom Ever mug I made for her for Mother's Day in the second grade. Did they plan for my dad to come over this morning to prepare me for my grandmother's arrival, not unlike how he stopped by last week to help my mother prepare by fixing up the guest room and installing bed rails?

"Coffee?" my dad asks, and my mom nods and then slips onto the stool next to me. He pours another mug, adds a generous helping of milk and sugar, extra light and sweet, the way my mom has always liked it, and passes it to her. "Do you remember when Abbi was six and she lost both of her front teeth and for about three months she had that adorable lisp and she would chatter on and on? And sometimes all we wanted was for her to be quiet so we could read the newspaper in peace? Now look at her."

My mom turns and appraises me, as if my dad meant it as a demand. She nods again, a little dreamy and slow. Takes a long, desperate sip of coffee. My usually chipper mother seems, if not quite gloomy, off somewhere else.

"I used to know everything that went on inside that head. Now, no idea," my dad says, and brushes my cheek with the back of his hand with such tenderness it's as if he imagines what goes on in my brain is something beautiful and precise. Funny, I was wondering what goes on in my mother's head. Even though I once lived within the confines of her body, even though her blood was once my blood, even though half of me is carved from the whole of her, my mom's thoughts are still impregnable.

As are everyone's, I guess.

"Right now I'm pretty sure she's thinking *Leave me alone, Dad*," my mom says.

"Ding, ding, ding, we have a winner," I say, though of course that isn't what I was thinking at all.

Later, I lie back on my bed with my phone perched on my knees and flip through the pictures from last night. I use my secret account, the one that only a few people know belongs to me, and I click to see what Friday night looked like for everyone else.

Julia has posted a short video of her and Zach on a porch swing in Tash's backyard. Her head is thrown back as if he has just said something hilarious, and his head is bent toward hers, and she's filtered it so that they are in color against a black-and-white background. A sweep of fairy lights twinkles behind them as they boomerang back and forth in a blur of romantic whimsy. The video, which already has 245 likes, tells a very different story from the one she told me last night.

"He's not interested anymore," she slurred, her head hanging from the car window to gulp the fresh air like a dog. "I think he's hooking up with Tash. Who can compete with her? No one, that's who," she said, and then she projectile vomited in one surprisingly graceful move. Most of it landed outside. The rest I cleaned with the same Clorox wipes that used to come in handy when I was Cat and Ramona and Kylie's designated driver last year.

On the way home, I thought a lot about how even Julia, who has mastered the bored tone of the truly confident, who I doubt has ever once thought about how to hold her arms, who even throws up with perfect aim, can look at a girl like Tash and feel intimidated.

As I scroll, I tell myself to stay away from this stuff. My Saturday-morning online ritual of vicarious socializing has turned masochistic, not at all in keeping with my mission this summer. Seeing other people's manufactured joy in glossy Technicolor, as addictive as that may be, tends to leave me feeling deflated.

It was sitting right here, with this same phone, in this exact same position, that I learned that Cat and I were no longer best friends.

It wasn't a total surprise. My friends often cut class—they stopped asking me to join in because I always said no—but about halfway through junior year they stopped regularly texting me to meet up later. Because of Instagram, I knew exactly where they were: always some senior guy's basement, always with their hands wrapped around red Solo cups, always with their eyes pink and their heads resting on the boys' shoulders like they were something too heavy to carry alone. A burden shared. True, I didn't love to party—I felt stupid even using that word as a verb instead of a noun—but that didn't mean I didn't want to tag along occasionally.

The outgrowing might have been mutual—I was as uninterested in their new activities as they were in the ones we used to do together and I still enjoyed (Netflix binges at Cat's house, coffee at the Blue Cow Cafe)—but the decision to go our separate ways was not.

Did I do something to upset you? I once texted Cat around Christmastime because I was too scared to ask the question to her face. I waited a full day and a half for a response, the whole time sick to my stomach with worry, and when one finally came, all she said was *Nope. Y?*

I had wanted her to tell me *Of course not*. I wanted her to tell me that *everything was fine*. I wanted her to tell me that she and the girls hadn't moved on. That's what best friends are for: to convince you that all of the nastiest voices in your head are wrong.

Later that week, we were all hanging out at Cat's house, and I was elated to find myself back there, after what seemed to be an inexplicable and long exile. This was about three months after the most recent *Where Is Baby Hope Now?* article and around the time a newspaper columnist pinned an entire war on me.

"What's it like to be famous?" Ramona asked me, and I got the feeling she was purposely stirring up trouble. Cat and I rarely talked about the Baby Hope thing—partially because there was nothing to talk about; it had always been what it was—and also because until recently, it was our only disconnect. Her dad *died* on 9/11. My whole family, me included, lived. In some ways, you might even argue we profited from it, if you considered being recognized or seeing your face on a tote bag a benefit. (I didn't, of course, but I could see how one would.)

"I'm not famous. Not really," I said, and Cat shook her head at me, like that was the exact wrong thing to say. Back then, it felt like I was usually saying the exact wrong thing, as if it were an art form I had studied and recently mastered by practice alone.

I thought we had long ago figured out our dynamic. I had assumed that friendship was static, not fluid. Ramona was our leader, Kylie was our echo, and Cat was our soul. Looking back, I'm not sure what my designated role in our foursome was. I was the kidneys, maybe—loyal, a little too practical, a little too earnest. Definitely no need for two of them.

Still, I do know who I used to be to Cat: her other half, her best friend, the one who had been by her side so long our child-hood memories were interchangeable.

And then, that Sunday, on a cold spring morning, after I had bought tangerine hair dye thinking that might be the answer, that my hair color would let me leap me over the divide that had sprouted up between me and my friends, I stared at my phone, and there it was, photographic evidence of what I'm sure I knew all along. A shared history doesn't guarantee a shared future. My best friend was no longer my best friend.

On my screen was picture after picture of a wasted Cat and Ramona and Kylie in various configurations all at Victor Sarmiento's party.

A happy threesome: big droopy, not even smug smiles, glazed eyes, arms thrown around each other's shoulders, a few taken with hands on hips, lips pursed, another with party-store mustaches on sticks. Cat's hair was purple, Ramona's pink, and Kylie aqua. Each picture was designed to scream *We. Are. Having. So. Much. Fun. Here. Without. You.*

When I had texted Cat earlier to ask what she was doing that night, she had written back: *Have to babysit.*

A three-word lie.

Cat knew about my secret accounts. They were her idea in the first place, the only way I could participate in any sort of online life without bringing out the trolls and the terrifying 9/11 conspiracy theorists. She was the one who had dubbed me absfabs35, set my location as Dubai, and taken a quick picture of the back of my head and set it as my profile.

So of course Cat also knew I would see those pictures. Even worse, I was sure she *wanted* me to see them, to send the message she could not bring herself to deliver out loud.

Here was my very first thought when I clicked:

Not *I hate Cat.*

Not even *They suck.*

Instead, I thought, *Okay, then. Moving on.*

I thought, *They do not even think you are worth wasting a paper mustache on a stick.*

I thought, *Time to start over.*

And so I did. I let them let me go. I didn't call Cat tearfully and ask what had happened to our friendship. I didn't even get angry. What was the point? We were friends and then we weren't. Not everything grows in tandem.

I know better than anyone that you can't always draw a straight line from the who you once were to the who you are now.

CHAPTER TWENTY

Noah

Phil is eating breakfast when I come downstairs: shredded wheat with half a banana (the other half saved in Saran Wrap), as he has done every morning I've known him. I was happy when my mom married Phil, not because I particularly like him or like living in his house, but because of the relief that came with realizing that making her happy was no longer solely my job. I pour myself a bowl of Lucky Charms; I like to imagine he's jealous of my wanton sugar consumption.

"Heard you and Jack went to a party last night. How was it?" he asks as he types on his work phone. Phil's a lawyer, so this conversation is probably costing someone $550 an hour.

"Fine," I say.

"You score?" he asks, without looking up. Is he joking? I don't think so. Joking is not something Phil knows how to do. Neither is laughing.

"You realize you're my stepfather and this is not a fraternity house. In 1995."

"Just making small talk," he says, and I look around for my mom to rescue me, but she's nowhere to be found. "Listen, your mother's worried about you."

"What this time?" Worrying is my mother's favorite hobby. She likes it even more than those spin classes where they yell at you, and she likes those an unhealthy amount.

"She thinks you need more friends." Again, he speaks while looking at his phone, and for a second I wonder if he's even talking to me. Then the brutality of what he's said hits me in the gut.

"Wow," I say. "That's harsh."

"I was glad you went out last night. When I was your age, I partied my ass off."

"Right." I have no idea what is happening right now, and I'm reduced to single-word responses. Phil wears suits during the week and khakis on the weekend, and his pajamas have piping and buttons. I've only seen him in a T-shirt once in four years, that time he had the flu, and it had a collar and a logo of a man riding a horse. If I had said *ass,* he would have said, *Language, please.*

It's like he woke up this morning and put on his to-do list *Try to connect with Noah by using bad teenage slang.* Normally, Phil doesn't even speak English. He speaks C-SPAN.

"Tell her not to worry. I'm fine."

"Jack's a cool kid. I like him. I do. And I think your bro-mance is super cute. But you need more than Jack in your life."

"Super cute," I repeat, and lean hard enough on the sarcasm that hopefully even Phil will notice. I wish I had brought my phone down with me. Then I could look at it, the same way he's looking at his, and I could pretend this conversation isn't happening. I'd text Abbi something like *Thanks again* or *Fun hanging out last night* or *See you at camp* or maybe just a subtle *Hey*. Definitely no exclamation marks.

Probably better not to text her at all. Play it cool.

"You need a girlfriend," Phil declares.

"Working on it." This is a lie unless you count my foot tap, which I don't, because that would be ridiculous. I have no idea how one goes about making something like a girlfriend happen. My plan is to figure it out my freshman year of college, when I won't be surrounded by the same people I've gone to school with my whole life. When there will be girls who won't assume they already know everything there is to know about me just because we both had Mrs. Navarrette in the first grade.

I wonder what Phil would say if I told him about my Baby Hope plans. He'd probably tell me I'm an idiot. That I should ask Abbi out on a date and forget the rest.

"Good. That will make your mom happy," Phil says with a hint of finality, like he's done delivering an unsatisfactory performance review.

"I'll keep you regularly updated on my progress and I'll circle back to let you know if I score," I say in my best businessman imitation.

"Oh, that's not necessary."

"I was joking," I say.

"Right," Phil says. "Of course." And then he goes back to his phone.

CHAPTER TWENTY-ONE

Abbi

"The plan is to meet after work. There's a 7-Eleven five minutes from here, so we are on for Slurpees and Twizzlers," Noah says first thing Monday, and bounces on his heels.

"Did you have coffee or something? You seem, I don't know, extra happy?" I ask, looking him up and down. He's unusually energized, which is saying something, because Noah always has a bit of a terrier quality to him, like he was born to be a camp counselor for four-year-olds.

"Just a beautiful day. Life is good," he says, and I consider teasing him that he sounds like a yogurt commercial. Also, when you let yourself really think about it, the world can be a cruel, dark place. We all know that buildings explode sometimes for no apparent reason. Or for complicated geopolitical reasons that will never quite make sense. And sixteen-year-olds get things like the World Trade Center cough, and some not-so-old people lose their memory.

And yet, he's right. I look around and see that I'm surrounded by so much wonderful mundane joy. Life is good, for the most part, which is why we are all greedy about wanting more of it.

"So can you drive?" he asks again.

"Sure," I say, and smile, which somehow makes him smile even bigger.

"Thank you," he says. "For doing this."

"You didn't really leave me much choice."

"I know. But still. Thank you."

"Your earnestness is making me uncomfortable," I say.

"It's also deeply uncool. Can I stop now?"

I shrug.

"Stopping," he says.

And then he lightly kicks my foot, again the dumb flip-flops—just because I'm aware of my flaws doesn't mean I have the power to fix them—and runs away.

Later, in arts and crafts, while we're making bracelets on picnic tables, Julia comes and sits down on the bench next to me.

"Sorry about your car," she says. "I don't usually drink like that."

"No worries. There wasn't much to clean up," I say, and string an *A-B-B-I* onto a pink thread and hold up my wrist for her to tie it.

"There's another party this weekend. This time at Moss's house, if you want to go," Julia says.

"Moss?"

"The Rangers' counselor?"

I try to picture him but come up blank.

"Redheaded dude who looks like Ron Weasley?"

"Oh, that Moss." I have no idea who she's talking about, but there's no need for her to know that. "Right. I'm in," I say, and then, because I can't help myself, I ask: "Are you only inviting me because you threw up in my car?"

Julia smiles this weird cryptic smile she has, the one that makes it seem like she keeps all of her best thoughts to herself, and then she spins my bracelet around so that the *A-B-B-I* makes a whole revolution around my wrist.

Like that's an answer.

CHAPTER TWENTY-TWO

Noah

Here is a complete list of everything I know about my father:

His name was Jason Michael Stern and he was born on February 16, 1968. According to his gravestone, he was a "beloved son, husband, and father," though I'm not sure that tells me much. You have to be a major dick not to make the "beloved" cut after dying in a national tragedy.

He ate pickle sandwiches. Random, I know, but my mom threw me this bone once when I was six. I've hoarded this morsel for years, the way I imagine some people collect emergency kits in their basements. Like it will come in handy later for reasons yet unknown.

My mom has always been stingy about my dad. As if he is a zero-sum game, not a dead person. Jack says his mom does this too, though his dad is alive and well with a new wife and three kids in Orlando. Jack's mom will only talk about him after three glasses of merlot, and even then she won't talk about him directly. Instead, she takes out her phone calculator and figures out how much he owes her in child support. Which is a long way of saying that Jack thinks it's not that my mom doesn't want to share, it's that she's still too broken to discuss him.

I don't buy that theory. My mother was a badass single mom for most of my life. She worked her butt off to give me everything I've ever wanted or needed and has never once complained, no matter how much wine she has consumed. When I was a shithead in the second grade and I begged for name-brand clothes even though I knew money was tight, she found a way to buy them for me. When she'd cook dinner, she'd always have me eat first, and only years later did I realize that she wanted to make sure I had filled up before she took her share.

I think my dad is where she finally drew the line. She wanted to keep one thing for herself.

Other known details:

My father, like me, was an only child, and his parents died in a car accident when he was a teenager. He majored in political science at the University of Michigan, was Phi Beta Kappa, and then worked as a trader. Based on the files in the basement, he was a superproud nerd.

He liked to do rabbit ears over my mom's head in pictures and dress up in ridiculous costumes for Halloween.

In what I think is the second-to-last picture ever taken of him, dated September 9, 2001, he's hugging my mom right after they've learned that I'd need open heart surgery. He looks unshaven and tired and bone-deep sad.

Last potentially relevant fact: when we buried him, the box was empty.

CHAPTER TWENTY-THREE

Abbi

Noah buys me Twizzlers and Skittles and Oreos and a Slurpee and he doesn't complain when the bill comes to thirty dollars. He whips out a credit card and swipes and signs like this is money well spent, and we gather our goodies and get back into my car.

"What's her name?" he asks, making himself comfortable in the passenger seat. He puts his knees up on the dash, like he's been here before. Like he's my regular copilot.

"Who?"

"Your Prius. I assume you named your car, no?" He rips open the Twizzlers and hands me one. "All good cars should have a name."

"Do you anthropomorphize all appliances or just motor vehicles?" I ask.

"My electric toothbrush is named Stan," he says with a shrug, and I can't help it. I laugh. "So, for your car, how about Betty White?" He taps his Converse to the song playing on the radio—something Top 40 that I would have been too embarrassed to leave on had Cat or Ramona or Kylie been in my car. Some of the few perks of my new life: I own the radio and my Netflix queue and my choice of nail polish.

"Nah."

"Chuck E. Cheese."

"Still nope."

"Stranger? That way every time you get in the car, you can say 'Howdy, Stranger.'"

Noah takes my Slurpee from my cupholder, helps himself to a long sip. I can't decide if I like or hate his overfamiliarity. How is he already comfortable? I've spent thirty seconds thinking about how to put my hands on the steering wheel. Does leaving them at ten and two make me look uptight? I'm also concerned the Slurpee is going to turn my teeth red. And I'm terrified of seeing Chuck Rigalotti in the flesh. I don't want to turn him from a photograph into a real-life person.

"Not even getting warmer." I decide on ten and two but with my elbows down: casual but safe. I plan to occasionally reach over with my right hand and sip my Slurpee through the straw so it goes straight to the back of my throat.

"All right. I give up. I hereby vest in you the power of full naming rights." He does some weird arm-crossing thing, like a knight with a long sword or maybe what people do in church. "Though since it was my idea in the first place, I retain veto power."

"Seriously?"

"No. Not seriously at all. You should know by now that at least fifty percent of the stuff that comes out of my mouth is nonsense."

"So you don't own an electric toothbrush named Stan?"

Noah shakes his head, and I feel the slightest snag of disappointment. I liked knowing such an intimate detail about him. "Life can really suck, right? So why not make it at least a little bit fun whenever we can? I mean, think about it. There are few things that a well-timed joke can't solve."

"What are you talking about?" I ask. "When has a well-timed joke solved anything?" I think about how my mom told me that a few weeks after 9/11, a magazine cover declared irony dead, like everyone had decided they were all going to stop laughing forever. It was one way of declaring that life would never be the same again. Turns out they were wrong and they were right. "Also, we are here tracking down nine-eleven survivors for a high school newspaper. That's like the exact opposite of fun."

"True. But you can be serious and funny at the same time. We need the serious to recognize the funny, and the funny to give us even a shot in hell at surviving the serious," he says. "It's a really simple theory if you think about it. They're mutually dependent, not mutually exclusive."

I sit with that thought for a minute, let it roll around in my brain, wonder what exactly that magazine meant by *irony*, a word that makes me think of hipster mustaches and cheesy T-shirts. Then I realize that I'm no longer nervous.

Noah is just another person in the world.

So is Chuck.

So am I.

CHAPTER TWENTY-FOUR

Noah

This could be a major bust. Before we even ring the bell, the sad, patchy lawn tips me off. Flyers flap in the broken screen door like half-dead birds. Not that I had high hopes for ol' Chuck. He was a total asshole on the phone. All angry snark thinly disguised as genial teasing when I said we'd have to meet after camp.

"Camp?" he repeated, incredulous. Like it was funny that we were children and also that children were icky.

"We're *counselors,*" I said, like that would make any difference. As if I actually had some dignity that he'd affronted. He's right to make fun of us. Pretty much everything about being in high school is embarrassing. Not only the hours spent jerking off behind locked doors, the days cooped up in windowless classrooms—not to mention the greasiness of it all. I'm talking our very existence.

We are a reminder to grown-ups of how far they've come and how much further they wish they could go.

I wasn't nervous in the car with Abbi, hadn't thought much beyond snacks and talking crap and trying to make her laugh. Standing at the door, though, I start to sweat and wonder what the hell I think we're doing.

This happens to me all the time. Things seem like a good idea until suddenly they're not.

Chuck opens the door. He looks identical to the picture he has on his website. Same fake, aggressive smile. Same flat, serpentine eyes. He does a faux grand sweep of his arm, as if he is welcoming us into his castle, not this small house that is in desperate need of a paint job and a cuddle.

He steers us to a couch that has a blanket half-folded at the end. The front windows are open, so the smell of manure mixes with Chuck's house's scent: the sharp smell of bleach. He's cleaned up, presumably for our benefit. The glass coffee table has streaks. The blue carpet has vacuum lines. His hair is wet and combed over, and though he is middle-aged, he looks perversely boyish, like he should be wearing footie pajamas.

"Wow. Baby Hope. Look at you!" Chuck says. He's strong, with the kind of muscles that seem like genetic accidents. Thick and ropy and ready to snap. "I've thought a lot about you over the years. Strange to be part of something like that together and to have never even met. Of course, it's different for you. All front and center."

He sits across from us on a beat-up leather recliner, the only thing that looks loved in this house. He rests his elbows on his knees and then claps his hands a few times, as if to get us started. He's wearing a Jets T-shirt, and that makes me like him even less, and then I feel bad because I realize this can't be easy for him. "You're the symbol. We're just background players. Glad to see you doing well."

"I'm fine," Abbi says, shy and friendly at the same time, but I feel her stiffen next to me.

"I can't tell you how many times I've wondered about what happened to you," he says, and it occurs to me that this is far from the first time someone has said this to Abbi. How weird it must be to know strangers have thoughts about you. No one has thoughts about me, not even the other kids at school. The only exceptions: Jack, my mom, and when my mom tells him to, my stepdad.

"That's really kind," she says with a rehearsed graciousness.

"It's not kind, it's the truth," Chuck says.

"Nothing happened to me. Not really," Abbi says. Her voice gets small, and I fight the urge to put my arm around her, to protect her. I know why I'm here, and I'm going to keep doing this until I get my answers. But that doesn't make the situation comfortable for her. Or make me right.

"You grew up! Just like you were supposed to all along! *Life happened to you.* They didn't take everything. Okay," he says, and claps again. "You kids want a drink? It's hot out there. I could use a drink."

Chuck gets up without waiting for our answer, heads to what I presume is the kitchen, and comes back a few minutes later with a bottle of beer and two cans of Coke. He puts the soda in front of us, the beer in front of himself. If I were my stepdad and judgmental, I would note that it's three-thirty in the afternoon.

"I assume you didn't stop by to say hello," he says.

"Thanks for taking the time to meet with us," I say. "I wanted to ask you a few questions. About that day. We're tracking down all the people in that photo." I make a conscious effort to keep my leg from bouncing up and down. I don't want Chuck or Abbi to know I'm nervous.

"Why?" he asks.

"I think it makes a great piece for our school paper. Finding out what happened to the survivors. Hearing their stories," I say.

"*Stories,*" he repeats with the same bite he used on the phone for the word *camp.* "I hate that. How we aren't real people to anyone. We are *stories.*"

He speaks to Abbi. Not to me. I don't remind him that even he admitted to wondering about what happened to Baby Hope. That the curiosity is universal.

Of course, now would be a good time to play my own 9/11 card. I could explain that I am also in the club, free museum admission and everything. That might buy me some of Chuck's goodwill, though probably not Abbi's. I don't know. For whatever reason, I can't seem to say it out loud. It feels too much like a lie.

"I didn't mean to insult you. I'm a journalist, and—"

Chuck laughs right in my face and then covers his mouth like he didn't really mean it. I think about the picture and how tired I am of no one telling me anything. How tired I am of being fifteen and dismissible. I decide to go with one version of the truth.

"Fine, I'm not a real journalist. You're totally right. I'm a kid playing dress up, and most of the time I'm a big idiot. But I wasn't trying to say you're a story instead of a person. I think our stories are actually what make us people. We each have a history. You know what I mean?" I ask. Of course he doesn't know what I mean. "Stories are like the . . . currency of connection. And all your stories woven together might tell some larger story about the history of our country from that moment to now."

My voice has turned earnest and pleading. Not the tonal

shift I was going for. I was hoping I'd sound like a bit of Sorkin dialogue. Fast and sharp and convincing.

"Who is this kid?" Chuck asks Abbi, and then finishes his beer in a single long gulp. "'Stories are the currency of connection'? You read that in some book?"

I wonder if Chuck used to have a good sense of humor. If it was grief that turned him mean and replaced the funny parts with derision. Or if, like his being muscular, he was born that way. No trauma required.

"No," I say. "As nerdy as it sounds, I actually believe it."

"My story," Chuck starts, and for the first time since we've sat down, he doesn't look ready to pounce. He looks deflated, like that single beer let all the air out of his body. "My whole story is that I lived. That's really all there is to say, isn't there? I made it out to live this life of glory and bliss."

His lips turn up into a quivering smile. I hate those sorts of setups—when someone tells a joke they don't want you to laugh at. We wait out an interminable awkward silence. Abbi and I both look at our feet. What can we say to that? *Actually, sir, your life looks chock-full of glory and bliss?*

"The thing is, I was one person before, another person entirely after. You're too young to know what that's like. How one day, one single day, out of the clear blue sky, can change everything. And then the strangest part—and I'm not even kidding—the strangest part is that afterward, I was—that I am supposed to be—grateful," he says, and unlike with the words *camp* and *story*, there is no sarcastic emphasis on the word *grateful*. Only a disbelieving wonder.

"I still can't wrap my head around that part. That in the wake of something like that, our expectations get so whittled

105

down. Doesn't matter that I haven't slept well in fifteen years. God forbid a car backfires and I take cover like I was in 'Nam or something. Let's not even get started on my relationship with my wife. Well, ex now. But still, because I wake up each morning again and again, I'm supposed to be grateful?" He turns it into a question, like he really wants to know the answer. Like we are here to solve a mystery for him and not the other way around. "You know what would have been better than surviving nine-eleven? You know what I'd be truly grateful for? If it had never happened at all."

I don't say anything and neither does Abbi. I'm clearly a shitty journalist. I should ask him what that feels like: having everything change in a day. I should ask him if 9/11 is the reason he got divorced, as if that sort of thing can ever be easily traceable to a single incident. I should ask him whether he knows the other people in the photograph. Instead, I remember Poet, my old neighbor's dog, who one Sunday afternoon got run over by some jerk driving while texting on a cell phone. I heard the crack of Poet's neck from all the way across the street. Afterward, he lay broken in the road, and if you squinted you could almost pretend he was a squirrel.

Still, there was nothing to be done about the sound.

"Here's what I think about when I let myself think about that day, which I don't. Not if I can help it," Chuck says, and it occurs to me suddenly that we are asking so much more of him by coming here than I realized. "I think about a billion tiny shards of glass showering down like a hailstorm in hell. A month after, I had to have a piece of glass removed from my leg. I didn't notice until it got super infected. My wife liked to bring up that story, like it was indicative of everything that was wrong with me. As if I'm the type of person who walks around with a gaping wound and doesn't realize it. Never seemed fair of her, turning that story around like that."

Chuck stands up and leads the way to the door, his way of telling us he's finished. I may have judged him too quickly, looked at his falling house and his chugged beer and his stupid quips and assumed I knew all about him. I wish I could think of something to say now, like *Thank you* or *I'm sorry* or *I promise not to turn you into a metaphor like your ex-wife.*

Also, *I understand why you are done talking.*

"Thanks for stopping by, Hope," he says. "If you ever need anything, I'm here."

"It's Abbi," she says in a voice so quiet I don't think he hears her.

"You guys seem like good kids, so I'm truly sorry if I didn't give you what you came for. I am grateful to be alive. I am." His voice cracks, and he squeezes his eyes shut, then opens them again. "Even now, it's not easy to talk about."

I've never seen a grown man hold back tears. I mean, I've seen it on TV, not only on the terrible network dramas my mom loves, but during live newscasts from disaster zones. Never in person, though. Never close enough that I've had to decide how to respond or learned that it apparently triggers my own tear ducts.

All that comes to my mind to say is *There, there*—a dumb word, repeated twice, as if to maximize its dumbness.

Abbi, on the other hand, seems totally in her element. She leans on her tippy-toes and throws her arms around Chuck's neck. He hugs her back, not tight, like I would have guessed. Casual and unwound, like he's happy for the comfort. Like she has done the exact right thing by hugging him.

Hugging him was not in the top one million ideas I had

for dealing with this situation. Number two, after murmuring *There, there,* was to run.

"We're going to be okay," she says, and he nods, like those words mean something to him. A benediction. She smiles up at him, all calm and grace, and he, to my shock, smiles back. Abbi's a natural.

"You're right. We are," Chuck says.

I stare at the ground, then at the takeout menus stuck in the doorframe. I think about all the questions I couldn't bring myself to ask.

CHAPTER TWENTY-FIVE

Abbi

"That was decidedly not fun," I say. We're headed back home, and a sad pile of our cherry-scented trash sits at Noah's feet. The radio plays a weepy ballad about getting your heart stomped on with a cowboy boot, and though like pastel hair, love seems to be the kind of thing that happens only to other people, the song echoes in my bones. That's what happens when I play Baby Hope for an afternoon—everything feels like a performance.

"This is not going to be easy, is it?" Noah asks.

"Nope," I say, and think about how horrible it was to sit there and watch the words tumble out of Chuck's broken mouth. It's so odd to be a fun-house reflection of other people's feelings. Or maybe not even a reflection. Baby Hope is an *amplifier*. I'm not sure of the right way to react when you see a grown man like Chuck go wobbly from memories. My instinct is always to comfort, to overstep boundaries I'd never even consider crossing in any other context. In my non–Baby Hope life, I don't go around hugging strange men.

Does Chuck cough too? I wonder.

"I appreciate you not saying *I told you so*," Noah says.

"I told you so," I say, and he laughs.

"So I have a theory that you can tell a lot about a person by the way they eat an Oreo," he says after rummaging through the bag and pulling out a plastic tray of cookies.

"You have a lot of weird theories."

"Do you carefully open them and go for the cream first? Or do you eat the cookie? Or do you defer to the Man and eat them the way they came? There are a ton of options here," he says, and there's something about him spewing pure nonsense that lifts the mood in the car. We are intentionally letting the hard stuff evaporate.

"That's three options," I say, playing along. "Not exactly a ton."

"Perhaps you only eat them alone in your underwear. Or on your birthday, the whole box in one go. Or maybe you dip them in milk as a way to evoke nostalgia for your long-lost childhood."

"It's just a cookie."

"Technically, it's two cookies with cream between them."

"So you think these things actually matter? How you like to eat an Oreo? You sure this isn't small talk?" I ask. I let my mind settle on Noah, who I know is trying to distract me, or maybe us, from the scene we have fled. Sometimes it feels like those towers are still falling and will never stop.

"This is not small talk! Details totally matter. Take your car, for example. She's still, as yet, unnamed. She's also immaculate, or was until I got here, and look at this little basket you have in the front: Tissues. ChapStick. Even a flashlight. What is this? Holy crap, do you keep Mace? That's genius."

"Are you making fun of me?" I ask.

"No! Not at all. I think people don't pay enough attention to the small things about each other. But that's the really interesting stuff." Noah takes his Oreo, manages to split it so that the cream is evenly distributed, and hands me half.

"I always eat the middle first, and then I regret it because then I'm left with the crappy cookies," I say. "For the record, I've never eaten an Oreo in my underwear."

"Interesting, and not just because you mentioned your underwear, though feel free to do that more often."

"Come on," I say, though the corners of my mouth rise and my face grows warm.

"My point is, your delicate undergarments notwithstanding, if you bother to add up all the details of a person, if you pay close enough attention, that's how you get to a whole," he says. His knees are back on my dash, and his hands make a hammock for his head. "And you're interesting to me because, believe it or not, I'd like to be your friend."

"Friend? Or blackmailer?" I ask. I don't think I've ever heard someone say something like that out loud, like it's an easy thing to admit, like there are no consequences to opening yourself up to rejection: *I'd like to be your friend.*

"I'm a blackmailing friend."

"Or friendly blackmailer."

"You know what I think?" Noah asks, and turns in his seat to look at me. His big glasses can't hide the look in his eyes, which, like this day, somehow holds too much: curiosity and playfulness and also pain.

"About how I eat my Oreos fully dressed or about the fact

that I'm joking along with my blackmailer may mean I have Stockholm syndrome?"

"I think people sometimes get you confused with Baby Hope."

"But I *am* Baby Hope."

"No, you aren't. You're Abbi Goldstein, a girl who, I'm learning, has a weird affinity for Wonder Woman T-shirts and flip-flops and keeps Mace and also an alarming number of asthma inhalers in her car and feels regret every single time she eats an Oreo. What's Stockholm syndrome?"

"It's when people who are kidnapped start to sympathize with their captors," I say.

"I did not kidnap you. For the record."

"It was me on the front page of the freakin' *New York Times* almost sixteen years ago," I say. "I am Baby Hope."

"No. It was a *picture* of you. Big difference."

"Is there, though? You said yourself that our stories are what make us who we are."

"You didn't write the Baby Hope story. I'm not saying you don't bear the burden of it, you obviously do, but you didn't write it. So it's not yours. Not really," he says, and I swat away the single tear that makes a slow, unexpected line down my left cheek.

That might be the most insightful thing anyone has ever said to me.

CHAPTER TWENTY-SIX

Noah

When I get home, my mom and Phil are sitting on the couch watching the news. Phil is typing on his laptop, immersed in work, as usual. I notice that my mom is crying next to him.

"Everything okay?" I ask.

"The world is a terrible, horrible, no-good, very bad place sometimes, and it doesn't need to be," she says, and then looks back to the screen, which shows the aftermath of another mass shooting, this time at a middle school in the Midwest. Forty-five kids dead in the span of a six-minute spree. I turn away. I've seen enough tragic shit for the day.

"You sure?"

"Come give me a hug. That will help," she says, and so I lean down and let her throw her arms around my neck. She inhales deeply—and I realize she's actually sniffing me, like I still have the comforting smell of the top of a baby's head—and I stifle my sigh at her overwhelming mom-ness.

"Your mother is too sensitive," Phil says, in a patronizing voice, like my mom is both charming and idiotic. Once I'm freed from her embrace, I resist the sudden urge to clock him in the face.

Forty-five kids dead.

I don't do anything, though, because I am me, and Phil is Phil, and also I've never hit anyone in my life, other than Jack in the third grade. If I actually did it, put my fist to Phil's nose, I think his number one concern would be whether he got blood on the couch.

I kiss my mom four times on the top of her head, which has always been our thing, and run upstairs to my room before I break something.

I don't let myself spend too much time thinking about how my mother married a bowl of oatmeal. How she is crying not just about those dead kids, but probably about my dad too. How in fifteen years there might be a me in that Midwestern town who selfishly decides his own personal questions are important enough to awaken half-sleeping wounds.

CHAPTER TWENTY-SEVEN

Abbi

I run straight to the guest room, anxious and eager to get a glimpse of my recently arrived grandmother. She's lying on the bed, the one with the new hospital-like guardrails you can pull up if necessary. Her arms are crossed and her hazel eyes are wide open. Still as a picture. She doesn't look any different from the last time I saw her, which was a couple of months ago over spring break. She has her long gray hair tied into her signature side braid, like a sister wife, and wears a faded black T-shirt with her lucky blue jeans.

"What are you doing?" I ask, because that's how it's always been between us. No need for formalities, the hellos and the goodbyes and the see you laters of life. We've always jumped right in.

"Playing dead," my grandmother says, her voice warm and friendly and clear and one hundred percent alive. I feel a rush of relief. With only two words, I can tell she knows exactly who I am.

"Umm, why?" I step farther into the room and catalog some more. Maybe there are a few extra strands of white in her hair. A few new lines on her forehead. Her hands, which used to be soft and playful, now look ancient and gnarled, hardened at the tips of her long fingers.

But the rest, the vast majority of her: same.

Or at the very least: familiar, recognizable.

"Just practicing," she says.

"Doesn't seem like the sort of thing you need to practice for."

"It's good to be prepared."

"No one has said anything about you dying," I say.

"Everyone dies, Abbi Hope. You of all people should know that." My heart clenches for a minute and I think: *She knows. Of course she knows.* I feel a burden blissfully unravel. And then I realize she's talking about 9/11, about the baby me. Of course she doesn't know about the cough.

"True. Seems silly to practice, though." I move closer. I want to hug her, to scoop her up like she's four years old and toddler-sized. I've never before felt that impulse with my grandmother. I used to crawl into her lap and sit on her like she was a comfy chair. I used to slip my snot-covered hand into her hand whenever I could reach, like Livi does to me.

I used to look up at her. Not down. Never down.

"Come over here and tell me everything," she says, and she starts to rise, slow and steady, a multistep process involving her elbows, then her wrists, and then her gnarled hands. Once she's up, she grabs me in a tight hug.

"You smell the same," she says, and it occurs to me that she's looking at me much the way I'm looking at her. Cataloging my changes.

"So do you," I say.

"I wish I could bottle up your smell. Weird to think that will go. Even my sensory memories are going to escape me." My grandmother's voice is resolute. She's the one who gave my mom her stoicism. In my mother it takes on a cheery perversion, but my grandma is all strong, clean lines when it comes to the difficult stuff. She's stating a fact, true words without any sentimentality. The day after my grandfather, her husband for over four decades, died, my grandmother climbed out of bed, brushed her teeth, walked downstairs and brewed a pot of coffee for the rest of us. Sliced bagels and set out the cream cheese and lox. Once we had all eaten and caffeinated, she clapped her hands and said, "Okay, where do we start?"

"Listen, I want to prepare you. Today is a good day. Tomorrow might be bad. That's how it seems to go with this thing," she says, and she's so much the same, so much my grandmother—she's taking care of me, again making everyone else coffee, when she's the one in pain—that I ache. "Your mom says I went out without pants. That's why I'm here."

"Apparently you gave the entire state of Maine a pretty good show," I say, and we sit side by side. I'm cross-legged, like my campers, ankle on knee. "But whatever. You have great legs."

"Totally," she says, stretching them out as if to admire them. Then she takes my hands in hers and stares at my palms. Traces the lines like there's something to be deciphered, like she's trying to make my details stay still. "I don't remember. It's like it happened to someone else. I asked your mom for a photo for proof. She showed me the police report. Fortunately, there were no actual pictures."

"I'm so sorry, Grandma." I try to imagine what that must feel like. To have whole patches of your memory vanish. Something empty that should be full. I try to imagine having to look at a photo to prove something happened to you, and then I realize that of course I've been doing that for forever.

"Don't be. Life with a capital *L*. So, tell me about you."

"Nothing to tell," I say. "You know. Status quo."

"I heard Cat dropped you." Despite myself, I laugh. With my grandma's martyrdom comes bluntness. When puberty first hit and my face erupted in acne, she'd looked at me and said, "Well, the good news is that awkward phases help with long-term personality development."

"People outgrow each other sometimes," I say, and though I don't mean it physically, I can't help but look down at my body. I could easily pass for twelve years old. I wonder if it's that simple. Not that I'm short, but that I didn't even try to keep pace with my friends. That they were moving faster toward adulthood—or at least one version of it—than I was. Which is ironic, considering what has happened since. All the ways time has now changed for me and zoomed forward.

"I say go find new friends," my grandmother says, and her hands move on to my arms, cradle my elbows, the slope of my neck. Like she's reading braille. "Ones that fit better."

"I'm trying," I say.

"Want to practice being dead with me? It's weirdly fun," she says.

"Sure."

And so we both fall backward, flat on our backs, and our hands clasp automatically. We may no longer be in her old house in Maine. I may no longer be six years old and entertained by something as small as putting a colander on my head. And yet, we find ourselves palm to palm, like always, each of us reaching for the other.

Together we practice. We keep our eyes open, though. Just in case.

CHAPTER TWENTY-EIGHT

Noah

Back in the safety of my room, I take out my phone, but I can't concentrate. Jack texts asking if I am coming over and I write back: *Long day.* I can't stop seeing Chuck and his cracked-open face. Or Abbi's eyes as she leaned in to hug him. Those kids dead on the news.

Crap. Today was brutal.

Jack's doppelgänger explanation is bullshit. Photographs don't lie. Still, there has to be a way to do this that doesn't take Abbi down with me. I wish I knew what that was.

I type: *Abbi, I'm sorry.*

I delete. Start over: *We don't have to do this.*

I try again: *I'm not really an asshole. There's something I should tell you.*

On the car ride home, we were able to move away from Chuck. The two of us hanging out in her little Prius, headed somewhere we didn't mind going. Despite everything, we had fun.

Not sure why I feel the heaviness again, like Chuck has followed me into this house and up the stairs and into my bedroom.

I cut and start over: *Thanks for today. You're the best.*

I click send and then power down my phone so I can't see if she writes me back.

CHAPTER TWENTY-NINE

Abbi

Three days after the Chuck interview, I'm surprised to find myself, of all places, in Jack's basement, sitting with Jack and Noah and nibbling on salami from an artfully arranged platter of fancy snacks that includes three varieties of cheese. But here I am on an old couch that looks passed down a few generations and has gaping holes that spit out fluffy yellowed guts, right in the middle of the two boys. We face a dark television set, and we line our feet up on the coffee table, like a picture on an indie album cover. Converse, flip-flops/glitter-toes, Vans. All dirty and well loved.

"So you going to Moss's party this weekend?" I ask about an hour into our impromptu hangout. I still don't know who Moss is, but I like the way it feels to drop his name, to let Noah and Jack think that I am the type of person who gets invited to parties. Which is silly because they know full well that I'm not. In fact, when Noah invited me over this afternoon, he actually said the words *You don't have plans after camp, right?*

"You're going?" Noah asks. I feel relieved that he doesn't sound surprised.

"With Julia. I bet it would be okay if you came too." I have no idea if it's okay for me to invite people to the party of a person I have never met. I suspect that as soon as we get there, Zach will work his mojo on Julia and I will again be left to fend for myself.

And who knows? Maybe Noah and Jack could become my real friends, which is something that would have seemed absurd to me even a week ago. Yet, here we are. Eating cheese and crackers and cured meats. Despite the blackmail, things are surprisingly not awkward.

Noah looks at Jack, and Jack looks back at Noah.

"That'd be great," both of them say, in unison. Then they laugh. In unison.

"We spend a frightening amount of time together, if you haven't noticed," Noah says.

"That's why we lured you over. We desperately need to mix things up." Jack runs his hands over his mini-Mohawk, not so much a nervous gesture, like Noah's hair rub, as a contemplative one. "Hey, you think I could invite Brendan to the party?"

"Who's Brendan?" I ask.

"So give me your take on this," Jack says, and leans forward. "There's this guy at the supermarket. He works a lane over. Everyone else thinks he's straight."

"He has a tattoo of a mermaid. A boobtastic one. On his bicep," Noah says. "I think it's fair to say *he* thinks he's straight."

"I never should have told you about that," Jack says.

"He has a tattoo? How old is this guy?" I ask.

"Tattoos. Plural. Seventeen. He's in community college,"

Jack says. "But, like, his tough outsides don't necessarily match his warm and mushy insides."

"Tell me more," I say, relishing this. I had forgotten how good it can feel to get out of your own head and become invested in someone else's life for a change.

"He's smart and nice, in a good way, not in an annoying way. He gives me these looks. I swear he finds excuses to ruffle my hair. I can't explain it. I get a vibe. It's not often I meet, like, good guys who give off a vibe," Jack says.

"What kind of vibe specifically?" I ask. "A gay or bi vibe?"

"The vibe that says *Let's go make out in the back next to the frozen fish because I think I dig you,*" Jack says.

"That's pretty specific. Why the frozen fish? What about the cup o'noodles?" Noah asks. "Or the aluminum foil?"

"Noah doesn't want me to be happy because then he'll be left all alone in his lonesome lonerdom of loneliness," Jack says.

"He's right," Noah says, deadpan. "Not about me being lonely, but about me not wanting him to be happy."

"So what do you think?" Jack asks me.

"I'm not going to lie and tell you that the mermaid tattoo doesn't concern me," I say with a smile.

"Okay," he says.

"If he doesn't want to make out with you by the frozen fish, there are lots of other guys who will. You're a catch of epic proportions," I say, not caring that I sound a little too earnest.

"No pun intended," Noah says, but we ignore him.

Jack leans back against the couch and turns to me. "Wow. That's so, I don't know, sweet of you. I feel tingly all over now."

"I'm good at pep talks. It's one of my fortes," I say.

"Seriously," Jack says, and it occurs to me that if you are

going to judge someone by their choice of best friend, a way better metric than someone's outsides, Jack reflects well on Noah.

"Do I invite him to the party?" Jack asks.

"Maybe in a casual way? Not in an *I'm hoping we're going to make out* sort of way," I declare with the authority of someone who knows stuff like this, even though I do not know stuff like this. I'm surprised by how civilized things are in this basement of boyness. There is truffle in the cheese. I imagined that we'd play loud video games, that I'd be inundated by the smell of socks, that there would be some awkwardness alleviated by staring at our respective phones. If we were at Cat's—the old Cat's—we'd be eating microwave popcorn straight from the bag and scrolling through Instagram.

"Asking for a friend here," Noah says. "What specifically would be the way to ask that would say *I'm hoping we're going to make out?*"

"I think it's all in the subtext. A certain look," I say. "Also, I'd stay away from the bad puns."

"Never. Puns are the tiny hill I'm willing to die on. So subtext like this?" Noah asks, and he stares at me with comically puppy dog pleading eyes and bats his long eyelashes. I crack up. "How'd I do, Abs?"

"Did you just call me Abs?"

"I did. Are we not there yet? To the Abs stage?" Noah asks, his face restored to normalcy. He holds up a piece of cheese and examines it from all angles before popping it in his mouth.

"There is no Abs stage," I say. "No one calls me Abs."

"Asking for a friend here," Jack says, "but what specifically would be the way to get to the Abs stage if hypothetically there were one?"

"You guys, I'm telling you there's no Abs stage," I say. "Not even hypothetically."

"I think there's an Abs stage," Jack says. "Definitely."

"We'll see," Noah says. "I'm optimistic."

"Do you normally put out fancy platters like this when you guys hang out?" I ask.

"I told you we went overboard with the cheese," Noah says to Jack.

"No, you didn't. You said we should get olives too," Jack says.

"He's right. I totally said that," Noah says, without a single trace of sarcasm. And then he smiles—a big goofy smile—right at me.

When I get home, my mom is drinking a glass of white wine on our front porch. She sits on the swinging bench, which until this moment I always assumed was purely for decorative purposes.

"What's up?" I ask, and point to the bottle, which rests next to her.

"Just enjoying the summer night. It's beautiful, isn't it?" My mom's voice has that weird dreamy quality again, like she's just gotten back from a meditation retreat. I find myself missing the chipper version of her even though her cheerfulness sometimes rings false and grates on my nerves. This Zen impersonator feels foreign. Did someone take away my mother's coffee and replace it with Xanax? Is she high? As far as I know, my parents don't get high. Not their style. They prefer endorphins from jogging or a caffeinated kick. If they were to dabble in drugs, it would be of the high-performance variety.

"I guess," I say, and sit down next to her on the bench. I ease down slowly, afraid the thing will collapse. The street is empty, and except for the faint buzzing of cicadas, it's quiet. The sky expands above us, an endless, deep thick purple.

"Want to hear something awful? Grandma told me that I've made her proud as a daughter. It sounded like she had things she needed to say. And you know what I did? I changed the subject to the weather." My mom takes another sip of wine and closes her eyes for a second.

"Mom, it's okay. She knows. . . ."

"I actually did that. I changed the subject to the weather. *What a hot summer we're having.* Like I couldn't be bothered to hear her out."

"You're allowed to be human occasionally," I say, and my lungs catch and stutter as if waterlogged.

"We aren't even having a hot summer! Sorry. This is harder than I thought it would be," my mom says, and I slip my hands into hers. She grips my fingers.

"What is?" I ask.

"Everything."

"Grandma?"

"All of it. When you pulled up in the car, you looked like a woman, not a girl. And to be honest, before now, I never really let myself imagine it. I dunno, after everything, I've been weirdly superstitious. Like if I let myself see you as an adult, something would snatch you away. And now the world is going to."

"Mom."

"No. It's a good thing! That's what's supposed to happen. I keep thinking about that horrible shooting. The forty-five parents at that middle school getting calls that their kids were never coming home. I'm so, so tired of always worrying about our world splitting into a before and an after again."

I ignore the icy feeling climbing up my back, the image of a shard of glass embedded in Chuck's leg, my cough that erupts just because I'm thinking about it. When I heard the news on the radio driving home earlier in the week, I shut it off.

An idea comes: *Tell her.*

My mother scoots me closer to her on the bench for her own comfort, not mine. I assumed that my plan this summer—my eight weeks of ignorant bliss—was a selfish one, me indulging my need for a little more joy in the *before,* but I realize with a start that it might also be the *right* thing, the *brave* thing, to let the truth stay buried for a little while longer.

My mother has finally allowed herself the fantasy of my growing up. So much guilt finally giving way to optimism. I will not be responsible for destroying her dreams. Not while my mom's already in the process of losing someone else.

"I'm not grown. I'm not even five feet." I kick up to show her my tiny size-four-and-a-half flip-flops. My toenails are painted with silver glitter. I'm wearing a string ankle bracelet a camper made for me. No one could mistake me for a woman.

"I didn't say you looked *tall.* Pretty soon you'll be on your own, though. Far away at college."

"We have a whole year," I say, careful to use a tone of not quite promising.

She pours more wine. Looks up at the sky, now more gray, finding its way to black.

"Mom, are you okay? For real?"

"This is what we experts call a midlife crisis. Nothing to worry about." She smiles and looks like herself. As bright and shiny as my sparkling toenails. Once again the person who used to give my boo-boos magic kisses whenever I fell. Who would sometimes sweep me up so fast, I wouldn't even notice that I'd touched the ground in the first place. Always with the same refrain: *You're okay, sweetheart. You're okay.* "By the way, your dad is coming over for dinner."

"Really?" My dad is never home this early.

"Well. Lasagna," she says, like that explains it, when what she really means is he's checking up on Grandma. I thought one of the reasons people got divorced was so they don't have to have dinner with each other's parents.

My mom pumps her legs back and forth, as if this is a playground swing, as if she thinks we can get somewhere if we push hard enough. I decide to lift my feet and join her. Who cares that we have nowhere to reach for? That our swing may become untethered and collapse? I'm looking for joy in this moment.

We push back and forth till the sky goes fully dark. Till it turns the color of goodbye.

CHAPTER THIRTY

Noah

There's this great episode of *Comedians in Cars Getting Coffee* in which Jerry Seinfeld and John Oliver fall in comedy love and talk about how they both have such a compulsive need to make other people laugh that it borders on sociopathy. No matter the circumstances, they're always looking for the funniest angle. In Trevor Noah's episode, he tells Seinfeld how stand-up in South Africa was illegal until about twenty years ago because telling jokes was considered a dangerous and powerful expression of free speech.

I'm pretty sure Jerry and John and Trevor would all agree with me that a really good joke could save the world.

CHAPTER THIRTY-ONE

Abbi

"Don't look now," Noah says, and I reflexively start to move my head, which happens whenever someone says the words *don't look now*. "But Cat is here."

I catch myself just in time. We are at Moss's party, loitering in the foyer because he apparently lives in a house on steroids and it's overwhelming. Two huge columns flank the entrance, each with a giant white marble lion at its side, both of which are currently wearing fluorescent pink Troll wigs. Naked statues spit water into the air at random, a chandelier the size of a horse dangles threateningly over our heads, and there's gold embroidered into the wallpaper. According to Jack, who it turns out might be one of those people who secretly knows all the good gossip, Moss's dad was the sixth investor in Snapchat and is now on the *Forbes* 400 list.

I shouldn't be surprised to see Cat. It seems like every teenager in New Jersey is here. Probably even some rich kids from Manhattan who tunneled their way over. Still, I bought into the fiction that my summer life with camp people would be like visiting Vegas—what happens there stays there.

"Can she see me?" I ask, holding myself perfectly still, like I'm doing the mannequin challenge.

"Why are you frozen? Move," Jack says. "Look natural. Be normal."

"I forgot how to do that." Again I have the arm problem. Where do they go? Up? Down? Do I cross them?

"She's here with that guy we saw her with the other night at the store," Noah says, looking over my shoulder.

"Hans," I say, and decide to put my hands on my hips, which I read in a magazine is flattering in photographs. I have no idea if it works in person.

"His name is definitely not Hans. Mike, maybe," Jack says.

"It's Hans in my head. Cat would never date a Mike."

"You're so much weirder than I thought," Noah says, and then does his cute hair-ruffle thing. He peeks over my shoulder again. "Wow, Cat looks wasted."

"You can tell from here?" I decide not to turn around. If I'm careful enough, we can avoid each other, like we did at school. At Oakdale, whenever I'd see anyone who even slightly resembled Cat, any flash of ubiquitous purple hair, I'd hide in a classroom or a bathroom.

The irony is not lost on me that my reaction to my friend's having outgrown me is super immature.

"She's throwing her arms in the air, waving like she just doesn't care," Noah says flatly.

"She was shit-faced last week too," Jack says. "I thought she was going to christen my car."

"Julia christened my car after Tash's party," I say.

"You're so not supposed to tell people about that," Julia says, popping up next to me. I assumed she was off with Zach, taking more photos to glam up her already glamorous-in-a-down-to-earth-way Instagram feed.

If you don't take a picture and post it, did it really happen? Cat used to ask. *No, no, it didn't,* she'd respond. And then she'd hold out her phone—she had the longest arms—and we'd all pose. Sometimes she'd even say *Duck faces, ladies.* Here's the strangest part: I would always listen. I would pout on command if Cat was the one asking.

"I'm keeping the drink I got you to make up for it," Julia says. She takes a sip of something that looks like Kool-Aid. Childishly red in a clear plastic cup. "Why are you standing so strangely?"

"My ex–best friend is over there."

"Oooh, I have one of those. They're seriously worse than bad breakups," Julia says, and then hands me her drink. "Fine, you need this more than me. And I say that even though Zach is making out with Tash in the corner."

I take a swig, and it burns going down. Definitely not Kool-Aid.

"Zach is a dick," Noah says.

"Totally," Julia admits. "And yet—"

"Can I ask you something?" Jack asks. "Is it his dickishness that makes you like him?"

"Who are you?" Julia asks.

"I'm Jack. Noah's friend. Abbi's too."

"It's not his dickishness. That's not really my thing. I like that he's full of surprises. Like you don't expect a guy in a fedora to be able to do a yoga headstand. Look at him. He's wearing overalls. I mean really? Overalls." Julia smiles as she says this, her voice thick with affection, even though we're all looking straight at Zach sticking his tongue down Tash's throat. They're no longer in a corner but in the center of the foyer, as if the party should revolve around them.

"I will never understand women," Noah says. He takes off his glasses and cleans them with the corner of his shirt, pops them back on. "If I wore overalls you guys would never let me live it down. Why does he get to wear them?"

"Do you *want* to wear overalls?" I ask.

"Not even a little bit, but that's not the point," Noah says.

"It's all about confidence," Julia says.

"But I have confidence!" Noah shouts, trying to make himself heard over the loud thumping music that has started playing. Is that a live band in the backyard? Who the hell is this Moss?

"Not enough to wear overalls, though," Jack says.

"Exactly," Julia says. "Exactly."

About half an hour later, one red drink under my belt, I'm feeling warm and loose and happy. Jack, Julia, Noah, and I wind through the crowds with linked arms, a merry band of new friends, and this way, with them literally attached to my limbs, I stop worrying about Cat. There must be at least three hundred people here. In the backyard, four kids with loud electric guitars pound away on a makeshift stage. The only reason this party hasn't been broken up by the neighbors is because I don't think there are any. Beyond the huge lawn, all I see are towering walls. I wouldn't be surprised if there's a moat.

"Have you seen Charles?" Julia asks once we've settled into a new spot, a little away from the music so we can hear ourselves talk.

"Lifeguard Charles?" I ask.

"Yup. Though I think he just goes by Charles in the wild," Julia says.

"Have you seen Brendan?" Jack asks. "He texted and said he might come. What do you think that means?"

"I think that means he might come," Julia says, who is now double-fisting the not-Kool-Aid because the line for the bar wraps around one of the verandas and is chock-full of grope-y drunk boys. "Who's Brendan?"

"The guy Jack is into who has a questionable tattoo and may or may not want to make out with him near the frozen fish at the supermarket where he works," I say.

"There are so many sexier sections," Noah says. "I don't get it."

"I'd pick the bakery," I say.

"Really?" Noah asks, like I meant it seriously.

"Is there a coffee shop? That would be my top choice. No rotisserie chicken smell," Julia says. "Or maybe I'd go the whole opposite direction. Lean into it. Sushi."

"I hadn't thought of sushi," Jack says, considering. "But it's not just about making out. I actually like him."

"How about produce? You'd get those awesome thunder sound effects before the spritzing," Noah says. "Very romantic, right? Like a summer rain shower."

"You're cute," Julia says, turning to Noah. "How old are you again?"

"Almost sixteen."

"Never mind," Julia says, and pretends to swipe right with her hand. "Too young for me."

Noah catches my eye over her head and exaggeratedly cocks his right eyebrow like he's scandalized. I laugh.

"Not even a whole year younger than Abbi, though," Noah says, and this time when he looks at me, he holds the eye contact, long enough that I feel it all the way down to my toes.

We sit on the back steps, me between Jack and Noah, and act like partygoing is a spectator sport. Julia found Charles, and now they're across the lawn chatting but not really chatting. More like the kind of close-face talking that is the flirty precursor to kissing. If I knew she wouldn't kill me, I'd totally stand up and cheer.

"I don't think Brendan is coming," Jack says, and leans all the way down to rest his weary head on my shoulder. I pet it because that's what you do with an adorable head like his.

"He might," I say. "And if he doesn't, I think . . ."

I trail off because suddenly Cat is right in front of me, and I can't for the life of me figure out why. We have an unspoken rule. She might not have ducked into as many bathrooms as I did last year, but I know she has done her part to avoid me. Why stop now? I moved on, just like she wanted me to.

Cat has a goofy smile on her face. Friendly, slightly amused. Like nothing has changed, like the calendar has rewound a full 365 days and we are at this party together.

"Hey!" she says, not a hint of fear in her voice. I wonder if drinking has made her brave before I remember that Cat has always been brave. Her favorite life hack has always been unearned confidence. *If you act like you know what you're talking about, people believe you,* she'd say. *If you want something, ask. It's not that hard.*

This is a lie. It just wasn't ever that hard for her.

How long has it been since we've actually spoken? Months. Cat and I spent almost a decade and a half in continuous conversation, and now she's turned into a stranger. Except she's not, because months don't actually erase years, do they? I feel like all those words must still exist, like there's a towering pile of them somewhere, though I can't decide if they belong in a museum or a landfill. Who knows? Maybe they could find a home at the Baby Hope exhibit.

"Hi?" I'm not rude exactly, not as rude as I could be. Still, remembering how it all went down—how it felt to open up Instagram that day and to see confirmation that my friends had all left me behind—keeps me from tone matching. I wonder where Ramona and Kylie are and then realize I don't care.

"I'm surprised to see you here! I mean . . . it's cool that you are. . . ." Cat stops, steadies herself. Starts over. "I mean, just because we aren't best friends anymore doesn't mean, you know, that we can't be . . ."

"Can't be what?" I ask, and I'm genuinely curious. What can't we be? This seems as good a question as any, though I have a treasure trove of things I want to know from Cat: *How did we become so different without my noticing? When did you become someone who could so easily disregard my feelings?*

Or: *Do you miss me too sometimes?*

Or even: *Are you okay?*

Both Noah and Jack scoot closer to me.

Can't be what? will have to do.

"You know. People who know each other," Cat says.

"That's the problem," I say, looking straight into her drunk eyes, emboldened by Jack and Noah. Emboldened by the realization that Cat ended our friendship with a lie instead of an explanation. I deserved more than that, even if we'd have ended up in the exact same place. Turns out her answers aren't the only ones that matter. "I'm not sure I actually know you anymore."

Then I stand up, and so do Jack and Noah, and without saying anything else, the three of us walk away.

I mentally check "for once get the last word" off my bucket list.

"Thanks, guys," I say a few minutes later, after I've taken a moment with my head between my knees to catch my breath.

"We didn't do anything," Noah says. He rubs my back a few times and I close my eyes, and when I open them again, he drops his hand.

"I normally run away and hide whenever she's around." My face warms again, and as I sit up the wooziness returns. "Wow, totally didn't mean to admit that out loud."

"I get it," Jack says. "She's a little scary."

"She is, right?" I ask. "I think it's the overconfidence."

"Cat could totally rock overalls," Noah says, almost wistful. I wonder if he likes Cat and if that's why he and Jack gave her a ride home the other day. He seems like the kind of guy who would get massive unrequited crushes on cute, quirky girls like her. It's not like I don't understand. I've had a platonic crush on her almost the entirety of my life. I spent years orbiting Planet Cat and I never minded a single bit that she was the one who got all the attention. Preferred it, actually. She gave me cover.

I don't like the thought that Noah would want anything to do with her.

"Why am I such a wimp?" I ask. I knot my hair into a bun on the top of my head and fan myself. Could Cat possibly like

Noah back? He's not really her type—she always said she likes men, not boys—but Noah has a certain stealthy charm. Even Julia isn't immune.

"You're not a wimp," Jack says. "You seem really brave."

"Please tell me you don't mean the Baby Hope crap," I say.

"God, no," he says. "I mean how you seem to be exactly yourself wherever you are. You are the same person at a party as you are in my basement as you are at school. You know, I once saw you eat lunch by yourself on the bleachers last year. You didn't hide out and eat in the library like I do when Noah's not there. You could have, but you didn't."

"I have this weird thing about fresh air," I say.

"Screw Cat," Noah says. "Seriously, screw her."

"She's not a bad person," I say. "She's . . ." I trail off because I don't know what she is. *Selfish. Impulsive and decisive. Easily bored.*

"I don't think she even recognized me as the guy who drove her home last week," Jack says. "I think that tells us all we need to know." I don't say it—it's no longer my job to defend her—but it doesn't really tell us all we need to know, because the old Cat might have been self-obsessed, but she was also funny and kind and strong. Which I realize now is why we never had the talk about us growing in different directions. That would have required a cruelty she didn't possess.

"You know what I think? I think the reason high school sucks is because it feels so small. Like a too-tight turtleneck," Noah says. "And even if you are brave enough to molt, there's all these people around you still, like, holding up and showing you your old skin."

"That's both beautiful and gross," Jack says.

"But soon our worlds are going to get bigger. Like exponentially," Noah says, ignoring Jack's gentle teasing. He throws his head back and looks up at the sky as if examining its vastness. It's dark and cloudy, but I bet he's picturing it bright blue. "And then there will be so much more fresh air for you to breathe. There will be more room to just be."

"I meant the fresh-air thing literally. Not like a metaphor," I say, and nudge Noah with my shoulder to let him know that I'm also gently teasing. I understand his point, though. You would think that the cough would help put all this stuff in perspective—a small thing versus everything. I think Julia might be right. Heartbreak is heartbreak. The fact that it already hurts less doesn't mean it doesn't matter. "So what will college feel like, then? A loose tank top? A poncho?"

"A cape," Noah says, and grins his goofiest grin. "I think once we break free of this place we're going to wander the whole world in capes."

"Way better than overalls," I say. Suddenly this moment is bursting with all the warm goodness of being surrounded by people who get you—a feeling I've been lacking as of late— and Noah and Jack both throw their arms around my shoulders and pull me into a group hug. Though I literally can't breathe smooshed between them, no fresh air to be found, I close my eyes and smile.

CHAPTER THIRTY-TWO

Noah

Here's my plan: I'll take the two pictures from my backpack and present them to Abbi side by side today at camp. I won't be all dramatic, like a prosecutor on TV. I'll slip them out, super casual and calm, and say *Hey, do you see what I see?*

The unidentified man in the University of Michigan hat.

The picture of my dad hugging my mom on September 9.

Same stubble and tired eyes. Same face.

But whenever I spot Abbi across the soccer field, or by the plake, or in the arts and crafts cabin, her hair pulled back in a ponytail, her arms around little Livi's shoulders, she smiles at me, warm and open and bright, like we are finally on the same team. Like we've pulled past obligation, past her equating me with blackmail, and moved on to fully solid ground.

A leap closer to the Abs stage.

I run through every scenario. I imagine her repeating Jack's theory about doppelgängers. I imagine her saying exactly what my mom said when I asked her: "Noah, that's not your dad, because that guy obviously lived." I imagine Abbi getting furious and calling the whole project off. I imagine her slapping me across the face, which is ridiculous. She's way more likely to knee me in the nuts.

The only thing I can't imagine: her telling me I might be right.

Her grabbing my hand and saying *Let's do this. Let's go find your dad.*

The photos stay in my bag, unseen, right where they've been all along.

CHAPTER THIRTY-THREE

Abbi

"I saw that six-pack and assumed that anyone who takes the time to shred their body like that must be dumb. I was wrong," Julia says to me. We are dangling our legs in the water at morning swim. At the other end, Lifeguard Charles presides over the plake like a king. "He's really smart. He goes to Wesleyan!"

"Wow," I say.

"Right? I don't know why I was so fixated on Zach. Did you see him meditating this morning at check-in? Come on. If you're actually serious about meditating, you don't do it with six hundred kids running around. He's always working so hard to craft his image. I think he thinks it looks like he's not trying at all, but it's the total opposite," Julia says, and then splashes her legs to cool off. We are in the middle of a heat wave—103 degrees and humid—and my lungs feel sluggish. My cough has been coming in frequent fits today, rough and hacking, so I keep tissues and a water bottle with me at all times. So far no blood, but I feel it pulsing through my veins, too close to the surface. Like it's waiting for the right moment to burst through. "Charles is on the swim team."

"That explains his stomach," I say, and steal a glance at him. He looks outrageously handsome without his T-shirt and in his red lifeguard shorts. His bare chest is accessorized by a whistle on a pink lanyard and what it turns out is the exact right amount of chest hair—and if you had asked before this moment what the exact right amount of chest hair is for a guy, I admit I wouldn't have been able to answer. He doesn't look like an actual real-life person who wakes up with morning breath or gets wedgies or occasionally stubs a toe. Nope, he's like an advertisement for youth, or maybe milk. Staring at him now, basking in his glow, I find I'm not into him. Not despite his perfection but because of it. Unlike Julia, I never assumed he was dumb. I assume he's boring.

Still, no doubt, people like Charles get to live forever.

"Yup," Julia says with a smile. And then lower, in a whisper, "We hooked up."

"I know," I say. "I was there."

"Indulge me here. I just want to say it out loud again. Make it a little bit more real."

"Oh, it was real. You guys weren't exactly discreet."

Julia splashes me and then smiles too. She's not at all embarrassed. And why should she be? If I were her, I'd want the whole world to know. I'd put up a video on YouTube. In fact, *that* is the sort of thing that should make one worthy of a *People* magazine sidebar. Julia and Charles hooking up would be much more interesting to read about in a nail salon or while getting your hair done than *Whatever Happened to Baby Hope?*

"We're going out for pizza tonight," she says, her voice giddy.

"Oooh, I see some pepperoni in your future," I joke.

"Sausage," she says. "Zach was pepperoni. Charles is . . . one hundred percent organic artisanal sausage."

"Look at us, bro-ing out."

"I know, right? Maybe we should do some catcalling." Julia puts two fingers in her mouth and manages an impressive whistle. "Your turn."

"No way," I say.

"Just compliment him or something. Look! He likes it. He's practically preening."

"Ooh la la," I shout, but not nearly loud enough for Charles to hear. "I could shred some cheese on those abs and make me some tacos."

Julia bursts out laughing, which it turns out is all the encouragement I need to make a fool of myself.

"I'd like to shred some lettuce on you too," I say, this time too loudly. "Your abs are the first step to making a delicious and healthy snack."

Lifeguard Charles looks up at me, and his face freezes into a slightly demented smile. He has heard every word.

I don't care, though, because Julia and I are laughing so hard, we have tears streaming down our faces. Worth it.

After camp, Noah is waiting by my car. He lifts two shopping bags in greeting.

"No Slurpee, unfortunately, because we would have faced a melting crisis, but I did get us fully snacked up for our mission," he says, and then we climb into the car and resume our positions. His knees on the dash. Me at the wheel. This time, I don't bother thinking about my elbows.

"I'm optimistic about this one," Noah says while he enters the address into his navigation and then plugs his phone into my charger without asking. Mr. T's voice directs me to turn right. "She was super nice when I talked with her. Actually excited to hear from me, which is a first."

Today we are visiting Sheila Brashard, whom I've always thought of as "second from the right." I've never met her, never even thought about her much until Noah started this whole project. Apparently, she lives in Ridgewood, which is a couple of towns over. In the Baby Hope photo, her eyes are huge and scared and her mouth is in the shape of an O. You can tell she's well aware that her life has suddenly morphed into a horror film.

"Can I ask you a question?" I ask. We're cruising along with the windows down, and the wind blows my hair off my face and then whips it back again.

"Always."

"What would you do if you were told you only have, I don't know, like six months to live or something like that?" Not sure why I choose to ask Noah, of all people. Maybe it's because he has big plans and I doubt he's ever once thought about death stealing him greedily in the night. What he lacks in Charles's kind of hardiness, Noah makes up for with his own tenacity.

He too will live forever.

"That's pretty morbid."

"So are these interviews."

"What we're doing is *historic*, not morbid. Still, if I only had six months to live, I guess I'd have two choices. Either go out in a blaze of glory, like do all the crazy things I've been too chicken to do before, or I could use those last six months to solidify my legacy." Noah says. The casual lightness in his tone makes clear he is someone who has previously considered this question but only in the hypothetical.

You'd think I'd have weighed these options. That would have been a good use of those middle-of-the-night cough-inspired freak-outs. I have not. I have considered traveling—seeing what the world looks like outside of this tiny corner of New Jersey—but not much else. I'm not brave enough to take on anything resembling a "blaze of glory," and no matter what I do, my "legacy," whether I like it or not, is already set in stone. If I somehow manage to win an Oscar or a Nobel Prize in the next few years, which is, of course, impossible, the headline of my obituary will still read *Baby Hope Dead at 20*. I'll no doubt end up in one of those news headers on Facebook or worse, one of those terrifying *New York Times* text alerts. I wonder what it will do to Chuck Rigalotti's already broken heart.

"You're so ambitious. What about, like, embracing your last bits of normalcy? You know, spending time with the people you love?" I ask, and then instantly regret my word choice. Not because I'm talking to Noah in particular, but because he's a boy and it's weird to use the word *love* in front of him. A rhetorical trap.

"That too, I guess." He breaks off a Twizzler and spins it around like it's a key chain, then knots it into a bow. Presents it to me like a gift.

"Except for your whole overalls phobia, you seem pretty fearless. What are all these big things you're too scared to do?" I ask.

"Bungee jumping. Skydiving. I kind of want a tattoo," he says. I pull onto the Garden State Parkway. Like always, I feel a catch of fear as I merge lanes. If the on-ramp to a highway feels scary, the blaze of glory route is definitely not for me.

"I don't see you as the tattoo type," I say.

"I don't see myself as a tattoo type either, whatever that means, which is kind of why I want one. Also, I want to shave my head." Now that I'm safely comfortable in the right lane, I hold out my hand for a candy refill. He drops three gummy bears into my palm.

"Do not shave your head. You have good hair."

"Thanks. How about you? You have six months to live. Go."

"I don't know. I don't really want to bungee jump or skydive or even get a tattoo. I definitely don't want to shave my head. Maybe I wouldn't do anything? Maybe I'd just keep chugging along until I stopped," I say, and feel the thrum of blood in my veins. My heart pumps its reliable beat, beat, beat. I ignore the crush of my defective lungs, which I picture not unlike a collapsed bridge. I ignore the inevitable wave of fear and dread that washes over me with its creepy gentleness. "I'd find joy in the smaller, mundane stuff."

"That's the saddest thing I've ever heard."

"It is?" I ask, unable to keep the hurt surprise out of my voice.

"It really is," he says softly.

CHAPTER THIRTY-FOUR

Noah

Sheila Brashard's kitchen smells like lemon and sugar. She cradles a mug in the shape of a bespectacled owl and motions us to help ourselves to the freshly baked cookies laid out on the wooden dining table. Her house is the exact opposite of Chuck Rigalotti's, and reminds me of home. Not where I live now, which has the antiseptic feel of a rich guy's bachelor pad, but the cottage my mom and I used to live in pre-Phil. Cozy and deliberately mismatched. Joy found in cheap and cheerful kitsch.

Sheila looks like the moms at our school (though I don't think she's an actual mom, because I don't see kid crap around): middle-aged and professionally dressed, the kind of person you would stop and ask for directions but otherwise ignore. When we walked in, she gave Abbi a hug, then held her face between her palms and murmured: *"Oh, honey."*

This should have been awkward but somehow wasn't.

"Let me start by explaining I have a theory that one of the

healthiest ways to deal with the worst things in life is to find the humor in them," I say, and pull out a spiral notebook.

"Makes sense," Sheila says, like she's game for wherever this interview will take us. I decide I like her, even if, as with Chuck, it turns out she's a Jets fan and the whole thing is a total bust.

"He has lots of theories," Abbi says.

"I still can't believe you're the real Baby Hope. It's kind of surreal to meet you finally. I have that photo framed in the house," Sheila says, and takes a cookie and begins to slowly break it into smaller pieces on a plate. I have my first question all primed and ready to go—*What was the funniest thing to happen to you on 9/11?*—but now that it's on the tip of my tongue, now that I'm watching her desecrate what looks to be a delicious treat, it feels too invasive.

"Really? I've never understood why anyone would want that photo, especially someone who was actually there," Abbi says. She's sitting cross-legged on the chair and looks comfortable here. Like she and Sheila have known each other for years, which I guess, in a way, they have. "Wouldn't you rather forget?"

"I wish that were possible, but I lost my husband in the attacks. Best I can hope for is to shift my perspective. You know those tattoos that people get that say something like *Be grateful*? It's kind of like that," Sheila says.

"For the record, if I got a tattoo it wouldn't say *Be grateful*. Just so you know," I tell Abbi, but she and Sheila ignore me. As they should.

"I find the photograph empowering. The world literally exploded and I survived," Sheila says, and then points at me. "He has a theory that we need to laugh through the worst things in life. I have a theory that experiencing the hard stuff is how we grow to be a better version of ourselves. That's how we keep it from being a waste."

Sheila reaches out to pat Abbi's hand. I wish I could do that. Touch Abbi casually. Like there's nothing scary about it.

"Where's the picture?" Abbi asks.

"In the master bathroom." Sheila's sly grin again reminds me of my mom. It's a *Do not underestimate me* smile. It's an *I'm more interesting than I look* smile. "The bathroom is where everyone is most themselves, right? So that's where it goes. Where the purest essence of me can see it."

"I've never thought of it that way. That the picture could be empowering," Abbi says.

"Tell us about that day," I say.

"What do you want to know? Mitch, my husband, worked on the ninety-fourth floor of the North Tower. Everyone died. *Everyone.* I never got back a single body part. We had a funeral for a casket full of photographs, which in retrospect makes absolutely no sense. A picture is not the same thing as the thing. We didn't get so much as a finger. I worked on the seventh floor of the South Tower, so I ran. That's what you can see in the original photo, me second from the right, though in my bathroom version, I'm cropped out, which might make it less weird that I have it? I don't know. I have my limits, I guess. In the original, though, it's me running barefoot because I kicked off my heels. Now I don't go anywhere except in sneakers. For work, I got these black ones that I pretend look like dress shoes," Sheila says. I can't help it. I look at her feet. She's wearing fuzzy slippers, which makes me feel better until I notice that they have a solid rubber sole.

"Did you keep in touch with anyone from the picture?" I ask.

"Of course not," she says.

"He's convinced we have, like, this secret communication channel," Abbi says.

"I'm surprised some morning show hasn't staged a reunion or something," I say.

"Lucky for me, the media has only ever been interested in Baby Hope," Sheila says. "The rest of us got to fly under the radar."

"How about at the time? Did you talk to any of them then?" I ask, unwilling to let it go so easily.

"Nope. I ran my ass off. Screamed the whole way. I've never been so scared in my entire life."

"How about this guy in the back? The one with the University of Michigan cap?" I ask, but she cuts me off.

"You know what you made me realize? With your theory? I'm stronger, but I laugh a lot less now," Sheila says. "Mitch used to crack me up all the time. He was hilarious. Every time my friends set me up with someone new—all these old, bald, divorced men—I think, *You're not as funny as Mitch.* Which is unkind, I know. But I was so lucky to have him."

Her eyes brim with tears, and yet she's smiling. I think, *This is the first time in my life I've seen someone simultaneously experience gratitude and pain.* Whenever I've asked my mom about my dad, she's always looked hurt and angry. Like my curiosity is a criticism. "He was better than everyone else, and that's one of the reasons I try to be better too. But not laughing so much is the hardest part. Not because I'm not okay now. I am. It's been fifteen years. Things get easier. You learn how to carry your grief. Still, everything was more fun with Mitch around." Sheila shakes her head back and forth once, then twice, as if to dislodge a memory, but then she looks up at us, helpless.

We watch as the balance shifts to pure grief. I think, *Maybe it's better that I don't have memories of the person I've lost. Maybe it's been unfair of me to ask my mom to give me some of hers.*

"We used to hold hands all the time. People used to tease us that we were like newlyweds. Oh, God, I miss that. You know how much I wish I could have buried even one small part of him? I would have taken a finger," Sheila says, and rests her forehead on the table and wraps her hands around her stomach, giving herself over to the pain. "Seriously. I can't tell you what that's like. When you find yourself bartering with God over body parts."

CHAPTER THIRTY-FIVE

Abbi

"All right, okay, so yes, I teared up," Noah says once we are safely back in the car. "You should know I'm a sap. I also cry at toilet-paper commercials and those videos of soldiers coming home and surprising their families."

"If you hadn't felt anything watching that woman cry over her dead husband I'm pretty sure that would mean you were a sociopath." I make no move to put the key in the ignition. My arms are too heavy, my throat too tight. My chest sends little sizzles of pain straight through to my lungs. I'm reminded of all the reasons I didn't want to play Baby Hope with Noah.

"Why are we doing this?" I turn to face him. His eyes are now dry. I suspect he wiped them on his sleeve, as I did mine. I wonder what he looks like without the protection of his glasses. If his big, kind eyes seem even bigger. "I mean really? Why?"

"Which this? Me eating this whole bag of Oreos? I may not even share."

"Come on. *This,* as in ripping open old wounds. *This,* as in blackmailing me to do it with you." I'm full of big questions today.

My picture hangs above Sheila's toilet. She chooses to remember every single damn morning when she looks in the mirror. To take the worst thing that ever happened to her and transform it into something powerful and productive. To become a better person.

I'm not sure I am strong enough to do that.

I look at Noah, but he looks away.

"I won't tell anyone you're Baby Hope," he says, so low I almost can't hear him. Sheila gets up each day and laces up her black sneakers and takes a train into the city like a warrior heading into battle. And yet she's leveled by the memory of holding her dead husband's hands. I bet she, like me, dreams of empty boxes underground, of thick dust, of how the entire world can unravel in the span of a single minute.

All it takes is a tiny, inexplicable tear in the fabric of the moral universe.

I wonder if she ever looks at that Baby Hope photo and instead of remembering to be grateful, she gets angry about being left behind.

I wonder what Noah sees when he looks at that picture.

I wonder what tattoo he would really want to get.

I wonder why the hell we are doing this.

"I wouldn't have sold you out. If you don't want to do the rest of the interviews, I understand. I won't tell anyone at camp either way. I was never going to," he says. "I want you to know that."

My stomach hollows at Noah's words. He won't tell. Still, there's no relief, only a blast of regret. It turns out I don't want to stop doing this. I like riding in Go! (the name for my Prius that

I'm secretly trying out in my head) to previously unexplored parts of New Jersey with Noah. I like having him as my copilot. I like that he deposits only three gummy bears in my hand at a time, the exact right number that I can handle in a single bite. I like feeling part of something important in a way that's intentional, not accidental. I like thinking that maybe there's still a chance for me. That, like Sheila, I can find a way to digest what has seemed indigestible.

If my mother were sitting in her therapist's chair, she might argue that this project is healthy, an unearthing. If my mom were sitting in our kitchen, though, she'd smile a fake smile and say "Eh, let bygones be bygones."

"Just tell me why," I say, softening, because I know that Noah lost so much that day almost sixteen years ago. His reasons must go well beyond this article he's planning. I'm tempted to touch his face, where there were tears moments ago. I feel an urge to trace a line with my fingertips, cheek to jaw.

I don't actually do it. Though I guess that would be one kind of blaze of glory.

"I think I deserve that much," I say.

"It's complicated."

"Please," I say. "I want to understand."

"Okay, so, not sure if I already mentioned it, but my dad died on nine-eleven."

Noah doesn't look at me as he talks. He stares out the windshield, at the closed garage door, at the old basketball hoop that presumably belonged to the family who lived in this house before Sheila moved in. I nod. Of course he didn't mention it. Of course I already knew.

"I guess I thought this would be a good way to learn more

about it. What happened. What that day was like. I need to learn about the survivors. It's not only me who's interested. That's why Baby Hope is so famous. Still. Even now. That's why I think that photo is so important."

Noah squeezes the bridge of his nose. The gesture is cute and sad and makes me want to tap his sneaker. I like how he refers to Baby Hope as something altogether separate from me. A symbol, not a person.

He didn't say *That's why you are so famous.*

He takes off his glasses, cleans them again with his shirt, slowly—what I'm learning is a nervous habit. I get to see his face. Same Noah, only bigger, brighter, more vulnerable. He pops them back on. Noah restored.

"The fact that everyone's still standing. It gives me faith," he says, like he's made some secret decision.

"But we're not," I say.

"We're not what?" he asks.

"All still standing."

"What do you mean?"

"Connie? The woman who is carrying me in the picture? Who saved me? She's dead." For some reason, saying Connie's name gives me the jolt I need to put the key in the ignition and start the car. Driving is a great excuse to not have to look at Noah anymore. It's becoming too much. He was born days before 9/11. Would it have been better if Noah had been five or ten years old when his father died? Or would it have been crueler for him to have been given an exact measure of what he's lost?

"I didn't know," Noah says. "I Googled her."

"She changed her name when she got married."

"I'm sorry," he says.

"I met her a few times, but I didn't really *know her* know her. I was really upset when she died, though."

"Why didn't you tell me at the start?"

I keep staring out the windshield. If I glance over, I don't know what I'll see on his face now. Pity? Resentment? Grief?

"I'm sorry about your dad," I say, a nonanswer, I realize, but somehow it feels way more important than explaining myself. Not that I could even if I wanted to. I'm not sure why I didn't tell Noah about Connie. I guess it felt like none of his business.

"It was a long time ago. I never really knew my father, so."

"That's really it? You want to learn about the survivors? And write, like, an inspirational piece? That's not so complicated." I remember all the questions Cat, who also lost her dad, used to obsess over. She later learned you weren't supposed to ask, not really. She once told me she wondered: Did her dad die instantaneously? Did he burn alive? Did he feel pain? Did he jump? Did he know he was going to die? Was he scared?

She asked the last one again and again: *Was he scared?*

I wonder if being sixteen has finally answered that one for her. Of course he was scared. We all are in the end. I'm pretty sure we all are in the middle too.

"I think I'm going to call my car Go! *G-O*, with an exclamation point. What do you think?" I ask, taking the dodge as soon as I see it present itself, like Noah does. We pick the easy joke over the harder answer. We are not so different, he and I.

"Brave, building the punctuation right into the name. It's a verb and a command all wrapped into one. I like it," he declares, leaning back in his seat. I can feel him regaining his equilibrium, leaving whatever he was feeling behind. "Can we please keep working on the piece? I can do some interviews on my own, or on the phone, but I've already set up Jamal. We need to keep Go! fit."

"Okay. One more interview," I say. He takes out the gummy bears and drops three into my open palm. I notice how his fingers barely brush mine.

CHAPTER THIRTY-SIX

Noah

"I'm ninety-six percent sure this Brendan thing is not just in my head. He apologized for not showing up at the party and bagged for me today on his break so we could keep talking," Jack says. "That must mean something, right?"

We're foraging in Jack's kitchen. Since Abbi isn't here, we're back to mainlining Cheetos straight from the bag.

"Don't listen to me. I know nothing," I say.

"Come on. You always have an annoying take. Or at least a theory. That's your shtick."

"Not today, man."

"Who are you and what have you done with Noah?"

"I've been humbled recently by raw human emotion." As soon as I say it, I realize I sound like Jack, all big words and euphemisms.

"I have no idea what you're talking about, and I speak fluent Noah."

"Abbi saw me cry," I say, and pretend to root around in the

bag. I'm embarrassed. Not as embarrassed as I was earlier, when I was *actually* crying in front of Abbi, but still. My cheeks warm. I feel the sudden need to bro out, like punch his arm or something. We should get back into the basement and play some Xbox.

"Whaaaat?" Jack says, and laughs. He grabs the Cheetos from my hands.

"The widow we interviewed talked about her dead husband. It hit close to home."

"So what's the problem?"

"You know the guy Abbi is obsessed with? The lifeguard? He would have been stone-cold."

"First of all, you've totally made up that Abbi has a thing for that guy. Secondly, why do you suddenly want to be like some stone-cold dude who can pull off overalls? Just be you." While he talks, Jack counts off his points with his fingers, which is his nerdiest habit, and usually I have no choice but to destroy him for it. Today, I let it go. "Did you tell her your whole dad theory finally? She deserves to know."

"Nope."

"You're an idiot."

"Yup."

"Did you get all mucus-y when you cried? Like did you snot all over her? Because, I'm not going to lie, there's no bouncing back from that."

"It was more like a low-key manly cry."

"You showed her that you have feelings. Good. As a rule, I think you should work on emoting more. All this bottling crap up is going to give you cancer or at the very least an irritable bowel. I need peanut butter." Jack grabs the Skippy from the cabinet and a spoon from the drawer and starts to shovel peanut butter into his mouth. "I think it's time to show her you're into her."

"Who said I'm into her?"

"We've been best friends for almost a decade. Do we really have to do this?" he asks.

"Fine. So what should I do?" I ask. "For real." I've been reduced to asking Jack for relationship advice. Jack, who's notorious for always falling flat on his ass.

"Woo her."

"Woo her? What, with my dorky banter and my inability to leave no bad pun unsaid? That's your plan?"

"Sure, that could work," he says.

"Was that sarcasm?" I ask.

"What do you think?" he asks.

CHAPTER THIRTY-SEVEN

Abbi

When I get home from my afternoon with Noah, I'm surprised to find Mel, Cat's mom, sitting in the breakfast nook drinking coffee with my mother. Fancy-looking chocolate truffles and an open bag of Stumptown make clear that my mom must have looted my dad's house.

"Hi!" I say, like I'm only thrilled to see Mel, not like she brings with her an avalanche of discomfort and mixed feelings. It's weird even by Oakdale standards that she's my second 9/11 widow of the day. Three if you count Noah by proxy for his mother. I don't remember the last time I was in the same room as Cat's mom, mostly because I didn't realize there would ever be a last time at her house. I miss the Gibson-Hendersons. I miss Cat's little brother, Parker, who was born obsessed with his big sister and always begged us to let him play too. We did, but Cat came up with wicked ways to torture him—made him walk the plank when we were pirates, forced him to paint our toenails and massage our feet when we played boss. I even miss Stewart,

Mel's husband, who walks around with noise-canceling head-phones and has probably said a collective total of fifty words to me in all the years I've known him.

I want some of Mel's famous challah french toast. I want to scratch their dog, Rusty, right behind his left ear. I want to help Parker with his word search homework. I want to rewind Cat to who she was before so I can go back to being such a natural part of their household that I can eat their cereal straight out of the box and if I'm still there at six o'clock, an extra dinner plate is automatically set at the table.

"Abbi! Come give me a hug! It's been too long!" Mel's arms are outstretched, her voice completely at odds with her face, which is streaked with mascara. She's been crying. *Haven't we all,* I think unkindly, a split second before I realize that it's not fair for me to be angry at Mel just because I'm angry at Cat.

Still. Hasn't she noticed I haven't been over for a while? Does she miss me too?

I give Mel a quick hug. I look at my mother over Mel's shoulder, and she widens her eyes at me.

"Hey, sweetie. Can I ask you a question? And please, be honest. I promise Cat won't get into any trouble. And you won't either." Mel wears a sad smile, pinched at the corners, like it hurts to hold it in place. "You don't have to cover for her. I just need to know the truth. Was Cat really with you the other night?"

"Which night?" I ask this like we still hang out all the time, like there's any shot that we were in the basement eating popcorn. Like I even know what she's talking about. It would be much better if my mother were the one to blow the whistle on this whole thing.

"Well, last Thursday, and then this past weekend," she says.

"I was with Cat on Saturday night." This is, of course, the truth. Or part of it, anyway.

"You were? Here?" Mel takes a sip of coffee, waits me out. She's known me since I was a baby. She'll wield her silence like a weapon until I talk.

As much as my mom complains that Mel's über-stay-at-home-mommy-ness makes her feel bad about herself, Mel's skills have been helpful over the years. She used to sew Cat and me matching Halloween costumes and help me with science fair projects. In elementary school, she'd film all the class plays, even the ones Cat wasn't in, add in cool graphics, and then email them to the parents who couldn't make it because of work.

She claims that the community rallied behind her after Cat's dad died and that she's happy to pay it all forward now that she has the time and resources. I can't lie straight to her face, which is almost as familiar as my own mother's.

"No," I say.

"Then where?"

"This guy Moss's house?" I say it like a question. I don't use the word *party*. That word scares pretty much all parents except mine. You say "party" to Stewart, for example, and he freaks out, starts asking for names and telephone numbers and addresses. When he used to ask where we were going, Cat would say "A bunch of us are hanging out," which we thought was an ingenious euphemism. Cat is forbidden to date until she is eighteen, an age that has always felt hilariously old. Of course, that hasn't stopped her. Not that she sneaks out to go on actual "dates," which connotes movie tickets and hand-holding and reservations. She sneaks out to be looked at and lusted over and then, if she feels like it, to hook up. Messy kisses and more, in cars or in boys' basements or in the backs of movie theaters, all of which we used to talk about afterward in graphic detail. *Technically I'm not breaking a single rule*, she'd say to me. *What I did was definitely not dating.* Come to think of it, I probably learned the art of the lie by omission by spending the last decade with Cat.

"Was there drinking?" Mel asks. I picture Cat unsteady on her feet, how she smiled at me like for a moment she might have forgotten the past year. My mom nods at me encouragingly, as if to say, *It's okay. Just tell the truth.*

"I mean, there were some people drinking. I didn't see Cat drink, if that's what you're asking," I say, attempting to get by on the technicality because I did not actually witness Cat bring bottle or cup to her lips. For a second there, I even considered playing dumb, saying something like *Well, even teenagers need to stay hydrated, ha ha*, but that would make me too much of a jerk. I like Mel. In eighth grade, she once used our emergency key to get the math homework I had forgotten and hand-delivered it in time for seventh period. Maybe I like her even more than I like Cat.

"I . . . ," Mel says, trailing off. She looks into her coffee cup. "I'm worried about her. She hasn't been herself lately." I think about Cat's face on Saturday night, when I said *I'm not sure I actually know you anymore*. She flinched. Despite that single flicker of fear and the drunken sheen, she looked exactly like the old Cat. Confident, undeterred, like the world bends to her and not the other way around.

"You know Cat and I aren't as close these days. You should try Ramona or Kylie. They'll know if something is going on with her," I say, because it occurs to me that I might be doing the opposite of protecting Cat by not saying she was drunk. Maybe her mom knowing more would be a good thing.

Mel doesn't answer, though, because my grandmother wanders into the kitchen. The left side of her long paisley night-gown is tucked into her underpants. She's barefoot and agitated. A woman in a uniform follows closely behind—her new aide, who seems unfazed by the fact that my grandmother is flashing thigh.

My grandma looks first at my mother, then at Mel, and then finally at me. There's an emphatic gathering of her shoulders, an enraged arch to her eyebrows, as if she is about to let loose with an inexplicable tirade, but then a sudden blankness descends on her face. She turns around and walks away as quickly as her body will allow. The aide follows.

"Not our best day," my mom says.

If I weren't so horrified, if I hadn't just experienced my grandmother looking right through me and seeing whom, I don't know, I'd laugh. Because *not our best day* is, if not a white lie, a complete perversion of the right words, *She's having a bad day*, and so perfectly encapsulates everything you need to know about my mother.

And probably now me too.

Mel leaves and I go upstairs to my room. As I walk by my grandmother's closed door, I tell myself that she's likely sleeping, that it's not a good time for a visit. I tell myself that I don't like to see people on my bad days either.

My phone beeps with a text from Noah, and I flush with an embarrassing amount of joy.

> **Noah:** Why can't you hear a pterodactyl go to the bathroom?
> **Me:** Why?

Noah: Because their p is silent!

Me: Groan

Noah: I'm sorry about this afternoon

Me: What's there to be sorry about?

Noah: Just everything . . . including that pterodactyl joke

Me: What are you doing right now? Besides texting me

Noah: Watching stand-up clips. You?

Me: Lying on my bed reading the poems taped to my
   ceiling

Noah: That's cool. I know nothing about poetry

Me: I know nothing about comedy

Noah: Want to get a burger after camp on Thursday? My
   treat. It will be an I'm sorry I'm an ass burger

Me: I don't really like ass burgers

Noah: Well done

Noah: Pun intended

Me: See you Thursday for burgers, ass on the side

Me: Ugh, I totally take that back. For the record, I wasn't
   trying for innuendo

Me: I meant since I didn't want "ass burgers," I just
   wanted burgers

Me: Never mind

Me: I'm going to stop texting now

Noah: Ha! You text exactly the way you talk

Me: I am a champion babbler, apparently, in all forms

Noah: I wouldn't put it that way. I think you have a lot to
   say. I want to hear it

Me: You sure are stealthy with that charm, Noah Stern

Noah: See you tomorrow, Abbi Goldstein

CHAPTER THIRTY-EIGHT

Noah

To: Vic Dempsey (VictorDempseyPhotos@smail.com)
From: Noah Stern (NoahStern01@smail.com)
Subject: Baby Hope photograph 2001

Dear Mr. Dempsey,

Thank you so much for your prompt response to my request for an interview. Unfortunately, it turns out "Baby Hope" is unable to attend as originally promised. I very much hope you will not cancel on that account. I guarantee that our conversation will be as quick and painless as possible. Thanks in advance for your time.

Sincerely,

Noah Stern

EIC of the *Oakdale High Free Press*

To: Noah Stern (NoahStern01@smail.com)
From: Vic Dempsey (VictorDempseyPhotos@smail.com)
Subject: Re: Baby Hope photograph 2001

No problem on the Baby Hope front. To be honest, I'm relieved. Sometimes I wonder if I've inadvertently ruined her life.

Vic

CHAPTER THIRTY-NINE

Abbi

My grandma is sleeping. My mom and I eat dinner at the kitchen island, chicken lo mein and beef and broccoli straight out of the cartons, and as usual, we trade halfway through. One of the perks of my being the only child of divorced parents: we get to keep things less formal because we are only a party of two.

"What was that about?" I ask.

My mom is nursing a glass of red wine, and her faraway eyes are back.

"What?" she asks. After work, my mom always changes into her exercise clothes. Today, she's in runner's tights and a tank top and her hair is pulled into her usual perky ponytail.

No doubt she ran before dinner, as she does most evenings. A five-mile loop through the outskirts of Oakdale. She prefers the residential side streets to the more popular runner's trail along the water, the one where you can see all of downtown Manhattan. We've come far enough from 9/11 that these views have again become a selling point for our town.

"What did Mel say to you?" I ask.

"Apparently Cat has been acting out. I told her it was typical adolescence. Probably also some delayed grief working its way to the surface." My mother takes a bite, and a noodle clings to her lip. I can hear the low whistle of my grandmother snoring from behind the closed door of her room. A soothing sound, her good or bad day rendered irrelevant by sleep.

"Am I going through a typical adolescence?" I ask, motioning for her to wipe her mouth.

"Sweetie, there's never been anything typical about you." My mom says it like it's a compliment. And maybe it is for the Zachs or the Cats of the world. *Purple hair, don't care.* One of the hardest parts of being Baby Hope is that I've never been able to blend, even when I want to, *especially* when I want to. "Mel's particularly worried about the drinking."

"I didn't want to say anything, but Cat was wasted the other night."

"Nice job not using the word *party,* by the way. Don't think I didn't notice." When my mom reaches over and tucks a piece of my hair behind my ear, I lean into her hand. She might drive me bananas with her relentless cheerfulness, with her reflexive optimism, but I can't imagine living in a household where I couldn't say the word *party* out loud. "Should she be worried about Cat? Is there more to this than I think?"

"I honestly have no idea. Maybe?"

I take a breath. Seeing Mel has made me rethink everything. I should tell my mom the truth. If I have newfound courage, this is what it should be used for. She has the right to know about what's going on with me. We're running out of time.

I can tell her without using the words *9/11 syndrome*. I can speak in euphemisms, like she does.

Not a good cough.

I can tell her in a way that doesn't burden either one of us, that allows me to still have this summer. I can tell her slowly, an easing toward action, the most casual of baton tosses. I can suggest she take me to a summer appointment with Dr. Cohn, the pulmonologist I've been going to for years for my asthma, instead of waiting till the usual September check-in. She can handle that. So can I. No need for either of us to go straight to the endgame. I can make us both believe that everything will be okay.

I feel a stab of pain in my chest.

"Mom?"

That's when the cough starts again, low and tight, and I reflexively stuff it down. Make a face like I swallowed my water down the wrong pipe.

When I catch my breath, I'll confess to her. I will. No more lies.

My mother's cell phone rings. Her face brightens when she looks at the screen. Her haziness dissipates like fog under sun.

"It's Dad!" she says, and springs to her feet. She looks down at her clothes, then glances out the window, as if she thinks he can see her from out there.

I'm still coughing. I grab a napkin, cup my hand around it to shield it from my mother's view. She looks happy. No need for me to ruin her good mood.

I'll tell her later. This can wait one more day, surely.

"You okay?" she asks me. I nod, give her a thumbs-up, and point to the water glass. She takes one more quick look at me, then accepts the call.

"Hey." She answers low and flirty, but I don't hear the rest because she leaves the room.

Just in time for her to miss the first bloom of blood.

It's getting worse.

CHAPTER FORTY

Noah

R aj Singh answers on the first ring, ready and eager to chat. I am in my bedroom with the door closed. I don't want my mom to overhear this conversation. She'd want to shut the whole thing down.

"Your email took me by surprise. It's been years since anyone has asked me about that picture," he says.

In the photo, Raj is wearing a suit and has a messenger bag slung across his chest and a maroon turban on his head that has stayed straight despite the mayhem behind him. Raj's arms are outstretched and reaching, hands clawlike, as if they are desperate to grab something solid.

He looks young. Early twenties at most.

"I'm sorry Abbi—Baby Hope—isn't here with me, but she said to say hi."

"Tell her hi back," Raj says good-naturedly.

"I realize this can't be easy to talk about," I say to ease our way into my pad full of questions. I'm less nervous today. Raj is a disembodied voice, not a real person with a house and a possibly broken life. There's nothing to look away from.

"Nah, it's been fifteen years. I can talk about it." He speaks with a heavy New York accent. *Tawk* instead of *talk*. I try to imagine what he looks like now. I assume he has wrinkles. That he has traded in his messenger bag for a briefcase and an aluminum commuter mug. "It's weird. It feels like a whole lifetime ago, and also like last week."

"Tell me about that day."

"My girlfriend broke up with me that morning. Out of nowhere. She was suddenly like, *This is not what I want.* I was heartbroken. You know what I was thinking about while I was running? If I make it out of here alive, I'm going to ask her to marry me. I'll buy the biggest rock I can afford. I'll get down on one knee in Central Park. So interesting where your mind takes you when you think you are going to die. I made big plans."

"Did you propose?"

"What can I say? I was young and stupid. I bought the ring. Got her to Central Park. And on the trees were all those flyers. You were too young, so you don't know. But all over the city, everywhere you looked, there were these flyers of the missing. Families who couldn't find their loved ones—"

"My mom made one for my dad," I say. I don't mention that she used a photo of him holding me as a baby when I was in the ICU, that I imagine she thought my nasal tube would garner extra sympathy, if not a second look at his face. That there's still a pile in a box in our basement and that I keep a copy folded in my desk drawer. My mother talks so rarely about my father, you'd think I was the product of an immaculate conception or a sperm bank. I like the tangible reminder that I once had a dad.

"Did he make it out?"

"No."

"I'm sorry. Most of them didn't, which is what made those posters extra eerie. After a while, I think people were posting them not with hope, but almost to tell the world what they'd lost. As a testament or something," Raj says.

I picture all of New York City papered in missing posters, like a freaky death collage. I wonder about that impulse to want to make other people stop and pay attention to your pain, and then wonder if that's what my whole nailing-a-9/11-joke thing is about. If we are all like my campers, eager to pull up our pants legs to compare our scars.

"So you proposed! That's impressive," I say, because I don't want to think about those posters anymore. About how, like Sheila said, the picture isn't the same thing as the thing but there was nothing else left for people to show.

"She said no."

"Crap. I was so hoping this story was going to have a happy ending."

"Don't worry. It does. She was like, 'I know this horrible thing happened, but I'm not going to ruin the rest of my life just to make you feel better.' Turned out to be the best thing that ever happened to me, because a couple of years later I met my wife, and she's amazing. We have identical-twin girls, and they're beautiful, man. I'm so blessed. Everything happens for a reason."

"You really believe that? Everything happens for a reason?" I ask, because I can think of no good reason for those towers to fall, or for a kid to shoot up a middle school. Any conception of God I have doesn't allow for that sort of unimaginable horror.

"I have no idea. Maybe. Sometimes. Who knows? Maybe I got out of there to make those two perfect girls. Maybe they'll be the ones to fix the world."

"Tell me what it's like to be a symbol. Do you ever get recognized?" I ask.

"You mean because I'm in the Baby Hope photo?"

"Yeah."

"Never. I'm a guy in the background. No one ever notices me. I know this isn't what you meant about being a symbol, but you know what? That day completely changed how I move through the world. I'm now a symbol, not a person, because people are freakin' idiots," Raj says, and laughs one of those sharp, bitter laughs that isn't a laugh at all but its opposite. That always makes me sad—the idea of laughter, what I sometimes think of as the only good thing in the world, or at least the best thing, co-opted into a nervous tic.

"What do you mean?"

"I was born and raised in New York. After that day, for the first time in my life, I didn't feel safe walking around in my own city because of my turban. People still don't know the difference between Sikhs and Muslims. Not that it's right to attack anybody, don't get me wrong. One night I got chased by these big dudes with baseball bats. If I had a penny for every time I got called a terrorist or told to go back to my own country since nine-eleven, let's just say I wouldn't have to save for my kids' college educations." He pauses, and I hear some noise in the background. A woman, presumably Raj's wife, telling his daughters to put away their phones and do their homework. "That day feels like a before-and-after for me in terms of opening my eyes to that shit. I mean, I got it on the playground as a kid, sure. But that morning changed everything."

"That's horrible. I'm sorry," I say.

"Like I tell my girls, better to walk around with your eyes wide open than closed, right?"

"Do you keep in touch with any of the other survivors in that photo?" I keep my voice casual, like it's any other question. Like I'm just moving our conversation along. Like I have nothing riding on it.

"Course not." *Bust.*

"This is going to sound random, but did you happen to know the guy running behind you in the picture? The one in the University of Michigan hat?" I hold my breath and wait. I cross my fingers because I know no one can see me.

"Blue Hat Guy!"

"Yeah."

"No, I didn't talk to him. I didn't talk to anyone. Didn't even notice him until later, when I saw the picture on the front page of the *New York Times.* I went to U of M, though, so when I saw it I was like *Go Blue!* I was really glad he made it out."

"Yeah, me too," I say.

CHAPTER FORTY-ONE

Abbi

Noah and I sit across from each other at the Burgerler, the only burger joint left in Oakdale now that our town has turned fancy and seems to prefer food trends served in bowls, like acai or poke. On Sunday nights when I was a little kid, my dad and I used to make a ritual of this place. We'd share onion rings from a red plastic basket and conquer the maze on the paper placemats with crayons. Last time we were here, maybe a year or two ago, he warned me that should anything happen to him, all his important documents are kept in the safe in his closet. I have no idea what spurred my dad's sudden concern about his own mortality, but it dawns on me now that I won't have much to leave.

Noah clears his throat and I shake away my morbid thoughts. Time for all that later. I'm determined to focus on the right now, on Noah with his hedgehog hair and glasses and mischievous grin, his spoon already in his hand, like he's ready to do battle.

"Tell me three things I don't know about you," he says after we have a mock mini-fight over a particularly gooey bit of chocolate syrup that I bet comes from a metal can. We've ordered an ice cream sundae, the kind with three enormous scoops and whipped cream and a maraschino cherry on top. Chocolate. Vanilla. Strawberry wedged in between. Childhood in a glass bowl, down to the rainbow sprinkles.

Is this a date? It feels kind of like a date—we're sharing one dish, it's just Noah and me here, and there seems to be a thick wall of flirtiness between us—but then again, I've never been on an actual date, so I'm no expert. All my boy experience has been vicarious. Stories told by Cat, occasionally Ramona and Kylie too.

I win our chocolate battle. Only because he lets me.

"Three things?" I ask.

"I read about it in a book. Seems like a good way to get to know someone. Having to choose three things. You start, Abbi."

"Okay. One, sometimes when I can't sleep, I get up, make my bed, change my pajamas, and start all over again. I like to give myself the illusion of a do-over."

"Does it work?"

"Not really, but it burns up some time."

"That's not nothing," Noah says.

"Two, despite my whole sweet-tooth-and-red-food fetish, for me, it's all about the french fries. Three, I have this weird obsession with Mary Oliver. She's this poet, and she can spin words into magic. She has this great line that asks what you're going to do with 'your one wild and precious life.' How cool would it be to know how to use words to make the world—life—feel, I don't know, more manageable, I guess?" I ask.

"That's exactly why I'm obsessed with comedy. That's what it does for me," he says, and I feel my heart beat a little faster. I like that he has a nerd-boy hobby. I like that it means something real to him.

"Okay, your turn," I say. "Three things."

He shrugs.

"No fair! I told you stuff," I say.

"Nah, it's not that. We don't need a gimmick, that's all. You're really easy to talk to," Noah says.

"Thanks." My cheeks warm, and the back of my neck tickles from the compliment.

"Okay, here's something you might not know: I almost died when I was a baby too. I mean, all of our near-death experiences can't be as dramatic as a terrorist attack." He stops, smiles at me. "But I was born with a heart defect. My parents didn't think I was going to make it."

Noah rattles this off like it's no big deal.

"Are you okay now?"

"I have a checkup at the cardiologist once a year, and if I get a pat-down at airport security I have to tell them about my pacemaker, but that's about it. I got lucky. Just like you." He clicks the metal of his spoon against mine again, a version of cheers.

I study his face for a moment, the parts I haven't spent much time exploring. I wonder what he would say if he knew about my lungs. Am I still lucky? I've always thought so. Even now.

Would telling him give me the courage to tell my parents? He could be my practice run. Because that's one of the things I like most about Noah, how I feel stronger around him.

"I look at it that way too. That we got lucky. Instead of the other way around—that we were unlucky in the first place," I say.

"Exactly," he says, and looks me right in the eye. I force myself to look back, fearless. Okay, not fearless, but I refuse to let the fear win. It feels like a moment, this eye contact, with these goofy smiles on our faces, because I'm pretty sure when we're talking about luck, we're talking about being here with each other.

This is the sort of bravery I need more of in my life. This courage to look right back at him.

Under the table, I feel our shoes line up. His, mine, his, mine. Our ankles touch, spring apart, touch again. Then he holds his feet against mine, so I force myself to stay still, to keep the contact going.

My lungs tickle in the best way possible. Tiny zings of excitement shoot through my body.

I think this might actually be a date.

CHAPTER FORTY-TWO

Noah

I should have taken her to that cool new sushi place on Main. It has candles on the table, even in the afternoon. No crayons and paper placemats. Made it straight-up obvious that we aren't just hanging out. I place my shoe next to hers and hold it there, but I can't tell if she notices.

When Abbi excuses herself to go to the bathroom, my ankle feels lonely.

I text Jack because I don't know how to sit here and wait for her to come back.

Me: She's in the bathroom
Jack: How's it going?
Me: Legit good
Jack: So what's the problem?

Me: Should I say something? About you know, my
   feelings or whatever
Jack: That's adorable
Me: You're not helping
Jack: I've told you all along to tell her how you feel
Me: No. You said I shouldn't have befriended her in the
   first place
Jack: I've evolved. She's cool
Me: How do I say it?
Jack: Speak from the heart
Me: My heart doesn't talk. It beats rhythmically because
   of an implanted electronic device
Jack: That is so literal
Me: Should I tell her she looks pretty today?
Jack: Use beautiful. No one likes pretty
Me: Okay. She's coming back. Anything else?
Jack: You got this, dude
Me: Was that sarcastic?
Jack: Honestly? Still deciding

Here's the thing. I do not *got this*. When Abbi walks back to the table, she looks even better than before. Her lips are shiny, her hair is spilling over her shoulders, and she's smiling, like this one-on-one thing across a table is no big deal. I try to mirror her casualness by looking at my phone's screen, as if I'm not creepily tracking her with eyes. As if my stomach isn't sitting on the floor.

CHAPTER FORTY-THREE

Abbi

In the bathroom, I gave myself a pep talk: *You are awesome. You do not need tangerine hair or to know about random bands like Oville to be interesting. You are enough. Also, you are amazing at pep talks!*

I reapplied my tinted lip balm, which is as close to lipstick as I get without feeling self-conscious. I once tried on Cat's signature red and lasted only three minutes before wiping it off. I know because she timed me.

When I return to the table, I try to saunter over—move with a confidence I do not feel. Noah's forehead is crinkled and he's leaning over his phone and I realize it doesn't matter how I walk because he's not paying attention.

"Everything okay?" I ask.

"It's just Jack."

"You look deeply concerned," I say, smiling. Do I sound flirty? I want to sound flirty.

"Nah. It's nothing," Noah says, and puts away his phone.

"Hey, you look prett—nice—I mean . . . beautiful." He looks down at his hands. My heart folds in on itself, and my body warms in a slow wave from my toes to my face. He called me beautiful. *Beautiful.* Which is so much better than pretty. I'd be embarrassed that I'm blushing, except so is he. We are so bad at this. I prefer it that way. I can't imagine sitting here with someone who knows exactly what to say and how to say it and doesn't freak out even a little bit. Because, like me, Noah is totally freaking out. I can tell.

"Thanks."

"You're very welcome."

Then I don't say anything, because I don't know what to say other than *Thanks again,* which is totally not the right thing. Normally I'd jump to fill the silence, but my mind has gone strangely blank.

"I made things weird, didn't I?" Noah asks as he points at me with his spoon. A drop of strawberry ice cream slides onto the table.

"I wouldn't say *weird,* necessarily."

"Then what would you say?" Noah has morphed into Noah again. Flushed, yes, but his reliable smile is back, playing at the corner of his lips. We are totally flirting. I can't be reading this wrong.

"You might have made things *different.*"

"Different bad? Different good?"

"Different good, I think?" I take a bite of ice cream, and suddenly hear Cat in my head: *Lick the spoon suggestively. Guys love that.* I decide to ignore her. To be me instead. "But definitely different."

"They say change is good."

"Change *is* good. Well, except climate change."

187

"Right. Climate change is bad. Very bad. And apparently so is menopause, which my mom calls 'the change' too," he says.

I burst out laughing.

"Shall we talk more about my mother's menopause? I figure I already made things awkward, why not keep going?" Noah asks. "She gets hot flashes. Mood swings."

"Please stop."

"Stopping."

"You're weirder than I thought."

"Hey, that's my line."

"It's a good line," I say. *I'm not so bad at this,* I tell myself. Cat used to argue that the reason I never had anyone to hook up with was that I didn't know how to flirt. That I'd get nervous and tongue-tied, that I needed to learn how to at least *appear* confident. I used to insist that the problem was the stupid photo—no one wants to kiss someone they could picture as a baby. Still, deep down I believed Cat. Baby Hope was just a good excuse.

Right now, though, my reflexive self-consciousness has seeped away. I might be nervous, and a tiny bit tongue-tied, and still miles away from confident, but that doesn't seem to matter. It's me here, flirting with Noah and cracking up.

"Okay, subject change. How about a lightning round?" he asks.

"Okay. Go for it."

"Coke or Pepsi?" he asks.

"Dr Pepper."

"World Series or Super Bowl?"

"Not into sports."

"Right? Boring. Coffee or tea?"

"Coffee."

"Dogs or cats?"

"Dogs. A hundred percent. Cats are creepy." He leans across the table and high-fives me.

"Words or emojis?"

"Words. I find emojis too vague. I need an emoji dictionary."

"I know what to get you for your birthday." My heart squeezes a little, thinking about my birthday, how loaded that day is, how if Noah were to remember the connection, he'd realize it was the same day his dad died. That's the fastest way I can think of to kill whatever might be going on between us. Noah doesn't seem to notice, so I do something I'm not used to. I let it go.

"*Harold and Kumar* or *Van Wilder: The Rise of Taj*?"

"I don't know what that question even means."

"We have some serious work to do on your comedy education," he says.

"We do," I admit.

"Well, then." He stands up and holds out his hand. "Shall we get started on that?" A dash of shyness creeps into his voice. That's when I realize he's asking me to watch a movie at his house. Today. As in right now. For a moment, my precious words fail me. I want to say something clever: *That depends. Will there be coffee? Do you have a cat?*

All I manage to say out loud: "Sure."

Noah's house is what my mother would snidely call a McMansion, which is to say it's new and huge and refuses to blend in this neighborhood of mostly single-story ranch-style homes. For reasons unbeknownst to me, whenever we drive by a new one, my mom, who rarely expresses extreme emotion other than joy, goes off on unhinged rants about how much she despises them.

Once I made the mistake of asking, "What did a McMansion ever do to you?" and I got a long lecture about how the influx of big money to Oakdale is killing our community spirit. These new houses are the reason the family-owned hardware store has been taken over by a fancy cheese shop. Somehow it all relates back to 9/11 and to us again falling prey to the greedy maw of capitalism. To how we are watching the world repeat the mistakes of history in real time, though I don't quite understand what exactly I'm supposed to be watching and not repeating.

"I'd take a wrench from old Mr. Seever over a thirty-dollar wheel of Manchego from a faceless corporation, wouldn't you?" she said, and I was too tired to point out that we had both of those items at home. In our kitchen. At that very moment. (The cheese had been stolen from my dad's, but my mom was the one who took it.) Not to mention in the last few years, my mom's practice has been booming because of the new Oakdale. Money apparently breeds dysfunction, which is great for her business.

Oddly enough, Noah and I are almost neighbors. His house, which I've unknowingly driven by a gazillion times since it's only three blocks from mine, has double-height ceilings and sleek furniture and dark hardwood floors. The only family pictures were obviously taken by the professional photographer at his mom's second wedding. Noah must have been ten or eleven; he's wearing a suit and has a mouth full of metal. Do his parents hate him? It seems inhumane to keep his awkward stage on display.

"Wow, look at this place," I say, a vague statement, because its enormity requires a comment, if not a compliment. Unlike both of my parents' houses, there's no kid art framed on the walls, no evidence beyond the wedding photos that anyone under the age of forty lives here. I don't dislike it for the reasons my mother would—I'm not particularly protective of the

Oakdale community spirit, and I don't have particularly strong feelings about capitalism or like the use of the word *maw* in any context. I feel a surprisingly lonely vibe here. The house doesn't seem like the sort of place that could grow a Noah.

"I hate it," he says flatly. "We used to live on the other side of town in this tiny cottage, but when my mom married Phil, we moved into this monster. You could have fit the old place into this room. But I don't know, it felt like home," he says, and then plops down on the couch. "It was the only place I ever lived until this." I follow and stand next to him. I need to decide how much space to put in between us, and my self-consciousness returns. Do I sit close to him since we've acknowledged things might be "different," or do I safely sit on the opposite side? I panic and plop down somewhere in between.

"Where's my cheese platter?" I demand. Noah laughs, stretches his legs out, and grabs the remote control.

"Are you ready to watch genius in action?" he asks.

"Yes," I say. "Yes, I am."

Then we proceed to watch a movie.

A whole movie.

From the beginning to the end of the credits.

I sort of chuckle at what I think are the right places, and I occasionally smile at Noah and pretend I'm enjoying what he apparently believes is a groundbreaking film about getting high and looking for hamburgers.

I spend a lot of the ninety minutes thinking about the space between us. A foot and a half, maybe more. I feel a tingling nervousness, and still I make no effort to move closer.

Neither does he.

I replay what happened. Him telling me I look beautiful. How our entire afternoon felt like a date, the air heavy with something unnamed. I have no idea what is happening on the screen, although I have surmised that the entire thing is about two guys named Harold and Kumar who are trying hard to get to a White Castle and for some reason Neil Patrick Harris, playing a douchey version of Neil Patrick Harris, keeps getting in their way. I have never been to White Castle, so I'm having a little trouble relating. Also, isn't NPH like a dad now? How old is this movie?

On top of all that is one more question I can't get out of my head: Why isn't Noah leaning over and kissing me? I spent the drive over imagining how it would feel. His mouth on my mouth, or my mouth on his, how I hoped nature would take over and I'd know which way to cock my head, as Cat promised long ago. How it could be one of those moments that stick, like that eye contact at the Burgerler. Because first kisses are supposed to be like that: indelible.

My actual expectations are low. By definition, a first is a first. I aim for slight awkwardness and figuring out the mechanics and hopefully some nervous laughter. Still, sometimes there can be magic in the imperfect.

I consider turning to Noah, moving in close. Instead, I freeze.

Maybe I've misinterpreted everything.

Maybe he has no interest in kissing me. Maybe his comment was a friendly "beautiful," a throwaway, not a cosmic change in our friendship.

Or maybe it was a manipulation, a way to keep me going on our project.

Or maybe it turns out Noah doesn't make me that brave after all.

CHAPTER FORTY-FOUR

Noah

"So you and Abbi sat there and watched all of *Harold and Kumar*? Are you shitting me right now?" Jack asks, and I immediately regret having told him anything. We are at my house, and Jack sits perched on the kitchen counter while I raid the cabinets for something to eat. My mom usually hides the good stuff behind Phil's shredded wheat. My back is to him, but I can hear Jack cracking up. "You got all the way to the end, when they finally get their White Castle, and you just sat there watching John Cho and Kal Penn chow down? That is so sad, man."

"Leave me alone," I say. I grab some sour cream and onion potato chips. I think about Abbi on my couch. Her brown eyes. Her legs crossed, her toenails painted with glitter. How badly I wanted to touch her thigh. Kiss her. Tuck one of her curls behind her ear, which is a move I've always wanted to try and probably never will. Because I'm a coward. And an idiot.

"You should invite her over tomorrow to watch *A Very Harold and Kumar 3D Christmas* and then *Harold and Kumar Escape from Guantánamo Bay.* Everyone loves bad stoner comedies from a decade ago. They're super romantic."

"It's not funny," I say, my frustration turning straight to anger. I want to punch the wall. I want to rewind time and grow a pair. I want to become someone else entirely.

"You have no game, my friend," Jack says, and this time he laughs so hard he falls off the counter. I don't help him up.

> **Mom:** What's wrong?
> **Me:** Nothing. Jack's here
> **Mom:** What happened?
> **Me:** Nothing!
> **Mom:** Something happened. I have that mom ESP thing.
>   I can tell
> **Me:** Relax
> **Mom:** I am your mother and it was just you and me for
>   more than a decade in that hovel so I know you better
>   than you know yourself. Also don't tell me to relax.
>   That only makes me worry more. I'm going to call you
>   now
> **Me:** I'm fine. Crappy day. Please don't call
> **Mom:** When did your mother calling you become the
>   worst thing in the world?
> **Me:** Don't feel like talking about it
> **Mom:** While I already have you in a bad mood, I might as
>   well tell you that Phil wants to take you golfing on
>   Friday
> **Me:** Nope
> **Mom:** Come on. He wants to do some male bonding stuff
> **Me:** I have camp
> **Mom:** After camp

Me: Plans after camp

Mom: With Jack? That doesn't count

Me: With Abbi

Mom: Baby Hope Abbi?

Me: Her name is just Abbi

Mom: I didn't know you were hanging out with her

Me: So?

Mom: It's interesting. That's all. She's like the face of 9/11

Me: No one is the face of 9/11. It was a terrorist attack, not a Cover Girl commercial

Mom: Don't be glib

Me: She's my friend

Mom: You don't have to be friends with everyone

Me: The other day you were saying I needed to branch out

Mom: Please . . . be careful with her

Me: Be careful of what? Tell me. What are you so afraid of?

Mom: Nothing. I am not afraid of anything

Me: Mom!

Mom: Never mind. Got to go. Ziti's in the freezer

CHAPTER FORTY-FIVE

Abbi

We were ten years old the day they identified one of Cat's dad's ribs. She and I were on her bedroom floor playing our umpteenth brutal game of Slapjack in a row. That was pre–friend merger with Kylie and Ramona, so it was just the two of us back then. It was early December, and we had lucked out with a snow day. The cancellation had turned out to be an over-reaction. We'd only gotten a dusting, so instead of spending the afternoon building snowmen, like we had originally planned, Cat and I were inside in cozy matching pajamas, playing cards and goofing around at her house. We were good at entertaining ourselves and thrilled not to be at school learning about how a bill becomes a law.

When the doorbell rang, we assumed it was the UPS guy, Larry, who we liked despite the fact that he had a creepy mustache and a van and looked very much the type to offer little kids candy. Larry often delivered big boxes full of grown-up stuff to Cat's house—boring things like toilet paper or napkins—but Mel always allowed us to cut open the boxes and dance on the bubble wrap. That day, though, when we ran downstairs and threw open the front door, the two guys facing us were mustache-less and dressed in blue.

Afterward, while Cat's mom sat shell-shocked on the couch, rocking back and forth, the way she used to when Parker was a baby on her lap, the police officers let themselves out the front door, and the older one, the only one who talked, told Cat and me to "be extra nice to our mama tonight." He sounded Southern, though clearly the police should have known to send New Yorkers or at least officers from New Jersey to deliver the news.

When Mel told us to go upstairs, before the cops had said a single word, Cat and I ran into the kitchen and listened at the door with giddy anticipation. Neither of us realized it could possibly be something serious until it was, until the words were spoken, and by then it was too late to sneak away or to unhear them. I remember standing behind Cat, my chin barely reaching her shoulder, and wanting desperately to put my hands over her ears. To absorb this news myself so she wouldn't have to.

The police officer said that it gave some families solace to have these found parts returned to them—those were the exact words he used, *found parts*. Like Cat's dad's rib was an object—a thing—like a good find at a garage sale.

"People appreciate having something to bury even all these years later, because it gives them something akin to closure," he said. Apparently, the protocol was that going forward, should more bones be recovered, Mel wouldn't receive the courtesy of an in-person visit—there wasn't the manpower for that—but instead would receive a telephone call. Some families got calls every couple of months. A rib, then a fibula, maybe part of a toe.

After they left, Cat ran up to her room in tears, and I didn't know if I should follow her or stay downstairs. Parker, who was so little at the time, curled up at Mel's feet like a dog. He was scared and confused; he had thought police officers in his house would have been cause for celebration. Something fun. Like dress-up come to life.

"Did Cat's dad die all over again?" Parker asked, because he of course already knew that his father was not Cat's father, that Cat's father had died at a time he couldn't fathom, because none of us can properly picture the time before or after our own existence. What I didn't understand until that moment is that Parker was right: it turns out people can die twice.

Mel looked at him and started to weep. I scooped Parker up onto my hip and went into the kitchen to get him cookies and milk and called my mom from Cat's landline and told her what had happened. I remember realizing that this was my very first taste of adulthood. I didn't like it. I didn't like it at all.

My mom came straight over. She tucked Mel into bed and put on *Dinosaur* for us kids, which of course we were way too old for by then, but we watched anyway, until Stewart came home from work earlier than usual and took over.

A week later, and nine years after Cat's dad died, the Gibson-Henderson family held another funeral. This time there was a casket, though I knew there was only a rib inside.

I couldn't stop thinking about how lonely that single bone must be in the ground by itself forever.

CHAPTER FORTY-SIX

Noah

"Okay, it's the morning of September eleventh, which was ironically the most gorgeous day of the year—picture a blue sky, like blue, blue, blue. Not a cloud in sight. I walk to Century 21, which is this discount department store downtown. I need a tie for a job interview, not a big deal. Everything is normal. I have my camera; I always do. Then I hear that sound— loud, indescribable, metal to metal—the first plane has hit, and my instincts kick in. I whip out my lens and start running toward the crash." Vic Dempsey's speech has a practiced quality, revs up as he gets going, like we should ready ourselves for the punchline. The photographer who took the Baby Hope picture has clearly dined out on this story for a long time, which is both understandable and gross.

Jack and I are standing in his small studio in Maplewood, New Jersey, and Vic is talking while looking at a series of shots laid out on a lit table. In the photos, a tall, thin woman in a business suit carries a baby in a fancy leather handbag. Her hair is wild around her head, like she's standing in front of a wind machine. I don't understand the picture at all—she looks simultaneously frazzled and serene, and the baby looks like it might fall out. I assume it's trying to sell me something but I couldn't say what.

"There was an explosion, so you went closer, instead of getting the hell out of there. That's insane," I say. I've thought a lot about what I would have done had I been there. And no matter where I put myself—on the thirtieth floor of the South Tower, on the second floor of the North Tower, or even blocks away—all I can imagine is running. That's how it looks in my mind: like something in a rearview mirror. Something happening behind my back.

"Epic," Jack says.

"That's how I'm wired," Vic says, all super cool and casual. He's probably in his late fifties, has a shaved bald head and pouchy eyes. He wears a denim shirt cuffed at the elbows and tucked into stylish, faded blue jeans. *He's handsome,* Jack whispered when we first walked in, but I don't see it. Jack tends to confuse swagger with good looks. "My instinct is to document, and I will put myself wherever I need to be to do it. I couldn't *not* take pictures. The world *needed* to see what I was seeing."

"Do you happen to know anything about any of the other people in the photograph? Like the guy in the blue Michigan hat, for example?" I ask, and Jack sneeze-mumbles, *"Not your dad,"* low enough that Vic can't hear.

Jack has always thought this whole thing was a bad idea. Or a stupid one. He might be right, but it's too late now.

"Nah. My job is to take the pictures. That's all. I thought it was what our country needed at the time. *Hope.* Of course, I didn't know that was her name! I mean, it was all so fortuitous in its own bizarre way," Vic says. With his *nah*, the disappointment settles across my ribs like a blanket.

"Hope is actually her middle name," Jack says.

"Still. People liked that. A shorthand sentimentality. Simplifies things," Vic says. "Also the picture totally followed something photographers live by: the rule of thirds."

"What's that?" Jack asks.

"It comes from painting during the Renaissance originally. The idea is that the background of the picture tells a story, and you want your viewer's eyes to roam over the entire canvas. So the focal point should never be the middle. The image should be broken down into thirds, both horizontally and vertically, and the most important parts line up along the resulting axes. Here, look. Baby Hope *proves* the rule of thirds," Vic says, and points to a framed version he has hanging on his wall.

He traces lines to turn the picture into a grid and demonstrates how Abbi isn't in the center but along the right axis. If you had asked me before this minute, I would have sworn she was smack-dab in the middle.

"There's a rule of thirds in comedy also," I say.

"Sometimes it's called a comic triple," Jack says.

"Like an Englishman, an Irishman, and a Scotsman all walk into a bar, and then the joke is always on the last person. It wouldn't be funny if you just had two. Doesn't work," I say, realizing we are derailing the conversation and also not caring.

"We've tried," Jack says.

"Right," Vic says, and looks at us like we are the stupidest people he's ever met. "In art, though, it's a storytelling tool. Look at that woman, for example."

He points to Sheila, who I used to think of as Business Suit

Lady and who now has a name and a lovely house I can see in my mind and a dead husband whom I can't picture but like to imagine was as awesome and funny as she claims.

"Sheila," I say, and Vic shrugs, like he doesn't care. Like her name is the least important thing about her.

"See how your eye starts at Baby Hope and then loops around? You look at Sheila and wonder: What is she thinking? Who is she? What happened to her shoes?"

I look at the photograph again, and for the first time, I don't look straight at the guy in the Michigan hat. I let go of my own questions and consider the work in its entirety. Each person a story woven into a larger whole, not unlike our interviews, come to think of it. This is the inverse of the missing posters. A different kind of collage.

I look at Connie, who I will never get the privilege of meeting in person. I wish I could ask her what it was like to scoop up a baby that was not hers. Were there others she had to leave behind?

"It's beautiful," Jack says. "It's not just a photograph. It's art. And it's certainly not neutral."

I look at it again, this time through Jack's eyes. A single, ugly moment transformed into something breathtaking. Amazing how it morphs to the viewer. He's right: it's not neutral.

What does Abbi see when she looks at it? Does she only see the baby with the balloon, like I only saw the Michigan hat? Or does it feel wholly separate from her? Again, the picture, not the thing.

"Three thousand people died that day. Three thousand. This picture is meant to provoke and to force you to remember. I'm forever surprised by how quickly the world moves on and goes about its business," Vic says.

Fifteen years. I think about what Raj said, how it feels like a lifetime and also last week.

"It's a myth, this concept of a before and an after. Every time I see a perfect blue sky, want to know what I really think?" Vic asks. "I think there are only afters and after thats."

CHAPTER FORTY-SEVEN

Abbi

"Stop fidgeting," Noah says to me while I pose in front of the pink wall. This is, of course, the first stop of the Instagram tour of Oakdale. It's practically famous, or as famous as a wall can be in a small town in New Jersey.

"Sorry," I say. If we were touring for social media purposes, we'd next head to the Blue Cow Cafe, where they draw clover designs in their lattes and sell chunky fresh-baked chocolate chip cookies that look way better than they taste. But we are not. We are here at the pink wall because Noah wants to take my picture. Not for Instagram or Snapchat or anyone else. He wants it for when my name pops up on his phone.

Cute, right? So freakin' cute.

"I can't see your face," Noah says. We've stopped on the way to meet Jamal Eggers, who I think of as Last Guy on the Right, or sometimes, Glamour Shot. Because considering the context, *running for his life*, he looks amazing in the Baby Hope photo.

His sleeves are rolled up, his shirt is partially opened to reveal a muscly brown chest, and he's midstride. If we were to give him a thought bubble, it would say *I got this.*

If I hadn't brought all the shorthand emotion and sentimentality that comes along with a one-year-old trying to hold on to her red balloon in the middle of a terrorist attack, Jamal might have been the famous one instead.

Actually, it turns out he's famous anyway, and for way better reasons. He's a well-known Broadway actor.

"We need to be at that guy's by four. We're going to be late," I say. I've spent the last forty-eight hours thinking about the fact that Noah and I have not yet kissed. Wondering how I managed to screw that one up, when everyone knows that going to watch a movie at a boy's house is total code for hooking up.

I've spent an equal amount of time trying to convince myself that I've dodged a bullet. I don't need relationship drama. What I do need are friends. Real friends.

"Okay," Noah says. He doesn't move, though. He stands there with his phone in his hand.

"What?" I ask.

"Nothing."

"Do I have something in my teeth?" I feel small, suddenly, and starkly illuminated against the vast pink background. Usually there are a few other people taking pictures, so there is company among this silliness. The wall feels strangely empty.

Noah walks toward me, still holding his phone like he's going to take my picture, but with a strange, determined look on his face. For one inexplicable second, I worry he's going to tackle me.

"Too close," I say, assuming he's zooming in for artsy effect, and I cover my face with my hands. He stops when we are less than a foot apart.

He drops the phone into his pocket and reaches up and pulls my hands down so that he is holding them in his.

"There," he says.

He doesn't touch his camera. He looks at me. I force myself to look up at him, force my eyes to meet his eyes. Because if I don't, then this won't happen. I might not know much, but I know that. If I don't look at him, if I am not brave, we may well spend the rest of my very short life debating whether we like *Harold and Kumar Escape from Guantánamo Bay* better than the original, and that's not really how I want to peace out.

I look up and he keeps looking at me, and then he steps even closer. When I breathe out, my chest brushes against his.

I'm not staring at his eyes, I'm looking at his mouth. He moves in closer, and then he kisses me, once, lightly, on the lips. Sweet and gentle and so perfect my knees buckle.

"What do you think?" he asks, and for once, I'm speechless. I nod, which is the closest I can get to what I really want to say, which, is, in Oliver-like fashion, *Please, sir, I want some more.* Noah reaches his right hand into my hair, behind my ear, and brings me toward him, and he kisses me again, surer this time. I'm kissing him too, and my back is up against the pink wall, and when I hear a car honk as it drives past, I barely notice.

Real kissing. My thoughts aren't thoughts anymore. I'm all sensation. Chills and butterflies and warmth in an addictive swirl. A tiny moan escapes, and I'm not sure if it's Noah or me or maybe both of us in tandem.

I realize I do not want to die in a blaze of glory. I don't care much about my legacy. I was wrong too to think I'd just chug along until I stopped. I want to kiss Noah for as long as I'm allowed. Honestly, if I have any say in the matter, this seems a spectacular way to spend the rest of my one wild and precious life.

CHAPTER FORTY-EIGHT

Noah

Abbi melts the moment she sees Jamal Eggers. I get it. He looks like an action-movie hero—white T-shirt, cut arms, shaved head. I showed Jack pictures of Jamal last night—not the Baby Hope one, but ones on his IMDB page—and after then going down a YouTube rabbit hole of watching him sing on Broadway and star in a Hallmark Christmas movie, Jack said, *Oh my God, I want to have his babies.*

I'm not really worried about Abbi and Jamal. We just kissed. No, we *made out* is a better way to put it—kissing suggests timidity—and if she enjoyed it even half as much as I did, I'm safe.

"Never thought I'd get to meet you properly. But here you are. You look happy. That's great," Jamal says, and takes Abbi's hand and gently kisses the back of it. Like with Sheila and even Chuck, this could be awkward or creepy or both, but somehow it turns out to be none of the above. He comes off sweet and gentlemanly. I want to take lessons. "I don't know if anyone else said this too, but I feel sort of protective of you. Like you belong to us survivors, you know?"

"Thanks, I guess. The whole thing is still weird," Abbi says, and her cheeks flush an adorable pink.

"I didn't mean it like you're a mascot or anything. It does this old man's heart good to know you're okay, that's all. You matter to me." We are in Jamal's loft apartment in Hoboken, and though I don't usually notice things like furniture, this place looks like it could be in a magazine. A futuristic sculpture stands by the front door. Delicate blue vases of various heights sit on a metal table. The floor-to-ceiling bookcases are filled with hard-back books organized by color.

"Thanks. I'm good. I mean, there's . . . Yeah, no, I'm good. Come on, you're not really old," Abbi says, and I think, *Don't be fooled by his muscles—yes, he is.*

"Turned forty a few months ago. Suddenly you discover you're not going to live forever. You would have thought I'd have figured that out a long time ago, but nope." Jamal sits back and lets his long arms drape along the back of his couch. Is he trying to show off his biceps? Because he is.

"Are you okay? I mean, are you healthy?" Abbi asks.

"You heard about Connie?" he asks.

"I did," she says.

"Nothing like that. At least, not yet, if that's what you're asking. I have asthma, and I caught pneumonia last year, but nothing major. My husband thinks it was my midlife crisis manifesting itself. Between you and me, I'd rather have gotten a Porsche."

We laugh this time, and a word I've never before used in my life, a word my mother loves, pops into my head: *charisma.* I kind of want to have his babies.

"It's strange. Realizing you're almost halfway there, halfway done with life. And to know how goddamn lucky I've been. Noah, you said you had questions. Ask me anything. I'm an open book."

"Can you tell us what you remember about that day, especially from the moment in the photo and onward?" I ask.

"I ran for my life and didn't stop running until I was over the Brooklyn Bridge. Luckily, at the time, I was training for the marathon. That came in handy," he says.

"Did you talk to any of the other people in the photo?" I ask.

"That day? No way. We were all running for our lives. You only think of us as a unit because we were captured together in that one single moment. We didn't know each other before. We were all strangers."

"What about afterward?" I ask.

"At the first anniversary, I met a few of them and thought we should try to form a support group or something. Thought we'd understand each other. For a while afterward—for a long time, if I'm honest—I had nightmares. Still do sometimes. You were too little or I would have invited you to join," he says, looking at Abbi.

"You guys got together for meetings? Like all of you?" I ask, and for the first time, I feel like maybe this could pay off, like I didn't sucker Abbi into this mess for no reason.

"Only a couple of us. Most weren't interested. I got this guy Chuck. And of course Connie. This was years ago. She was good people, Connie. The best. Chuck wasn't my favorite," he says. "Realized we didn't have that much in common after all."

"How about the guy in the University of Michigan hat? Did you know him?"

"Why are you so interested in Blue Hat Guy? What about Pencil Skirt Lady?" Abbi jokes.

"I care about Pencil Skirt Lady too," I say.

"I know nothing about Pencil Skirt Lady. But yeah, I know a little about Blue Hat Guy," Jamal says, and as he points to the Michigan M on the photocopied picture I've brought, I feel a shiver zing its way up my shoulder blades, like a cold finger writing letters on my back.

"What do you mean?" I try to sound normal, but my voice comes out strangled and tight.

"I didn't know him or anything. But a friend of a friend knew him. I heard the story later."

"Do you know his name?" I ask.

"Nope. But apparently he stopped to help someone. And then he turned around and went running back in. It didn't occur to me to do anything but run away. Not once. I didn't even stop to help Connie, and she was carrying a baby! I've spent years in therapy working that out. I'm so sorry, Hope," Jamal says.

"It's Abbi, actually. And you have nothing to be sorry for."

"You tell yourself that if the shit hits the fan, you'll be a hero. But I was no hero. I've had so much luck in my life. So much damn luck. I get to sing on Broadway! And all these amazing people didn't make it out. So many amazing people, better people than me, that's for sure. All those firefighters and police officers and that guy in the blue hat. They all ran straight into the belly of the beast. No fear. I was so scared, I pissed myself. Literally. That may be too much information," he says. So many words, one after the other, delivered in his clipped stage-actor diction, and yet they make little sense to me. I keep hearing one phrase over and over again: *He turned around.*

"Just to be clear—you know for a fact that the guy in the University of Michigan hat ran back in? So did he . . . um, do you know what happened to him?" I don't want to know, not yet. I've been waiting forever for an answer, and suddenly, it all feels too soon. It turns out I don't want the truth. That isn't what I was looking for at all. All I wanted was confirmation of my greatest, stupidest hope: that my father is alive.

Not answers. A miracle.

I wish I could time travel a few hours. Back to when my biggest problem was wondering how to kiss Abbi without making a fool of myself. Or to immediately afterward, when I mentally high-fived myself for that smooth hand-in-the-hair move. When I felt happy, like I could stand in front of that wall with her forever.

I loved kissing Abbi.

I do not love being here, discovering that I was both wrong and right.

I do not love that I did this. On purpose. Separated my own life into a before and after. When I knew and when I didn't.

"He's gone," Jamal says. The room starts to spin, and I feel the sweat gather behind my neck and knees. I steady myself by staring at one of the blue vases. Tears start to form behind my eyes and so I bite down hard on my tongue.

I want to throw those vases against the wall. One at a time.

"He knew he was on a suicide mission. You don't run back in, maybe more than once, thinking you're going to make it out. He knew what he was doing. That guy haunts me. What went through his head when he went back? What made him turn around? What does that feel like—sacrificing your life for other people's?" Jamal asks.

"Maybe he wanted to go out in a blaze of glory and leave a legacy, you know? He got to do both at once," Abbi says.

"That's really stupid," I say.

"Excuse me?" she asks, and even through my haze, I can hear the hurt in her voice.

"I'm not saying you're stupid. But that anyone would do that. That's really stupid." I picture the vases shattering in an explosion of glass. I hear what it would sound like: a sudden eruption. I imagine getting impaled by the shards. Them embedding under my skin. Maybe not even noticing till later how deep the wounds are.

I see blood. I taste it too.

"He's a hero," Jamal says.

"No, he's not. He's a fucking moron," I say.

CHAPTER FORTY-NINE

Abbi

We've been driving for fifteen weirdly silent minutes.

"I need to get home," Noah says.

No candy has been passed. No jokes made. No words spoken. I guess he deeply regrets the kissing.

"We're almost there," I say. My chest hurts, like my breath keeps getting caught on a jagged edge in my lung. I wish I could rewind us to the pink wall. I wish we had taken a picture to post to the Instagram feed in my mind, even if it now feels like a lie.

What did I do wrong? I wonder.

"Do you think my mom will be there?" It feels like Noah is speaking Spanish, a language I've studied in school but still don't know, beyond basic sentences like *My name is Abbi. I went to the beach. The beach is hot.*

I've never met Noah's mother. I have no idea about her schedule.

"You're right. It's almost five. She should be there," he answers himself.

He stares out the window. He's in a galaxy far, far away.

"Sorry, I'm . . . I don't feel so good." Noah doesn't look sick. His knee is bopping up and down and he's picking at his cuticles and he's still all filled up with that energy I envy.

What I think but don't say: *Didn't back there feel like the best kind of beginning?*

For a second, I consider whether this awkwardness is about the interview. But it was the easiest by far. No tears. No widows. When Jamal hugged us goodbye, he even smelled famous, like fresh laundry and money.

When we left, I was feeling stronger, like maybe we'd all be okay. Like we'd find some sort of Hollywood ending.

Nope.

I pull into Noah's driveway, shift the car into park. Force myself to look right at him.

"My mom's here," he says, and grabs his backpack and runs out of the car and into the house without saying goodbye.

CHAPTER FIFTY

Noah

"Noah, is that you?" my mom asks without turning around when I walk into the kitchen. "Don't tell Phil, but we're going to count the french fries as a veggie tonight."

She stands in front of the giant stove, shaking pans and stirring stuff. Since Jamal, I've been on autopilot. Key in the door, bag at the foot of the stairs, shoes off. A coldness radiates out to my fingertips.

I'm the fucking ice man.

"Did you know?" I ask, my voice so flat it's like it's been run over. Too many emotions and thoughts. Only choice I have is to power down. "Did you?"

My mom turns around, sees my face, and then crosses the room to take my hands. They are shaking. My whole body is shaking.

I feel vacuumed out. I feel almost nothing.

"Noah, honey? Hey, what happened?"

"Did you know?" I demand again. I won't say it out loud.

I shouldn't have to. If there was ever a time for her ridiculous mother ESP to work, it's right now. I shouldn't have to say out loud, *Hey, Mom, have you been lying to me for my entire life? Did you know it was Dad in the Baby Hope picture all along? Did you know he went back in? Or worst of all: Did you know I thought he was alive all this time?*

Turns out I'm the butt of the longest joke ever told. I just had the punchline backward.

She looks me straight in the eye. It strikes me that I can't remember the last time I really looked at my mother. A bit of new padding hangs from her neck, and a white hair sprouts from one eyebrow. She's dressed in what she calls "loungewear," which is another word for fancy sweats. She's still my mom, just an older, more tired version, and since she's my comfort, always has been, I reflexively relax at her touch. And then I remember what is happening.

I don't know if I want to hug her or hurt her.

"Yes," she says. "Yes, I knew."

CHAPTER FIFTY-ONE

Abbi

"He kissed me and I thought he was into me but then he ran away. What is *that* about?" I ask. I'm sitting on the newly rediscovered porch swing with my grandmother and her aide, Paula. My grandma seems to be having a good day. Paula has a thick Brooklyn accent and the sort of comforting brashness that makes you think she'd be good in a crisis or on a reality show.

"Well, not for nothing, but how was your breath?" Paula asks, making it clear she's not here to make friends. I cup my hands and sniff.

"Not bad, I think? But this was hours ago."

"You guys are morons," my grandmother declares, not unkindly, though not particularly kindly either.

"Thanks a lot," I say.

"No, seriously. We always underestimate the narcissism of the young."

"Worrying about my breath makes me a narcissist?" I ask.

"Garlic lingers, you know," Paula warns. "When I make pesto, my husband says he can smell it on me for like a week."

"Maybe it was something I said?" I ask, ignoring my grandma and turning to Paula.

"Gloria Steinem would roll over in her grave if she heard the way you're talking. Why do you assume *you* did something wrong?" my grandma asks.

"Gloria Steinem is still very much alive," I say.

"Whatever. Then it's just feminism that's dead."

"Touché," Paula says, but she pronounces it like "tushy." Already my grandma and Paula seem to have come to some sort of agreement about how things are going to be between them.

"You assume whatever happened to Noah is all about you. I get that, but it's the definition of narcissism," my grandmother says, and smooths the frizz on the crown of my head with her palm, like she used to when I was five. "Focus on the self is an essential part of growing up. It's not really your fault that you're so stupid."

"To be honest, I bet it was your breath," Paula says. "It happens."

"Maybe what's-his-name really was sick. Maybe he remembered he left the stove on. Maybe he got an emergency text. There are a gazillion reasons why he could have run off that have nothing to do with you," my grandma says, and then crosses her arms in her no-nonsense way. Paula subconsciously copies the gesture.

My grandmother has always had that effect on people; since childhood, all I've wanted to do was sit at her feet and learn.

"I have a talent for ruining good things," I say. "That's not narcissism. It's a fact."

"Ha! Wow, so narcissistic *and* melodramatic. Add in moody and you hit the teenager trifecta!"

"You're just being mean," I say, though I'm smiling. I feel soggy with love for my grandmother. I want to tackle-hug her, pin her down like a thumbtack on a wall map. I want to hold her old hands, make her fix me in place too. It may be narcissistic and also dramatic, but in my mind two words echo: *Don't go. Don't go. Don't go.* I can't lose her.

"Sorry not sorry," Paula says, and whips out a file she must have been hiding in her pocket and starts to shape her fingernails. "But, girl, you need to buy some Listerine. Solves this problem, easy peasy lemon squeezy."

CHAPTER FIFTY-TWO

Noah

A few hours later, my mom knocks on my door and doesn't wait for my *Come in*. Probably because she knew she wasn't getting one. I'm lying on my bed, staring at the ceiling. She sits at my feet, doesn't make eye contact.

"Do you remember when you were little, how we used to cuddle in the mornings before I went to work?" she asks, and takes my bunched-up blanket and folds it into a perfect rectangle. "That was the only thing that got me through losing your dad. The way you'd curl your little body against mine. You used to not let me turn around because you liked looking at my face. I mean, you were always bursting with so much sweetness. You'd hold my hand when we were walking from room to room. I felt like the luckiest unlucky person in the world. I might have lost him, but I had you. Do you remember any of that, Noah?"

I don't answer.

"Of course not. Those are the sorts of memories mothers

hold on to, not sons." She shrugs, wipes a tear from her cheek. Clears her throat and starts again, calm this time: "Your father saved six people, including a pregnant woman. Seven if you count her baby."

I stay quiet, because I don't trust myself to speak. The anger takes root. I should be feeling grief instead—though it's hard to miss something you never had. I want to put my fist through the wall. I want my knuckles to bleed. I want to unfold that damn blanket.

"He was so close to coming home. So close! You can see it in that horrible photo, which I hate, by the way. *Hate.* It's like being slapped in the face every time I see it. He's running toward us. You were so tiny then. With that literal broken heart. You, in that little hot box, with wires and breathing tubes and the bruises all over. That should have been enough to keep him putting one leg in front of the other. That should have been enough. Why wasn't it enough?"

My mom starts to weep. She gives up on wiping away the tears. Lost cause. I do nothing to comfort her.

"He went to work that day to get his lucky hat. 'I'll be back in no time,' he promised. 'In and out.' We were both so scared for you. We were desperate. He thought the hat would help. He needed to feel like he was doing something."

"You lied," I say. Two words. I can manage two words. They come out like spit.

"I don't know how to explain this."

"Try," I demand. I close my eyes, one sense down. There, easier. "You didn't not just tell me. I asked you straight out and you lied."

"I couldn't do it, Noah. I'm still so angry at him. So unbelievably angry, which isn't fair. I know that. How was I supposed to tell you about all those people showing up at our door to say thank you, as if I deserved gratitude for what your dad did? As if I were happy that they got to live when he chose to die? I wanted to slam the door in their faces. Even the pregnant woman, with that swollen belly and those swollen eyes. I even begrudged her. 'God bless you,' she said to me, sitting right at our kitchen table, your dad's and mine, and I laughed right in her face, I really did laugh, like it was funny, because what I wanted to tell her was *God has nothing to do with this. God has left the building.*"

My mom stands up, as if we are done, as if we don't have almost sixteen years of lies between us. She sits back down, wipes the still-flowing tears with the arm of her shirt.

"We ran into that lady once. In a mall, right in front of Macy's, and her baby wasn't a baby anymore, though she was pregnant again. He was around your age, five-ish, and you looked at each other, peeking around our legs. Before either of us could say a word, she started to cry, like *she* had the right to cry, *not me,* and yes, I realize no one has a monopoly on pain, but *still*. Her son had a mom *and* a dad and soon a baby brother or sister. She wasn't doing it alone. I picked you up and ran to the parking lot. Once we got into the car, I broke down, I lost it, and I swear I'll never forget this. You, all buckled up in your little seat in the back, said, 'Mommy, why was six afraid of seven? Because seven ate nine!' You were trying to make me laugh. Even then, you were you, Noah."

"You lied," I say again, because the other words—*Why didn't you tell me?*—are too hard right now. I don't want to hear stories about me as a baby. I've seen the pictures. I used to be adorable. Who cares? Nothing lasts forever.

"I didn't want you to feel that somehow we weren't enough

for him to come home to. I couldn't bear that. I wanted you to not to have a single bad feeling about that pregnant lady. Was that wrong? Because that's the truth. I didn't want to infect you with those feelings of betrayal."

"It didn't work," I say.

"What didn't work?" she asks. "What do you mean?"

"I thought he was alive. All these years. I thought he was there at the World Trade Center, that he survived and decided not to come home, probably because I was so sick. I thought he left." I choke out the words, realize I'm not as far gone as I thought, because the embarrassment rips its way through my body, slices the numbness right in half.

"I didn't . . . I didn't realize. Oh, Noah." She reaches to hug me, but I turn around. I can't watch the pity flash across her face. I cover my head with a pillow, like a little kid. "You're just like your dad. Your eyes and the shape of your mouth and your insatiable curiosity and, oh God, your sense of humor. How you want to make everything a lighter burden to carry, and not just for you, but for everyone else. Maybe even more for them. You are all love and magic, like he was. It never occurred to me that if I didn't tell you the truth, another myth would take its place. I'm so sorry."

I feel no relief. Her apology bounces off me. What did I think was going to happen with this whole Baby Hope photo search? Did I think I'd discover my dad was still alive? Seriously? And even if he was, what was I going to do? Track him down?

Things stay lost. I thought I'd already learned that lesson.

"You know, it took me years to realize that it had nothing to do with us. Your dad didn't turn around and save all of those people because he didn't want to come home. Or because we weren't enough. Your father turned around because that's who he was. Extraordinary. He was a hero. He never had a choice."

"We all have choices," I say, and then I get up and pack a bag.

CHAPTER FIFTY-THREE

Abbi

I play it cool when I see Noah at camp. All *Hey, what's up,* super casual, not at all like my grandma, Paula, and I spent hours last night analyzing his behavior. Not like I've replayed that kiss a million times in my head and want some more *pleasethankyou-verymuch.* I can do this platonic-friends thing. No hard feelings. No feelings at all. Not a one.

My heart is not hiccupping. That yearning I'm feeling is merely hunger, not longing.

It's all cool.

I'm cool.

"Hey," he says, and does his best guy nod. I wait for him to say something, anything else, even a *Yesterday was a mistake, let's just be friends,* to which I had the response all prepared: *Totally agree.* He looks rough today, hair all over the place. Before he has a chance to speak, Uncle Maurice, Knight's Day Camp's fearless leader, breaks out a bullhorn and starts shouting instructions.

Today is the start of Color War, which I've been looking forward to since I took this job.

"All groups are to be split in half, designated blue or red, and then paired with their opposite gender counterparts. Junior counselors go with opposite junior counselors. Senior counselors with opposite senior counselors," Uncle Maurice announces, and I hear Julia mutter under her breath: *"Crap."* Clearly, she wants to spend the day with Zach about as much as I want to with Noah. Which is to say not even a little bit.

I don't even want to look at Noah—no need to stare rejection right in the face—so I look over at Zach, who looks at Julia, who looks at me because she doesn't want to acknowledge Zach. And around we go in this exciting game of avoiding each other.

"I'm on Abbi's team," Livi declares, and upon hearing this, the rest of the girls line up behind Julia.

Little traitors.

We divide everyone into equal groups. Uncle Maurice hands me ten red kid-sized T-shirts that have the camp logo, a graphic of a Knight, and then pauses and quietly hands over one more kid one for me. I pull it on over my tank top and try not to stare as Noah takes off his shirt, which looks old and battered and says University of Michigan, and carefully folds it. He then slips on his adult-sized camp shirt. His abs, while nowhere near Charles's level of chiseled, are not as boyish as I would have guessed. There's a possibility this guy actually does crunches when he's not watching comedy specials. Or at least *while* he's watching.

"Hey," Noah says. He's walked over to me, and he's standing so close, I can feel his breath on my ear. I try to squash the hope that takes flight in my chest. "About yesterday. I'll . . . Can we talk later?"

There it is. Over before it even began. I guess it's a credit to him that he wants to discuss things as opposed to letting me know via the cold shoulder. He doesn't really owe me anything.

"It's fine," I say, flushing as I remember that this morning I gargled not once, but twice with mouthwash. Just in case. I ignore the sadness that crashes over me, a cold, unpleasant shower of disappointment. "Friends?"

I put out my hand for him to shake, like this is the start of a job interview or something, and he looks at my hand and then up at me, like he has no idea what that gesture means.

"Sure," he says, keeping his hands in his pockets, which means mine is left dangling, and I awkwardly drop it. "Right. Friends."

"So Color War," I say.

"Color War," he echoes, as if to say, *I see your intense discomfort right now and I have no desire to save you from it.* Which is pretty crappy of him, considering he's the one who ran away yesterday, not me. He's the one who wants to "talk." If he wanted us to be together, there wouldn't be the need for a conversation. We'd continue what we started.

"We're going to kick the blue team until they're dead!" Livi says, interrupting our weird showdown. Her whole tiny body vibrates with excitement. "We're going to be the winningest!"

"I like your enthusiasm, but we're not supposed to actually kick the other team. Or, you know, kill them," Noah says, charmed by Livi, which in turn charms me despite myself.

"Not actually kill 'em dead," Livi explains, and shadowboxes the air before progressing through an array of karate moves. "But boom, pow, wham, boink 'em!"

"That was some impressive onomatopoeia," Noah says,

smiling at Livi, and then he pauses only a half second before mock-punching my shoulder.

We're back to being buddies. I tell myself I don't mind. I tell myself you can't lose something you never really had.

The blue team is going down. We're in the middle of an aggressive game of musical chairs—it turns out I'm a ringer—and I'm distracting myself by getting completely swept up in the competitive spirit. Red paint decorates my face. My hands still burn from tug-of-war. My voice is shredded from screaming. The scoreboard is officially tied, and we're moments away from learning who won the day's Color War.

After a particularly brutal seventh round, most of my fellow reds have been eliminated. Only Livi, Noah, and I are left from our team. From the blue, there's Zach and two boys whose names I do not know and who I intend to beat, despite the fact that they are four years old and the cutest.

The music switches on, and we begin to circle again, moving increasingly faster in our weird squat-run so that our butts are ready to find the nearest chair. The song swells along with my heart. For the first time in my life, I understand all those sports fans who cry over things like the Super Bowl. I'll admit it: I want to win. I want to win more than I've ever wanted to win anything in my life.

This feels much bigger than the first day of a silly camp Color War. This is about giving Livi a taste of victory after no one wanted to be on her team. This is about giving me a taste of victory too. Some sort of cosmic sign that I will be okay for now, that this heartbreak is temporary, that I'll survive summer's end.

The music stops. I drop to the nearest chair and manage to beat the two blue boys, who end up falling onto my lap.

"You're out!" I scream, exuberant, punching the air, until I see that both Livi and Noah have been left standing too. Shoot. It's just me and Zach for the last round, and victory now rests solely on my shoulders. A crowd has gathered around us— a bunch of the older kids and even Lifeguard Charles—and the cheering grows louder.

I can do this, I tell myself. *I will do this.*

I think tactically. I'm about half of Zach's size, so I can't meet him with brute force. I'm going to have to be sneaky and fast.

The music starts—a girl-power pop song, one of my favorites, one that I danced to in my room before the start of camp, one that promises I'm better off without him—and we start our rotation around the single chair. I'm breathing heavily, enough to feel the burn in my lungs, sharp and tight. I ignore the pain.

"Go, Abbi! Go!" Livi yells.

"You got this," Noah says, calm and fierce at the same time.

"Take him down!" Julia screams, crossing team lines to root for me.

I watch Zach's hairy knees as we move, and listen. I know this song, have air-drummed to it enough to know when the absence of music means an extra beat or dead air. Then, as the singer promises to come back stronger, louder, better, there it is, a millisecond of a pause and the music stops. Zach starts to lower his heavy body onto the chair, and so I do the only thing I can. I slip right under him and land first.

I win.

The crowd goes wild. Everyone is screaming. Zach still sits

on me, but I'm so excited that I barely notice. The chair, this victory, is mine. All mine.

After a moment, I push his back to get him off me, but he doesn't move. I push again.

Suddenly, my disloyal lungs decide now would be a good time to revolt. They don't even give me a chance to revel for a few minutes. I cough deep and hard and it hurts in a way coughing is not supposed to hurt. I feel like I've dislodged an organ.

"Get off of her!" Noah yells, right up in Zach's face. I cough more. I feel the blood vessels in my face fill. Too hot. "You're hurting her."

"Seriously, move," Julia says as Noah grabs Zach by the collar and lifts him off me.

"Relax, brother, I was playing," Zach says. "I was barely sitting on her. She's fine."

Except despite the fact that I've been freed, I can't get any air. The coughing gives way to a whooping wheeze. The world blurs and I see explosions of light.

"Help!" Noah screams. "She has asthma!"

"What?" Zach asks.

"Someone call an ambulance," Noah says.

Ambulance? No. This isn't happening. *I'm fine*, I want to say. *We won Color War! Please don't ruin this for me.*

I want to tell him *This will pass. It always does.*

I want to say *I know what this is.*

I want to say *I still have one more month.*

No words come. I'm trapped in one of those nightmares where you can't scream.

I try to grab hold of something solid as I fight for consciousness, and Noah takes my hands.

"It's okay," he says, squeezing tightly. His voice is faux calm, betrayed by an unmistakable undercurrent of panic. "They're coming. Put your head between your legs. I promise you're going to be okay. Breathe. Abbi, please breathe. Breathe."

I lean forward. The air only comes in tiny squeezed-through doses, like air is something solid and hard and impassable. I can't get nearly enough. I have no idea how long I've been sitting here. I picture my inhaler in my bag, which feels hundreds of miles away. All that empty space between us.

"Breathe," Noah says again. "I'm here. Breathe."

"What's happening?" Livi asks. "Did Abbi eat red paint?"

That's the last thing I hear before everything goes dark.

CHAPTER FIFTY-FOUR

Noah

Abbi's blood is on my shirt and on my shoes and I have no memory of how it got there. I call Jack from the emergency room, my hand shaking so hard I have trouble pressing the buttons.

"On my way," Jack says.

"They won't tell me anything. They took her behind the swinging doors and told me to wait. How am I supposed to wait?"

I pace up and down in a loop, step over the bleary-eyed and the sick. A little kid with a shiner vrooms a Matchbox car up the back of his seat while his mom tries to wrangle an ice pack onto his face. I ignore the nurse who keeps pointing at the No Cell Phones sign. This place feels postapocalyptic: already on alert and resigned to defeat.

I can feel the adrenaline rush through my veins, and feel enraged at the useless energy. I want to *help her, goddammit.*

"Abbi's going to be fine," Jack says. Nonsense words. A

sentence that has as much value as when people find out my dad is dead and say, *I'm so sorry. I didn't know.* As if their knowing has any bearing on the matter.

"There was blood everywhere. I mean, I thought she was going to die right on the field. I've never seen anything like it." I don't tell Jack that I said a prayer under my breath, that it felt like I needed to mark the divide between when Abbi was okay and when she wasn't. That when she passed out, I thought, *This is it. This is how it looks when people die.*

"She's going to be fine," he says again.

"She was blue. In the ambulance."

"Noah," Jack says. "Take a breath."

"I thought she was going to die. Seriously. I mean, she still might. She could be dead back there, for all I know." I hear the hysteria in my voice, the crack on the word *dead.* In the ambulance, she opened her eyes and looked at me, and I held her hand and said over and over: *You're going to be fine.* I wonder if she thought the same thing I did when Jack said them: that the words were as hollow as lies.

"My ETA is T-minus three minutes," he says. "Sit down. Relax. I'm almost there."

"I'm going to strangle Zach with my bare hands. Break both of his arms. He's never going to do one of those stupid headstands again."

"I promise we can tag-team body-slam him WWE-style later. But right now, you need to sit down."

"She said she just wanted to be friends." Like my shaking hands, it seems I can't control the words coming out of my mouth. I ignore the pressure mounting behind my eyes.

"Abbi said that?"

"No. Your mother. Of course Abbi! I'm such a fuckup. My dad was a hero, and what do I do when faced with my first real life-and-death situation? I panic." I lean against a wall and bend my body in half. Head to knee. A prayer that is not a prayer but an apology.

"I don't know. Sounds like you did everything right."

"I almost threw up in the ambulance. No one knows that. Don't ever repeat that."

"Ambulances are nauseating. Lots of twists and turns. And sometimes you sit backward," Jack says. "Did you sit backward?"

"Thank God I didn't puke."

"Dude, you got this hero thing all wrong. Who cares about whether you puke? It's about getting in the ambulance anyway despite knowing that you might blow chunks on the girl you are secretly in love with," he says. "That takes courage."

"Are you running right now?"

"Yup. I can drop little wisdom bombs and run at the same time. I'm a hero too."

"Tell me she's not going to die. She can't die, right?" I ask.

"She can't. She won't. Not going to happen," Jack says.

"How can you know that? People die all the time."

"Not Baby Hope."

"That's a bullshit answer," I say, and the mom of the kid with the Matchbox car gives me a dirty look. I mouth *Sorry*.

"Okay, how about this. There's no way that in less than twenty-four hours you could make out with a cool girl, find out your dad, who you thought was alive all these years, is definitely, a hundred percent dead and like this major hero, and then have your almost-first girlfriend die, who also happens to be, like, this national icon. That would be too ridiculous, even for you, Noah."

"That actually helps," I say.

"Good. I'm walking in now," Jack says, and then before I can even say thank you, he envelops me in a tackle hug. I quietly start to cry.

CHAPTER FIFTY-FIVE

Abbi

My first thought when I wake up, after *I'm not dead,* is *I bled all over Noah.* I'm not proud that this is where my brain goes first instead of the much more logical and empathetic *My parents must be devastated.* Maybe my grandma is right about my narcissism.

I have a tube in my nose and an IV hooked up to my arm. I'm wearing a hospital gown, though I have no recollection of changing clothes. I do remember being rolled from room to room. X-rays, a CT scan. Not sure when I fell asleep. I assume they medicated me, that perhaps there are some good drugs dripping into my veins right at this moment.

My mother stands next to my bed, staring at me intently, and I get the distinct impression she's been in this position for a while. Possibly hours.

"Abbi? Oh, honey." My mother's clenched face softens and releases. "How are you feeling?"

"I don't know. Embarrassed, I guess." My mom laughs a snot-filled laugh because she's also simultaneously crying.

"I meant physically."

"Okay. Tired. I have a headache. Where's Dad?" I ask mostly to get her to stop looking at me.

"Daddy's right here," my father says, and the fact that he calls himself *Daddy* when he's been Dad for a long time now breaks something on my insides.

I turn my head toward him, slowly, since I'm afraid of disrupting all my attached machinery, and I notice that his eyes are as puffy as my mother's. If I could, I'd jump out of bed and perform a tap dance, anything to make them both feel better. To prove that I'm going to be fine. But when I breathe, it feels like pressing a bruise. Standing would be impossible.

"Guess what? You won Color War," my mom says. She's decided to play this cheery, despite her tear-soaked cheeks. I'm okay with that. I'm familiar with this script. It's much better than the alternative. "Nice work."

"How do you know?" My voice sounds clear, if a little rough. Like I'm at the tail end of a cold. Not like I'm dying.

"There were a bunch of camp people here. You should have seen the waiting room," my mom says, and then starts counting on her fingers. "First of all, Julia and her boyfriend, I think? A mom and this cute little girl dropped off a bunch of pictures she drew for you. A boy who was quite dapper and kept apologizing. He also tried to get everyone to hold hands and send you positive energy, which was awkward."

My mom chatters and floats round the room as she talks, picks up random objects and then puts them back down. A clipboard. A vase. A remote control. "Let me see, what else? You have a ton of flowers."

238

"Noah and Jack are still out there," my dad adds. "They've been here all day. They seem like nice boys. Kept offering to get us coffee. Kept calling me Mr. Goldstein. Then their friend with lots of tattoos showed up. He brought cookies!"

Apparently, my dad is as nervous as my mom. All verbal diarrhea.

I'm in a hospital bed. My parent's look scared and tired and so unwaveringly sad.

So this is it, I think.

"Listen, I just want to say . . . I'm sorry. I'm so, so sorry." The sobs start low, behind my defective lungs, and try to push their way out. "I should have told you. I wanted one last summer—"

"Oh, baby, don't cry. It's going to be okay. You'll be able to go home soon, I think. They need to do one more test." My mom sits down next to me and links our hands. Her face is wet again. Still, she smiles. She looks deranged. "But you're going to be fine. I know it. It's—"

"Wait. Should have told us what?" my dad asks, and I consider changing the subject, reversing back to my mother's false promises. There's no real need to confess. I'm here. The truth—the fact that I'm sick—is no longer a secret. What difference does it make that I knew this was coming?

And yet, I realize I don't want to be like Cat, who pushes her way into my mind even at this moment, though this time she brings with her an epiphany: I don't want to get by on half-truths and twisted language, on the filtered picture rather than the real image.

"It's . . . it's been going on for a while. The coughing. The blood. I didn't want to worry you," I say.

"Worry us!" my mother yells, and my dad and I both jump. My mom never yells; we've moved from loving sympathy to rage in mere seconds. I feel dread climb its way up my spine vertebra by vertebra. "This is your health. Are you serious? You didn't tell us?"

"Mom," I begin.

"How long?"

I shrug. "It wasn't that big a deal. I mean, it was, but it wasn't? I didn't think I needed to say anything until . . ."

"Until what, sweet—" my dad starts, but my mom interrupts him.

"Tell us, damn it! The doctors will need to know. How long?" She's on her feet again, pacing the room, her fingers balled into tight fists. I look over at my dad, but he has his dropped his head into his hands.

"Don't be mad," I plead. I knew they'd be upset, but I figured they'd take the news in their usual calm, martyrlike way. Also, and it pains me to admit this, I thought *seeing* me sick would mean they couldn't really get mad. You know, because of the whole limited-time-left thing.

"Abbi, sweetheart, please tell us how long," my dad says, and the tremor in his voice betrays his calm tone.

"I'm sorry. I'm really sorry. Not long. Maybe about six weeks–ish? But it wasn't so bad. I was going to tell you in the fall. I needed the summer. I wasn't ready. Don't hate me."

"Of course we don't hate you," my dad says at the exact same time my mother says, "There's a tumor."

I feel the floor of my insides give way.

Turns out there's a big difference between knowing and *knowing*.

"I thought we agreed we'd talk about the best way to approach—" my dad says, but my mom rolls right over him.

There's no containing her. Her anger bounces off the four walls; I can feel it, like a current.

"Do you have any idea what this means? Tumors grow. The earlier you catch them . . . Oh my God, you should have told us." My mom is no longer whirling around the room. Instead she stops abruptly, and folds over herself. She reminds me of Sheila Brashard talking about her husband, but about a thousand times more hysterical.

"I'm sorry," I say again. "It wasn't . . . I didn't think." I sound like a little girl. Maybe this is what dying is like. Moving backward through time until you're not there anymore. Until you disappear from a room.

"We don't know anything yet," my dad says, and covers my mother with his body, folds himself directly over her, as if to bear her pain for her. "They need to biopsy. None of us should jump to any conclusions."

"Right. We shouldn't jump to conclusions," I say. I'm fully aware of my own hypocrisy. We all know where this came from. We all know how this story ends. This part is not a fairy tale. From the first moment I saw blood, I've never for a second thought things could be otherwise. You don't get to be a survivor twice. You don't.

A tumor.

My mom shakes off my father's embrace. Looks at me in the bed. Slowly scans the length of my short body from the oxygen tank to the tube in my nose and down to my feet. Shakes her head.

"I can't do this again," my mom says. "I'm sorry."

And then she walks out of the room.

CHAPTER FIFTY-SIX

Noah

My mom calls me twenty-seven times. I send her to voice mail. Then she starts texting. Because of course she does.

Mom: PICK UP YOUR PHONE. PLEASE. I'm worried. You haven't been home since YESTERDAY!!!

Mom: Noah! You can be mad at me and still give me the courtesy of telling me you're not dead. I don't ask for much.

Mom: Please text back two letters: OK.

Mom: I'm losing it. Seriously. Don't do this to me.

Mom: I saw the news. Is Abbi okay? Are you? What's going on?

Phil: You okay, bud? Your mom is really freaked out.

Phil: Noah? Please let us know you are okay. I'm worried too.

Phil: This isn't funny. We're your parents and we're scared. Call. Text. Send a smoke signal. Anything.

Me: . . .

Phil: Those three dots mean you are there, right?

Me: Did you make a joke?

Phil: What?

Me: The smoke signal thing. That was a joke

Phil: Sort of. Not a very good one. Are you okay? Feel free
to answer in Morse code.

Me: Another joke

Phil: I'm trying.

Me: I'm at the hospital waiting to see Abbi

Phil: Your mom is a wreck. Been worried sick all night.

Me: Tell her I'm still angry

Phil: She says she understands. You have every right
to be.

Phil: For what it's worth, she didn't tell me either.

This unravels me. I think about my mom and Phil, how
every night before bed, she slathers on her hand cream and he
uses his Waterpik, and how, most mornings, she pours him his
bowl of shredded wheat. I think how two lives can be braided
together so tightly it doesn't leave enough room for the truth.

Did she think he couldn't handle it either? Or did she realize
that by telling him and not me, I'd feel doubly betrayed when I
inevitably found out? My brain feels like it might spontaneously
combust. This day has held too much. I still have Abbi's blood
on my shirt.

Phil: Please come home tonight. You guys can talk this all
out.

Me: Ask her if it's true that he liked pickle sandwiches or
if that was a lie too

Phil: She says yes. 100%. She also says to tell you that
your dad once entered a pun competition. She says
that's a real thing. Competitive wordplay.

Noah: What?

Phil: Apparently it's kind of like improv. She said your dad
sucked at it and didn't get past the first round but it
was hilarious and terrible and you would have loved it.
She said she has a million more things she wants to
tell you about him and that you need to come home to
hear at least the first three.

Noah: I'll be back later

Phil: Good. He sounds like a cool guy. I'd like to know
more too. Your mom needs to work on talking about
him.

Noah: Is this still Phil?

Phil: Don't sound so surprised. I've been in therapy for
years. I'm very self-actualized.

Noah: This day has been very confusing

CHAPTER FIFTY-SEVEN

Abbi

My dad and I are staring at a television screen mounted on the wall of my hospital room, not talking. We're watching our second episode of *Judge Judy*.

"I'm in love with your mother," he says, suddenly, breaking our uncomfortable silence. His voice drips with misery. My mom left about an hour ago. We have no idea where she went or when she'll be back.

"What?" I ask to buy time as my brain catches up with this revelation, which, like the announcement about my tumor, isn't so much a revelation, actually, now that I think about it, as a confirmation. I have no idea how I'm supposed to feel. Of course, kids of divorce often fantasize about their parents getting back together—I did it for years—even though everyone says that those reunions don't happen and that hoping for them is like expecting someone to rise from the dead. And yet, here we find ourselves, one-half of the way there.

"I'm in love with your mother. Again. Or still." My father

doesn't look at me. Judge Judy screams at the defendant and jabs at her with a heavily ringed finger. I can see the spittle forming at the corner of her mouth, the peculiar benefit of watching her in HD. I wonder for the tenth time if Judge Judy is pretending to be angry, if her entire show is pure shtick, or if she truly cares that the lady with the teased hair did not pay the cost of ruining her cousin's wedding dress with regurgitated merlot. I want to yell at the screen and tell them to stop fighting, that life is too short, and then I remember that I once read somewhere that the litigants get paid to be there.

Like pretty much everything else, none of it is real.

"Does Mom love you back? I mean, I know she loves you, but does she love you in like, you know, that way?" I ask. I have no idea why my father has chosen this moment, while I'm immobilized by an IV in a hospital bed and my mortality hangs in the balance, to discuss the intimate details of his and my mother's relationship. Then it occurs to me that maybe it's because he knows we're running out of time and for him, unlike me, that realization has turned him honest. Maybe he subscribes to Noah's blaze-of-glory theory, and this is how we're going to go out—with big, life-changing declarations. Maybe he wants to have another wedding, and soon, so I can be well enough to attend. I could be maid of honor.

Just after the divorce, there was nothing I wanted more— one house, one family, dinner on proper dishes that we put in the dishwasher afterward. And then, around twelve or thirteen, I stopped wasting birthday wishes on that sort of nonsense. I know people whose parents have had ugly, bitter divorces, whose parents can't be in the same room together, who have to eat Thanksgiving dinner twice so no one is upset. I was grateful that my mom and dad seemed to still like each other. I'm

246

relieved now by the idea that they'll have each other to lean on after I'm gone.

"I don't know. Things have been . . . There's been something new between us lately," my dad says, and his voice breaks. "I shouldn't be telling you this. I'm scared. I'm so unbelievably terrified about what's happening, and I know your mom is too, and her running away, that wasn't only about you. I mean, it was mostly about you, but not totally. Last night, I asked her if I could move back home. Great timing, right?"

Again with the nervous talking and the oversharing.

"What did Mom say?" I ask.

"She said she'd think about it. That it was a lot of change at once, because of your grandmother. We didn't know that twelve hours later you'd be hemorrhaging on the soccer field." He makes a weird sniffle-laugh sound. Our lives have always been absurd.

"I wasn't hemorrhaging," I say.

"Do you prefer *bleeding profusely?*" he asks.

"I do, actually." This time, we both laugh, no anxious sniffling, and for a second, it feels like old times, or pre-today times, when my dad and I could sit comfortably and chat and would not have to pretend to be engrossed in *Judge Judy* to avoid having to face up to my impending death. Overall, things were pretty good pre-today.

"When you have a kid, it's like letting your heart walk around outside your body. You never get used to it."

"It's going to be all right," I say, which is truer than *I'm* going to be all right.

"I know I should pretend I'm not scared, that that would be the right move parentally, but I can't. Abbi, you being sick? You won't know until you're a parent, but holy crap, it's our worst nightmare. Let me have your tumor. Please hand it right over. Forget the results. Even the biopsy scares me. That's surgery."

My dad looks at me, and I'm afraid to look back. I don't want to see his eyes. Instead, I turn again to find that *Judge Judy* has been replaced by *Wheel of Fortune;* the host and the letter-turning lady both have terrifyingly frozen faces. Talk about living forever.

"I've been so naive thinking we paid our dues all those years ago. That we were so lucky. We got to do all our worrying at once. I've been the opposite of your mom. She's been extra worried about you," he confides.

His voice breaks, and I pretend not to notice. I pretend we are not both drowning in our own fear. On the screen, the woman in the tight dress turns the letter Z.

Sometimes, even though it's perverse, I think about the jumpers on 9/11. About two hundred people plunged out the windows of the Towers toward certain death. With the exception of a single couple, who held hands as they fell, the rest went one by one, as if they'd been waiting in an unfathomable line.

It's entirely possible that there was a line. That there's decency in the darkness.

The jumpers have mostly been erased from history. It's an unspoken rule that you don't talk about them, but I've never been able to understand the stigma. When I think about those two hundred men and women, I think only of bravery, of taking one last leap of faith, of reclaiming their last bit of power the only way they could find it.

At night, when I can't sleep, I sometimes think about an article I read once about a lady who, as she fell, had the presence of mind to hold down her skirt so she wouldn't flash the people below. I wish I had told Noah about her, how *she* should be the national treasure, not Baby Hope, because I realize that's how I want to die. Not on my terms—no one gets to die on their own terms—and not in a blaze of glory. I want to scoop up dignity wherever I can find it.

"Don't be scared. I'm not. I mean, I am a little, but this is life with a capital *L*, right? Surgery, shmurgery." I speak with a bravado I do not feel. I look up at the *Wheel of Fortune* puzzle, but the letters blur. I find myself irrationally annoyed about the preferential treatment given to the letter *E*.

"Dad," I say, and my voice grows serious. I decide there should be no fear, at least not about words. I want radical honesty. "It's *still* and *again*. As in you are *still* in love with Mom, and you are also in love with her *again*. Just to be clear."

My words are punctuated by the *tick-tick-tick* of the big spinning wheel on television. We stop talking for a second and stare at the screen to wait in suspense as the pointer lands: a lady named Tess in a leopard-print blouse cheers when she adds a brand-new washer-dryer wedge to her dollar total. A cardboard representation of the possibility of the thing. Better than bankruptcy, if not quite as cool as the Hawaiian vacation.

My mother once told me the most disconcerting part of being a parent is that you never get to settle into it, that your child is constantly being replaced with another version you don't recognize. She said she looks at old photos of me and asks, *Who's that?* I wonder now how it's impossible to feel our own incremental growth. How this theory of hers could help explain the disconnect I've felt since I've started high school. I am me and also an unrecognizable version of me, both at the same time. How it's possible I could have once been friends with

Cat and now am not at all. Four entirely different people: the two mes, the two hers. Our new configurations, for whatever reasons, unreconcilable.

It strikes me that Baby Hope only existed for as long as it took the photographer to take that picture.

"You'll have the biopsy; the tumor's going to be benign. This will all be over. But it's going to take us through a surgery to get to fine, and I'd like to fast-forward that part," my dad says, again to the television. This is hard work we are doing here, the not-looking-at-each-other, the pretending-to-truth-tell. He wants to fast-forward to another iteration of me.

But he doesn't know I'm going to be fine. No one does.

When I look up at the screen again, my brain fills in the missing letters, and I'm finally able to solve the puzzle, even before Tess.

I shout out the answer, as if to claim the small, well-deserved victory of being right.

CHAPTER FIFTY-EIGHT

Noah

"Put on channel four. Are you watching this?" I tell Abbi. I'm at home, in my room, in my pajamas. We're talking on the phone, which feels weirdly intimate. I can't remember the last time I made an actual telephone call, other than to Jack from the ER, but I needed to hear that she was okay. Her voice sounds lower and huskier than in real life.

"Details are scant at this time, but eyewitness reports say that Baby Hope, who was made famous by a photograph taken on nine-eleven and who now goes by Abbi Goldstein, was rushed by ambulance to Garden State Hospital after she collapsed at a nearby summer camp. She is sixteen years of age," reports Brittany Brady, the platinum-blond newscaster who is always outside and who always looks cold. "By way of background, the woman who saved Baby Hope's life, Connie Kramer Greene, died less than one year ago from breast cancer, a disease many believe was caused by her exposure to toxic chemicals on September 11, 2001. In just the last five weeks, two New York City police officers who were part of the recovery at Ground Zero have died of nine-eleven-related illnesses. No word yet on whether Abbi's condition is related to the attacks. One of Abbi's best friends, Cat Gibson, has kindly agreed to talk with us this evening.

"Can you tell us what went through your mind when you heard Abbi had been admitted to the hospital?"

"Best friend my ass," Abbi mutters.

"It was a complete shock. I've known Abbi since we were little, and I don't think she's ever even broken a bone. I'm really worried," Cat says through my television.

"Has she been sick recently?" Brittany Brady asks.

"Um, I don't think so? I mean, she's always had asthma."

"If Abbi is watching right now, what would you like to say to her?" Brittany Brady asks.

"This is so meta. Because you *are* watching," I say, and Abbi shushes me.

"Like to her directly?" Cat asks, and Brittany Brady nods. "Right. I hope you get better, Abbi. My mom told me about her conversation with you. You didn't have to cover for me about that, but you did—even after everything. So thank you."

"That was Cat Gibson expressing . . . ," Brittany Brady says, trying to cut her off, but Cat keeps on talking.

"Abbi, you're the brave one, not me. Always hugging all those strangers. Still, it's hard when the person who's supposed to know you best looks at you and only sees who you used to be. Come home soon, okay?"

The newscaster keeps her face placid while she forcibly grabs the microphone back.

"This is Brittany Brady reporting live outside of Garden State Hospital." Then the news goes back to covering the president's latest tweets threatening nuclear war and hence the destruction of humanity. I switch off the television.

"Just when I thought I was ready to hate her," Abbi says.

"Brittany Brady? She seems okay to me, though I think someone should really buy her a coat," I say.

"Cat!"

"Joking. Who knows? You're better off without her. I'm starting to learn that sometimes there aren't easy explanations for why people do the things they do," I say. "Also, I think sometimes people think they're protecting you when they're really protecting themselves." I look at the floor of my room, which is covered with boxes of my dad's old stuff. My mom hauled everything up from the basement, including about a dozen photo albums I didn't know existed. She wants to go through it all together, to, in her words, *introduce me to my father*. She seemed so hopeful, I didn't have the heart to tell her that I don't think he's in there. As Sheila put it, a picture of a thing is not the same thing as the thing.

"Sorry for bleeding all over you. I should have said that sooner. The most embarrassing moment of my life," Abbi says.

"Don't apologize. Though you did scare the shit out of me, figuratively speaking. And out of Livi literally." I open one of the albums, and my parents' wedding photo stares back at me. I close it. There's plenty of time for all this later. I'm no longer going to think of my dad as if he's only available in limited quantities that need to be rationed. He's dead, yes, but he lived for thirty-three years. I have a lot to catch up on.

"I heard Brendan came to the hospital?" Abbi asks. "Please tell me he and Jack are hooking up. I need some good news today."

"According to Jack, they've been doing more than talking by the frozen fish," I report.

"Yes!"

"Can I come visit you tomorrow morning? I . . . Yeah, can I come by?" I ask, and realize this is not suave at all. I've never been suave. I'm never going to be suave. Listen, my dad did pun competitions. I apparently have nerd encoded deep in my DNA.

"Sure," she says. I smile.

"I'm so happy that you're feeling better, Abs," I say.

"Thanks."

"Oh, crap. You failed my test."

"What test?"

"I called you Abs and you didn't correct me. Now I'm really worried."

"You practically saved my life this morning. I think I can let one Abs go."

"Wait, I can call you Abs now?"

"I guess."

"I knew it! There's an Abs stage!" I pump my fist in the air, even though I know she can't see me.

"There's no Abs stage," she insists.

"I never would have guessed that you'd have such an elaborate initiation ritual. I mean, I had to practically shower in your blood to get here. But it was worth it."

"Good night, Noah," she says, all mock-annoyed.

"Good night . . . Wait for it . . . ," I say.

"Waiting," Abbi says.

"Good night, Abs." I sigh with contentment, loud enough for her to hear. "It was so, so worth it."

CHAPTER FIFTY-NINE

Abbi

"I'm here," my mom says after we've both been pretending to sleep for at least an hour. My mother returned to my room around dinnertime, sheepishly donning her weariest divorce-smile and carrying a bunch of balloons, of all things, and now lies on the cot next to my bed. Despite arguing that I'm old enough to stay here alone for one night, that she and my dad should go home and talk, I'm relieved she ignored me. I didn't realize that once darkness fell, the fear would slice right through me. "I mean, I'm here for you. I'm not going anywhere. I panicked earlier. Residual PTSD, maybe." She pauses. "No, that's an excuse. It's seems so silly now, but I really believed if I worried about you enough, that that alone would keep you safe. Like my mother says when she reverts to Yiddish in an emergency, *Kinehora*. Imagining your future would jinx it. But the world doesn't work like that. It never did," she says.

I don't answer. I listen to the *beep, beep, beep* of the machines. Find comfort in their rhythmic reliability.

"After the first plane hit, Dad and I started running back toward the Towers. To get you. But we couldn't. There were cops, and all these people running in the other direction, and the roads were blocked, and it was impossible. Dad said that Connie would keep you safe—you were her favorite—and she'd been so excited about your birthday. She made you that crown. There was nothing to worry about, but of course this was before the Towers actually fell. We didn't know. No one knew," she says, and starts weeping quietly. "Sometimes the worst thing you can possibly imagine happens. It just does. But on that day, for me, it didn't. I mean, I thought it did, it almost did, it could have, but then you came home. My baby came home."

"And so many other people's didn't," I say, tears hot on my cheeks. I don't have to look over at my mother to know her face is wet too.

Tomorrow afternoon I will be knocked unconscious while doctors cut me open and tinker with my tumor.

Tumor. Tumor. Tumor.

Say that five times fast and it still doesn't lose meaning. Believe me, I've tried.

A surgeon will slice off a piece of my lung and then send it to a lab for analysis. Even if it's malignant, the doctor, a middle-aged woman with gray-streaked hair and a cruel brisk efficiency, has promised there are *options*. That's the word she chose—*options*. Not one sounded even slightly appealing. Other drugs, chemo, more surgery. She talked about stages, which made me think of that time Cat went on a baby food diet and she'd stare at the little labels and restrict herself to only jars stamped with the number 1 or 2.

"It feels like the worst thing I can possibly imagine—you,

sick—is actually happening, and I don't know what to do. I'm so ashamed of how I keep failing to protect you. This isn't how it's supposed to be. You are a child."

My mother starts crying again, and I reach out my hand for her to grab.

"None of this is your fault. That's one of the reasons I didn't want to tell you. I knew you'd blame yourself," I say.

"I think that makes me feel even worse."

"*Mom.*"

"I have an idea," she says, and clears her throat. "Tonight, let's think happy thoughts. It doesn't have to be about tomorrow. Or all the ways I've failed you, because oh, man, have I screwed this all up. I'm going to close my eyes and just for tonight feel all the best things. How proud I am to be your mother. How you're the best thing that ever happened to me, even though I've never deserved you. How much I love you."

"I love you too." I decide denial has worked pretty well so far. Right now, while I still can, I will dwell on the good stuff. That which cannot be taken away, at least not yet. My parents again, still, together, always there for me. Swinging on the porch with my grandmother. Noah and Jack grabbing my hands in friendship. A waiting room full of people I had no idea cared. A stolen moment illuminated in pink.

In the morning, on top of my hospital gown, I put on a pair of oversized sweatpants and a too-small gray long-sleeve T-shirt with a shiny unicorn—what my dad picked out from my closet to bring me from home. I dab on some ChapStick. My unruly hair is pulled back into what I hope looks like an intentionally messy ponytail. The nurse refuses to unhook my IV, so there's nothing I can do about the creepy slow drip into my bruised arm or the blue under my eyes from not sleeping.

No doubt I smell like hospital and fear.

No doubt I look as terrible as I feel.

Even though Noah's exactly on time, I jump when he knocks on the door. My parents, who are slumped in the corner, greet him with the same kind of apologetic kiss-ass grins they used when they met with my guidance counselor about my college prospects. Fortunately, they quickly excuse themselves to get coffee.

"Why didn't you mention you were an expert at musical chairs?" Noah asks, and though his tone is jokey, there's a rehearsed air to the line, as if on the way over, he decided how he was going to break the ice.

"Hi," I say, and ignore his question. Instead, I smile. Noah being here changes the balance in the air, tips me back over toward gratitude.

"Hi yourself," he says back, and returns my smile. "So I have a speech prepared. I practiced on Jack last night, and it killed. Do you want to hear it?"

"Sure." I don't really want to hear a speech. I want him to sit down next to me on the non-IV side of my bed and lace his fingers with mine. I want him to tell me that if he could survive open-heart surgery as a baby, I can handle a lung biopsy.

I want him to tell me that I will not be assigned a stage. That I have been mistaken. This whole thing has all along been a comedy, not a drama. A silly adventure like *Harold and Kumar*, and just as nonsensical. I'll get another fairy-tale happily-ever-after.

For the first time since I coughed up blood and recognized

deep in the hollows of my bones what sort of story I was living, I allow myself to think of the possibility of an alternative.

But I know life isn't a Choose Your Own Adventure book. The sort of hope swirling in my brain is dangerous.

"Can I sit?" Noah asks as he takes the chair most recently occupied by my mom. Then he stands up again and decides instead to move to the end of my bed.

"You don't have to give a speech," I say. "We're good. Listen, you made it to the Abs stage. That's a pretty impressive accomplishment."

"Am I squashing your feet?" he asks.

"No."

"Good. I brought you gummy bears instead of flowers. Figured they were a more practical choice." Noah puts the candy on the rolling cart and then fidgets with the string of his hoodie.

"I hate hospitals. Look at that blue thing over there. That's for medical waste. I spent the whole night wondering what gross stuff has been in there and what's in there right now and I pictured it, like, oozing together, and climbing out and attacking me while I slept." I realize I should stop talking, let Noah say whatever it is he came here to say. That we could do better than discussing medical waste. But alas, I am me, and I am nervous.

"You have a vivid imagination," Noah says.

"I do."

"Well, so do I. Which is sort of what I came here to talk about."

"You came here to talk about your vivid imagination?" I catch myself, and then mime zipping my lips shut and throwing away the key.

He clears his throat.

"Since I was a kid, I've been telling myself a story. This is embarrassing to admit, because it makes me sound like such an idiot, but after a while, I started believing that story, you know? It went from an idea to fact without my noticing. Am I making sense?" he asks.

I nod. I tell myself stories too. We all do.

"I have a confession to make: the whole tracking-down-people-in-that-photo thing was because I wanted to prove myself right. It wasn't really about the newspaper. Or not only about it, at least. So Blue Hat Guy? That was my dad. His name was Jason Stern. I thought, until we spoke to Jamal, well, I thought he was alive," Noah says, and he coughs a little on the word *alive*. Like it was shameful of him to hope. I so understand that feeling, the cruel embarrassment that comes with wanting what cannot be, that I can't help myself. I reach out and grab his hand and squeeze. He looks up at me, surprised. "I thought . . . It sounds so stupid, and Jack has been telling me for years it was stupid. I never listened. I thought he used nine-eleven as an excuse to run away. Since I was sick as a baby, I figured it was too much for him. Everyone else in that photo survived. I assumed he had to have also."

I look over at our fingers, linked.

"I'm so sorry, Noah." I try to catch his eyes, but they are darting around the room. Looking anywhere except at my face. I wonder if everyone, if everything, dies twice. If that's how grief is: cyclical, never finished. The Towers are still falling. And falling again.

"That's why I needed to get home after we talked to Jamal. I realized that my mom must have known. She had always known. And she didn't tell me. My dad was this hero—he saved *lives*— and she kept it a secret."

"Maybe she had a good reason?" I say this without a single thought as to what that could be. I want to extend her the same courtesy I'm asking of my own parents—to understand I had my own reasons for not telling them everything.

"Actually, I think she did." Noah's eyes glitter, and he clears his throat. "I wanted to tell you the truth. Not only because you deserve to know why we've been doing what we've been doing, why I was so insistent, which was horrible of me, but also because I didn't want you to think I was running away from you the other day. I'm so sorry for all of it."

"Maybe you *should* run away from me. I've got a tumor. I'm dying," I blurt out.

Oh no. I had no intention of telling Noah this. In fact, I had every intention of *not* telling Noah this.

"What? Come on, you're not dying. Though, by the way, there's been a lot of talk that you OD'd."

"Seriously? I've never done drugs in my life."

"Wait a minute." Noah pauses a beat as he catches up in our conversation. "You have a tumor?"

"In my lung. They're going to biopsy it later today." I keep my voice calm and refuse to allow self-pity to creep in. If Noah can handle losing his dad twice, I can handle a simple medical test.

"You don't know you're dying. You don't know that for a *fact*." He says it with such authority, it's as if he thinks he can make it true by being emphatic.

"No one wants to say it out loud, but I'm sure it's because of nine-eleven. Lots of people are getting sick. Fifteen years seems to be the magic number for these types of cancers."

"Some people are fine. Lots of people. Jamal was the healthiest-looking person I've ever met and he's forty."

"I have a *tumor*." My imploring tone now matches his. I don't know why I feel the need to push the point when I never intended to make it in the first place.

In the early hours of the morning, after my mother had fallen asleep, I Googled *lung tumors*. The vast majority are malignant.

"What about if I know you'll be fine? What about that?" Noah asks.

"Honestly, I wish it were up to you."

A few minutes later, after we've turned the television on and off and waded through the awkwardness, Noah stands up, walks around the room one time, then comes back to the bed and sits down right next to me. Like he's thought about it and made a decision.

"You need to get better. You know why?" Noah asks.

"So you can drive me crazy by calling me Abs?" I joke.

"Because I don't want to be your friend. I don't. I'm sorry."

"You don't?"

"I don't."

"You're not sorry," I say, but I'm smiling.

"You're right, I'm not sorry. By the way, I like your shirt. I think unicorns are both over- and underrated, as far as mythical creatures go."

"What? Why?" I ask, and then realize that now is not the time to get derailed by a Noah theory, though I do, at some point, want to know what he thinks of narwhals. "I don't want to be your friend either."

Our eyes catch for a minute. Noah looks at my lips and starts to lean in, and for maybe the first time in my entire life, I know exactly what happens next.

Noah seems unfazed by the fact that we are in the least sexy place in the world and that I, fewer than five minutes ago, told him I'm dying. It's just him and me and the kissing—which isn't normal kissing. We've graduated to the next level some-how: accomplished kissing, two people who know what they're doing. My entire body hums with desire. Joy too.

I might be dying, but I'm alive right now.

The beeping grows louder and more persistent, almost angry, and Noah breaks contact to make sure I'm okay. At first, we have no idea what's happening, and I worry that it will be musical chairs redux. Blood and hyperventilation all over again.

But then it dawns on both of us at the exact same time and we burst out laughing. Among this collection of wires, I'm hooked up to a heart rate monitor.

CHAPTER SIXTY

Noah

My mom demands that Phil put away his phone tonight, so the three of us sit around the dining table, dishing pot roast onto our plates and half talking. I feel sorry for Phil that this meal is not billable, though I wouldn't be surprised if he has papers in his lap. My mother beams at me, like we're about to embark on some sort of happy familial breakthrough. Oh, crap. I better not be getting a half sibling.

"So I had a better idea for this weekend instead of golf," Phil says.

"It's a Christmas miracle." I hear my sarcasm and then try to break the bite in my voice with a smile. It's not Phil's fault that I despise his favorite hobby. It's not Phil's fault that I'm pretending to be eating when I'm really pissing myself with worry about Abbi. It's only even sort of Phil's fault that he's Phil.

"One of my clients got me two tickets to see some comedy roundup at the Apollo. You in?" he asks.

"That's awesome," I say. "Yes. But just so you know, you had me at not golf."

"We can go to the club after the show," Phil says, and I groan. I've been vocal about how much I hate Phil's country club, which is full of rich, entitled white assholes who live in McMansions like this one. It makes me terrified that my future looks exactly like my right now, only with a beer belly and a forty-minute commute. "I'm joking."

Until yesterday, my worst fear was never leaving this place. Now it's Abbi dying. Earlier, I Googled *lungs* and *9/11 syndrome*. Not my finest idea.

"How's Abbi feeling?" my mom asks, as if she can read my thoughts.

"She's really sick," I answer, and find that my throat closes around the word *sick*.

"I'm sorry. She's young, though. She'll be okay." My mom uses her best skinned-knee-mom voice.

"You don't know that."

"You're right. I don't," my mom replies, and I wonder if she'd have backed down so easily if we were having this discussion last week or the week before. She and I now live on less stable ground. She treats me like I could detonate at any moment. She's probably right.

"I'm not trying to be a pain in the ass. But you don't know," I say.

"You're worried. You should be. We get it. We are too," Phil chimes in, and I wonder if this version of Phil, iPhone-less and still with something to offer, has been here all along. It's possible I mistook unflappable for boring. He's such an easy target, with his collared shirts and workaholism and shredded wheat every damn day. "But I really do believe she will be okay."

"That sounds a lot like magical thinking. I'm kind of done with that." I cut my meat into smaller and smaller pieces, with no intention of eating them. I make track marks in my mashed potatoes with a fork. I consider building a spud snowman. Anything to not look up.

"Or it's good old-fashioned optimism," Phil says. "Sometimes there's a difference."

"Thanks for the tickets," I say, because I'm suddenly grateful that Phil is here with us.

"Wait, you do realize I'm coming with you, right?" he asks.

CHAPTER SIXTY-ONE

Abbi

As they put me under for surgery, six hours after I was scheduled, I feel myself slip into sleep. In my dream, I'm falling fast headfirst toward the ground. My body lines up with the building behind me in perfect synchronicity, and I don't need to look to know where I am. One World Trade Center smokes from the top, like the tip of a dainty cigarette. Paper blows around me in a tornado of documents: personnel files and receipts and contracts. These things kept in folders, once thought important, now exposed as meaningless.

Other than the roar of the wind, it's quiet, almost peaceful; the decision has been made. No choice but to give in and to let my body fall.

Of course it's 9/11.

Of course I'm Falling Man.

The ground comes toward me fast, and right before I slam into it, the image morphs again. Ash swirls, coats my face, like I'm swimming in paste. Am I Dust Lady? That would be the logical next step in this iconic photo nightmare. But then I see Connie, and she runs next to me and she's smiling. Alive! Connie signals that I should follow her with a flick of her thumb. I am again Baby Hope, except this time, I am not a baby. I am sixteen-year-old me, running for my life while the taste of death sits on my tongue like a cough drop.

I grip the string of a red balloon with my right hand, always with that damn balloon, but this time I'm not strong enough to hold it down. Instead, I find no matter how hard I try, I can't let it go, and so it lifts me up toward the blue, blue sky. As I rise, Connie shrinks smaller and smaller still, until she becomes nothing but a speck on the ground. Just another particle of dust for someone else to ingest.

And then I too am lost to the heavens.

I am terrified I might never wake up.

CHAPTER SIXTY-TWO

Noah

~~Baby Hope, my father, and nineteen jihadis walk into a bar. . . .~~

Still no news from Abbi or her parents.

CHAPTER SIXTY-THREE

Abbi

When I open my eyes, my grandmother is sitting next to my bed, and Paula, her aide, is sleeping in what I already think of as my father's chair. My chest feels like someone cut it open with a knife, which given the circumstances is totally appropriate. My inner elbow, where the IV attaches, throbs, and though I'm buried under blankets, I feel cold.

"Where's Mom?" I ask. I need to see my mother's face. Right now. I feel unmoored and confused and I don't care if wanting my mommy makes me sound like a whiny baby.

"Your parents stepped out for one second. They're going to be so pissed off. They've been waiting for you to wake up for forever," my grandmother says, and reaches out her hands and grabs mine firmly in her grip. "I don't know what you're playing at with this whole hospital thing, but just so you know, I'm the only one who's allowed to die around here."

"Grandma," I say, but then my lids close and I drift off for a minute. I open them again.

"I'm going to say some words that are scary to say, especially right now, but that I still need to say, okay?" she says. "I'll always be with you, even when I'm not."

"What?" Where is she going? Why does my mouth feel like I licked the inside of a toilet bowl?

"You know what I think about sometimes? I think about how all the little bits of me that I'm losing will somehow find their way to you. Like they are . . . what's the word . . . tangible. Like they are tangible things that can crawl from my bedroom to yours and so as I become less me, you will become more you, and I will continue to march on within you when I'm not me anymore. You're going to keep growing. That's how it's supposed to be." I can smell my grandmother, feel the knots of her fingers. Her words add up somehow to a feeling. A swell. "This is life with a capital *L*. It's not always pretty," she says, and she laughs the same laugh I remember from childhood, when we wore steel colanders on our heads while we chopped vegetables from her garden. A memory bubbles up: she always let me use the grown-up knives. "But you already knew that."

"Grandma?"

"Yes, sweetheart?"

"I'm going to be okay, though, right?" I ask even as I realize it's unfair to make her promise me something she has no control over, and something she cannot have for herself. And yet, still I ask.

"Of course you are," she says, and strokes my cheek. "Of course you are."

And this time I let myself sleep with the comfort of knowing I will again wake.

★ ★ ★

I don't know how much time has passed, but my parents sweep into the room, their arms overflowing with flowers. My dad has a bottle of something that looks celebratory tucked into his elbow.

"Abbi!" they scream in unison.

"Hey," I say, and look around the room. "Where's grandma?"

"Home."

"Really? I didn't hear her leave."

"Dad bought some carbonated apple cider, because he's a lunatic and counts chickens before they hatch," my mom says, and leans over my bed and kisses me all over my face, like she used to when I was a little kid. "The doctor should be in to talk to us any minute."

"Mom! Stop!"

"Sorry. You smell terrible anyway," she says, and the smile on her face wobbles and then fixes into shape.

She's terrified.

As am I.

It turns out there's an entire ocean between knowing and *knowing*. It turns out they are different states of being entirely.

I want to stay here, in my cozy before.

"You're going to be fine," my dad repeats.

"Let's wait for the doctor," mom says. "But either way, Abbi, you're a fighter."

If my poor mother weren't on the verge of a nervous breakdown, I'd roll my eyes. I once held on to a balloon while being *carried*. That does not make me ready for whatever is coming.

"Don't roll your eyes at me," my mom says.

"I didn't!"

"You did in your head. You have that teenager thing where you think I don't get you. I get you, Abbi Hope Goldstein," she says, and plops down next to me on the bed and points her finger right at my chest. "You *are* a fighter. I didn't know you were sick. You covered your tracks on that one. But all this stuff with Cat and the girls? You've been so tough. I knew you were heartbroken, but you kept right on, no complaints. Of course you should have told us you weren't well. We are supposed to protect you, not the other way around. After we get you out of this place we're going to start doing things differently. But don't for one second think you're not a fighter. You are the toughest kid I know."

"Feel better?" my dad asks.

"No," my mom says. "But I've had a bunch of Xanax."

"I was asking Abbi."

"That was quite a pep talk," I say, intentionally rolling my eyes hard so that both of my parents can see. Then a wave of panic hits. Dr. McCuskey is here. Her hair is pulled into a bun that's precariously secured with a pencil. She better have worn a scrunchie and a hairnet during my surgery.

"I'll get right to it. As you can see, Abbi handled the anesthesia beautifully. Once we were inside, we decided to do a full excision of the pulmonary mass, mostly because of the extremity of the symptoms—for example, the blood-streaked sputum," Dr. McCuskey says, and then pauses. She looks deliberately at my mom, then my dad, and finally me, the same way I checked my mirrors on my driver's test. Is she intentionally taking her time?

If I were a doctor, this is not how I'd drop big news. Instead, I'd bounce into the room and shout it out in basic English, as quickly as possible: *Benign! Malignant! Stage III!*

No need to keep us twisting in the wind.

Also, what's sputum?

"Vessels were found around the mass, which helps explain

the bleeding," Dr. McCuskey says, and the monitor starts to beep. My poor heart. Again the dangers of sneaky optimism. Sometime since this morning, I've let the possibility of my being all right sneak in. I realize how stupid that was. "But there was no sign of any other growth. All the blood work looks good."

"Okay," I say, in an attempt to encourage her to get to the point.

"Shhh," my mother says, and clamps her hand over my mouth.

"In short, the biopsy showed a *benign* clear-cell tumor of the lung. As usual, we sent a sample to an outside lab to verify, but I think it's highly unlikely the results will be different," Dr. McCuskey says.

"Yes!" my dad screams, his fists raised in victory, as if his beloved Jets scored a touchdown in the Super Bowl.

"I don't understand," I say. I'm having trouble making sense of her words, realigning them into English. "What does that mean exactly?"

"It means you're going to be fine. It means . . ." My mother stops talking midsentence and folds into herself. She drops her head between her knees. Her entire body shakes with sobs. She is keening, a word I didn't really understand the meaning of until this moment.

My dad looks at my mom, and then he too starts tearing up.

Dr. McCuskey clears her throat. My dad wipes his nose on a handkerchief he takes out of his back pocket. My mom sits up and pulls herself together.

"We need to check Abbi regularly. I'm going to order a chest X-ray every three months to start, and then every six months, because these sorts of growths don't always manifest with symptoms. Of course, if she is experiencing any coughing or

274

wheezing, I need her to come in to see me immediately. Is that clear?" Dr. McCuskey asks.

I nod.

"Are you telling me I'm not going to die? For real?" I ask.

"You are not going to die. At least, not from this," Dr. McCuskey says.

"Of course you're not going to die," my dad says, his voice thick with something like rage. "You are never going to die."

"Well, that's not quite true, is it?" Dr. McCuskey barks an awkward laugh. She releases the pencil from her hair, and we watch as her long gray curls cascade down as if in slo-mo. She is not the doctor I would have cast in the movie version of my life.

"You just said she's fine," my dad insists.

"She is. But let's address the elephant in the room, shall we? Most sixteen-year-olds do not get lung tumors. I mean, it can happen, but statistically you have a far greater chance of, I don't know, being struck by lightning. I don't know that that's true, but you get my point. I do think we need to assume this is connected to your chemical exposure as a baby. Of course, there are many complicated aspects of nine-eleven syndrome, and it's not fully understood. It can present in numerous ways—respiratory disease, cancer—and we don't know enough at this point to predict how or even whether it will manifest. I'm going to enroll Abbi in the World Trade Center Health Program. She's entitled to the benefits of—"

"So what you are saying is she's *not* fine," my mom says.

"No, she *is* fine," my dad says.

"Let me try this again," Dr. McCuskey says, but breathes out in that *God, give me the strength* kind of way. I get it. My family can have that effect on people. "Abbi is now tumor free. The tumor that we did remove was benign. We need to treat her health with excessive caution and be aware of the risks she faces. Things like this could pop up from time to time and could potentially be serious. We got lucky this time, but we don't know what will happen. Hence the monitoring. And she's entitled to health care. Got it?"

"So what you are saying is I can sleep at night, but no, not really?" my mother asks, her voice thick with hysteria.

"You can sleep. We can all sleep. We just need to be careful," my dad says. "We can manage that. Can't we?"

"So to be clear, I'm not dying?" I ask again, and Dr. McCuskey nods, I don't know if in frustration or confirmation or possibly a blanket yes to all of our questions, and leaves the room.

And that's when I catch up to my parents, and the good news hits me so hard and so fast I feel light-headed. Giddiness gives way to pure happiness, clear and profound and overwhelming. I laugh and cry at the same time, a loud eruption of water and guffaws and even an animal-like moan.

I'm not dying. Not yet.

The refrain repeats in my head. I'm unzipped, and the world and its infinite possibility seep in, life rushing to fill in all my empty spaces.

"That doctor needs to work on her bedside manner," my dad says, and then scoots into bed on one side of me, and my mother comes in on the other, and they close their arms around me.

We hug and cry and scream with joy until our voices are hoarse and our throats go dry, and even then we only stop when an unhappy nurse comes in the room and shushes us quiet.

CHAPTER SIXTY-FOUR

Noah

It's ten o'clock at night and Jack and I are at the twenty-four-hour diner drinking milkshakes and toasting Abbi even though she's not here to see us. My face hurts from smiling.

"I feel like we should switch the word *wart* with the word *tumor.* The stuff that can kill you should be called warts because those sound gross and dangerous and the things that look funny and grow on your toe because of bad gym hygiene should be called tumors. We have it all wrong," Jack says.

"Not laughing. New subject."

"So Brendan came over the other day and my mom freaked," he says.

"Why?" I ask.

"She was all, *Oh my God, where's Noah?*"

"Very funny."

"I'm so glad Abbi's going to be okay. I mean, I knew it all along, but it feels so good to know for sure," Jack says. "You know, things are looking up for us. Perhaps this summer will involve more than just you, me, and YouTube."

"That would be quite the plot twist," I say.

"Nah. We're both going to blow it," Jack says. "No pun intended."

CHAPTER SIXTY-FIVE

Abbi

Three days later, I'm back at home, in my own bed, again contemplating the ceiling, though this time Noah is lying down next to me. The door remains wide open, a surprising last-minute rule imposed by my mother. I guess the possibility of my having sex was only okay when it was a distant hypothetical.

"I still can't quite believe it," I say, and I trace my fingers lightly over my incision. "I mean, the doctor actually cut something out of my body. I'm not delusional."

"No one thought you were delusional," he says, and turns so he's looking at me. Now we are side by side, perched on our elbows. Mirror images of each other.

"I kinda did. I was convinced I was going to die. For real. And now it looks like I should be okay—"

"You will be okay," he interjects, and for a minute, he sounds disturbingly like my dad.

"It was all real, though. This actually happened. Baby Hope lives another day," I say, not sure if I'm kidding. Because there is bizarre relief too, in knowing that I won't be torn off people's walls in disappointment. I realize the irony of my re-surviving.

I think about the tumor, its taste of blood and fear and mortality, day in and day out, metallic and bilious and rancid, and how I was wrong. It will not invade and conquer and grate me into dust. At least, not yet. It was only a warning shot: *Pay closer attention*, it said. *You don't have the luxury of not.*

My future has come back to me, a gift returned to sender. My heart has unclenched itself from a fist to an open hand. But something happens when the story you tell yourself turns out not to be your story at all. You have to figure out what to replace it with. Something needs to grow in the space left behind.

Courage, I tell myself. That can fill me up.

"Those are my favorite kinds of punchlines. The curveballs that make total sense. Like you think the joke can only end with A or B, and somehow the comedian finds a C. Not that I think this was a joke. But you get me," he says, and I do. I get him. It's nice to apply some overarching rules to all this. I like to think in terms of story or even poetry. He frames it with comedy. But in the end, it's all the same thing.

Noah traces his finger up and down my arm, a lazy, tender stroke that thrums under my skin.

"How are you doing?" I ask, since I realize this week has not only been about me. Those damn towers play on a forever loop. He's not unscathed.

"I had a long talk with my mom. I feel weirdly okay. It turns out my dad didn't just die. He went out with like this amazing mother-effing ninja kick-ass hi-yah. He saved a freakin' pregnant lady. These are some epically good genes I have," he explains, and his smile is equal parts proud and shy and sad.

"I could have told you that you have some epically good

genes," I say in a mock-flirty voice, and reach out to touch his hair, because I'm totally allowed to do that. He rewards me with a small kiss on the nose.

"I looked up the technical definition of *benign growth* last night. It literally means something harmless that has grown or is growing," Noah says.

"What?" I ask.

"Right? Like when you think about it that way, it almost sounds like normal life. Like what's supposed to be happening to us," he says. Our eyes catch, and a warmth spreads through my body. Like he's holding me closer just by looking at me. "Anyhow, the other day at that party, I had it all backward. I said that I thought when we left Oakdale our life was suddenly going to get exponentially bigger. But I think that can happen without going anywhere. We don't have to wait."

"We can rock our capes now," I say.

"Exactly," he says. And then he kisses me.

CHAPTER SIXTY-SIX

Noah

Jack and I play video games in his basement, and as usual, his blue-haired anarchy girl is kicking my ass. I give up mid–space dino attack and pick up my phone.

> **Me:** I know I was just at your house, but I miss you already. Can I say things like that yet?

Jack pauses the game and sits next to me so he can read over my shoulder.

"No, you cannot say things like that yet. Try to play it cool for at least a minute," he says.

> **Me:** Also remember when you were dying? That was funny

"Too soon, idiot," Jack says, and smacks me on the head with a throw pillow. I ignore him and continue to type:

Me: Too soon?

Me: Sorry. Of course it's too soon.

Me: Abs?

While I wait for a response, my hands go clammy. Did I blow this already? All for a not-particularly-funny joke? I should have asked how she was feeling, like a normal person.

"You should have asked how she was feeling, like a normal person," Jack says, reading my mind, and if I didn't know he could kill me in one move, both on-screen and in real life, I'd punch him. My phone dings with a new text.

Abbi: Ha! I'm totally here! Never too soon. Miss you too.
Was fun hoping you were sweating it out there for a minute

"Holy crap. She's like the girl-Noah," Jack says. "I'd totally binge-watch the crap out of this rom-com."

"Shut up and go away," I say.

Me: You're evil

Abbi: I'm evil? Was I the one who just made jokes about someone potentially dying from cancer?

Me: I thought . . . humor helps

Abbi: I'm kidding! I totally get it

Me: Have I ever mentioned that I'm obsessed with finding the perfect 9/11 joke?

"Sharing one of your idiosyncrasies. Brave. I like it," Jack interjects. "Being occasionally vulnerable is key. I told Brendan my coming-out story yesterday, though of course I had to ratchet up the drama a bit."

"I think your mom is calling you," I lie, and motion upstairs. Of course he stays put.

> **Abbi:** Seriously? A 9/11 joke? That is so weird and so you and makes complete and total sense to me, you comedy nerd
> **Me:** Haven't gotten very far. Think the problem is I'm swinging too big. A joke is not going to save the world
> **Abbi:** Maybe not. But it could save someone in the world
> **Me:** You think?
> **Abbi:** Maybe even the person telling it
> **Me:** Look at you having theories too
> **Abbi:** By the way, tell Jack I can't wait to meet Brendan

"Let me take this one," Jack says, and successfully wrestles my phone out of my hands.

> **Me:** Abs! This is Jack. Listen, when you meet Brendan under no circumstances are you allowed to ask about the boobtastic mermaid tattoo
> **Abbi:** Did you save my life, Jack? Did I say you can call me Abs?
> **Me:** PLEASE LET ME CALL YOU ABS. I'll be your best friend. You can ask Noah if you need to see my references. I come preapproved
> **Abbi:** Okay. Fine. But only because I happen to be in the market for a new best friend. So what happens if the tattoo comes up naturally in conversation?
> **Me:** It will not come up in conversation

Abbi: What if I happen to mention to Brendan, "Oh man,
    I love tattoos. You know what I've always wanted?
    A woman naked on the top, finned on the bottom.
    What's your position on why I totally have this weird
    need to permanently ink my body with that mer-
    image?"
Me: I hate you
Me: That was Jack. This is Noah again. I don't hate you.
    Not even a little
Abbi: I don't hate you either. Not even a little

I feel myself smiling like an idiot, and I'm powerless against it. Before Jack can say anything, I pick up the controller and restart the game. I set fire to an alien overlord and shoot off a rocket. I keep my eyes on the screen and my thumbs busy as I wait for him to make fun of me for my shameless lovesickness. Which is fine and inevitable and fully deserved.

But for once, Jack holds back. Instead, to my surprise, on-screen anarchy girl takes a break from her ass-kicking to lean over and give me a celebratory high five.

CHAPTER SIXTY-SEVEN

Abbi

"Here are the rumors about you in order of most repeated: one, drug overdose; two, you were hit by a bus; three, you tried to kill yourself; and number four, my personal favorite, you had a bad reaction to shots of human growth hormone," Julia reports on my first day back at camp while we distribute the cupcakes I brought in for the girls. I can only hope that my collapsing and being taken away on a stretcher will not feature in their future therapy sessions. I've been out of a camp a week, like a month in camp time, the entirety of which I have spent watching TV and texting Noah and Jack. As much fun as both of those things are, I'm thrilled to be back at work. "You should have seen this place the day after. Swarming with news trucks."

"Basically my worst nightmare," I say, relieved that the media interest, after an initial flurry of activity, has died down. Dr. McCuskey, at the request of my parents, issued a statement that I had been released from the hospital and was expected to make a full recovery. Other than the outrageous rumors and a few random Baby Hope memes on Twitter and Facebook, and yes, I was a punchline on the *Daily Show* (Noah loved that one), most people seem to have forgotten about me. Which is just the way I like it. "By the way, it was none of the above."

"I know. I'm happy you're okay," Julia says, and throws her arm over my shoulder and squeezes. "It wasn't the same here without you."

"Oh yeah?"

"Totally. I had to clean up, like, three floaters."

"Funny."

"What's it like being Baby Hope? I've been wanting to ask you that since the second day of camp," Julia says as she loops around the table handing out napkins. She gives two to Livi, pauses, hands over a third.

"Wait, you knew?"

"Of course I knew. We all did."

"Seriously?" I ask.

"I don't know if you've heard of it, but there's this really cool thing called the Internet? Some people even have it on their phones now," Julia says. "You're kind of a big deal in my family. My dad's a history professor at Princeton, and he does this whole lecture about that picture and how its popularity is connected to our love of the myth of American resiliency. Also, my little sister and your frenemy Cat work together at Pizza Pizza Pizza over in Mapleview."

"Why didn't you say anything?"

"You obviously didn't want to talk about it. I don't buy my dad's argument, by the way. I think you were a cute little white baby with a balloon. Everyone loves balloons." Julia shrugs, takes a bite out of her cupcake, like being Baby Hope is no big deal. Like who I am doesn't change anything and it never did. "I was dropped by my girls junior year too. It's a thing that happens sometimes. It sucked. No real reason. They got like sucked into field hockey and I wasn't on the team and whatever. But want to know how I got revenge?"

"How?"

"I made better friends. *Real* friends. Ride-or-die friends."

"To answer your question, I have no idea what it's like to be Baby Hope. I mean, I've only ever been me. That's sort of like me asking what it's like to be you," I say.

"Fabulous. That's what it's like to be me."

"I never doubted it for a minute," I say. And when she offers to show me pictures of Lifeguard Charles without his shirt on and oiled up at the shore last weekend, I do not say no.

"Are you okay now?" Livi asks me as I help her into her swimsuit and slather her with sunscreen.

"I am. I got the card you made me. I put it on my desk at home," I say, and offer her a tissue to clean her always-running nose. She opts for my shirt instead. Just leans right in, all casual, for the nuzzle-wipe. I admire her shamelessness.

"You scared me. Please don't do that again." Livi pouts and puts her hand on her hip, in that exaggerated, practiced way of little kids. No subtlety.

"I'll try not to," I say, and she envelops me in such a big hug, she knocks me back.

"Did you know I have a picture of you as a baby in the bathroom at my house?" Livi asks.

"You do?"

"Yup. Every time I poo in the potty, I look at you. Isn't that the craziest?"

"The craziest," I say, and happily take her wet, snotty hand as I lead the group to the plake.

When I walk to my car after camp, Noah is already waiting in the passenger seat. I climb in next to him, and he grins.

"Open your hand," he says, and when I do, he drops three gummy bears into my palm.

"Since we're done with the Baby Hope stuff, what do you think about starting a new project?" I ask. Last night, when I should have been sleeping, I stared up at my ceiling and kept rereading the Mary Oliver poem I taped there. The meaning kept morphing, not unlike how a chair can turn into a monster in the dark and then right back into a chair. While I read and reread, an idea began to form.

"What did you have in mind?" he asks.

"It's a little strange."

"You're a little strange. That's why I like you," he says.

"Full disclosure: It will not help you get into Harvard. It does not in any way involve comedy. And you cannot write about it for the *Oakdale High Free Press*."

"You are really selling this thing," Noah says. "I have one question: Will it involve spending more time with you?"

"Absolutely. It will definitely involve spending more time with me," I say.

"Sold," he says, and leans in for a kiss. I'm struck by how natural it all feels, Noah sitting in the seat next to me, his lips pressing against mine, how he has turned from stranger to lifeline in mere weeks. My arms wrapped around him like they know exactly how they should be.

"And Go!" I add. "It will involve spending more time with Go!"

"You know how I feel about Go! and her entirely superfluous exclamation point," he says, now planting tiny, delicious kisses on my neck.

"And also . . . my grandma."

Noah abruptly stops the kissing. "Oh. We were so not on the same page just then about the word *project*," he says, laughing, and though his lips are no longer on mine, his fingers draw devastating circles on my thigh.

"What were you thinking?" I ask.

"No comment," he says, and now it's my turn to laugh. "Seriously, though, tell me what you have in mind."

"I want us to do a series of interviews with my grandmother and record some of her best stories and memories before they all get eaten up by her dementia. I want to literally make them into tangible things. Do you think you can help me?"

"Let's do it," Noah says, and my whole body tingles. "I really like the idea of hearing someone's best memories instead of their worst, for a change."

"Right?"

"Right," he says, and this time, I'm the one who leans in for a kiss.

"But I have a favor to ask first," he says, his voice suddenly a little nervous and shy. "I have one last person I need to visit. Will you come with me? Please? You don't have to be Baby Hope. You can be Abbi."

"Of course," I say. "Anywhere."

CHAPTER SIXTY-EIGHT

Noah

We are in the pregnant woman's living room, though of course she's not the pregnant woman anymore. Just like Abbi isn't Baby Hope. Sixteen years changes things.

Her name is Charlotte Dempsey, and she has four children, and works part-time at the local library. "That face! I'd know it anywhere."

When we did our interviews, everyone seemed to be mentally drawing a line from the baby in the photograph to the girl in front of them and measuring the vast distance between the two. This time, Charlotte is connecting me to my dad, which I assume is less of a line and more of a hop, skip, and a jump.

"I was so happy when you called. I mean, I only knew your dad for four minutes, but I have a lot to tell you about him anyway," she says. We are sitting across from each other on faded gray couches in a house cluttered with happy kid junk.

"Thanks," I say, and feel a stab of the sort of envy my mom must have felt when she saw this woman at the mall. If there had been no 9/11, would bedtime have meant rowdy pillow fights with a slew of brothers instead of only my mom and me and a library book? Who would I have been if we added up to more than two?

"You know that he was a hero. That goes without saying. Everyone was running one way, and he chose to run the other," Charlotte says.

"I like to run in every direction," says the youngest boy, who is putting together a Lego Death Star on the floor, looking up at me from under his too-long bowl cut.

"I bet you do, bud," I say, using my camp counselor voice. He nods at me seriously.

"That's Jaden, my baby. He's five. Jason is my eldest. He's fifteen, and then there's Joseph and John in between. I'm obviously outnumbered." She points to the family portrait on the fireplace mantel. The picture is a few years old and was likely taken at a Sears. It in no way follows the rule of thirds.

"We named Jason after your father. A friend told us that in the Jewish tradition, you can honor people who've died by using the first letter of their name. We knew your dad was Jewish and decided to keep going with the *J*'s. All my boys are named after him. We wanted to thank him every way that we could."

"That's really nice. I bet he would have loved that," I say, though it feels weird to speak on his behalf. I have no idea what my dad would have loved or did love much beyond what my mom has told me: his University of Michigan hat, pickle sandwiches, terrible puns, our family, and apparently, random acts of heroism.

"I'm so sorry for your loss. I told your mother right after it happened, though I realize now I was probably the last person she wanted to see. I never got a chance to give my condolences to you."

"Thank you," I say, and Abbi reaches over and squeezes my hand. "Honestly, I'm not even sure why we're here. I guess I wanted to put a face to the story I heard. I appreciate you taking the time to meet me—us, me and Abbi."

"I have this family, these four perfect, beautiful, pain-in-the-ass children who wouldn't have been born if it weren't for your dad. Every single day I think about your mom and you, because I realize your loss was our gain. I'm not going to sit here and pretend there's anything fair about that. I was the last person he rescued. There were people before me, but I was the last," she says.

"Five other people," Abbi chimes in. I haven't wrapped my head around that number yet. What about the three kids Charlotte had afterward? Should we add them to the tally, or do they get erased by the ones my dad never got to have with my mom? And what do these numbers mean, anyway? My father was a hero, regardless of whether you can count the people he rescued on one hand or two.

"When your dad found me, my clothes were on fire. He used his jacket to put out the flames. Wrapped me up like a burrito, scooped me up, and got me out of there. While he was carrying me, he asked my name, and when I said Charlie, because that's what I go by, even though I'm technically a Charlotte, you know what he said?" she asks, and we shake our heads, because of course we have no idea what he said. What could you possibly say in a moment like that? *Nice to meet you, I'm Jason. Lovely day for a run.*

I picture it for a moment: My dad carrying this woman in

his arms. He looks like an action hero. His face smudged with grease. The ultimate badass dragon slayer.

I feel myself swell with pride.

"Your dad said, and I swear I am not making this up, he said *Liar, liar, pants on fire.*" Charlotte smiles tearfully at us. "The whole world was burning down, I didn't know if I was going to die, I was scared I might lose my baby, and he managed to make me laugh. A hysterical laugh, maybe, but I laughed."

I look at Abbi and Abbi looks back at me, and huge grins overtake both of our faces. I feel unadulterated joy.

"His last words were *Liar, liar, pants on fire*? Like he was making a joke about you being literally on fire," I say, to make sure I understand exactly what she's telling me. "He said that? Out loud? To you? On nine-eleven?"

"Yup," Charlotte says. "I know it sounds inappropriate, but I swear, it was the perfect thing. I was terrified and his silly joke brought me back to myself. He made me feel better. He reminded me that I was *alive.*"

That word *fate*, which reared its head when I saw Abbi at Knight's Day Camp all those weeks ago, pops into my brain again, and this time it doesn't even make me feel a little embarrassed or uncomfortable.

For the first time in my entire life, I feel a direct connection between me and my father. When I was younger, I thought of him as a question mark—an entirely unknowable entity, or worse, a void. Recently, he's morphed into a comic-book superhero—spandexed and fearless—which has felt equally untouchable. But now I realize that it's unfair to distill him down to a single decision—turning around—as enormous a legacy as that may seem.

"Wow," Abbi says.

"I know," I say.

"Your dad told the first nine-eleven joke ever. *Ever*," she says.

"And it killed," I say, with the confidence of knowing that my dad, whoever he might have been, would have loved that terrible pun.

"Groan," Abbi says, but she's smiling.

I think about my father's last words. Only slightly more hilarious than heartbreaking, and grounded wholly in the truth.

The perfect punchline.

I could laugh or I could cry.

I choose to laugh.

CHAPTER SIXTY-NINE

Abbi

Later, at home, my grandmother and Paula are eating pizza in the breakfast nook, and my mom perches on the counter. My dad sits at the stool around the kitchen island.

"Are you guys staging an intervention or something?" I ask, and grab a slice from an open box. "What's going on?"

"Your ChapStick is a little smeared," my grandma says, and smirks.

"The Noah problem wasn't about you after all, I hear," Paula says.

"What Noah problem?" my mom asks. "Why am I the last to hear about everything? How are you feeling, Abbi? Any coughing?"

"Nothing bad," I say, which is the truth. My incision has started to heal. I can imagine my lungs again being just another part of my body one day, like my belly button or my knees. Something I don't think about much, beyond my asthma.

"There was no Noah problem. There was, at one point, a Noah misunderstanding. All's good."

"All's good, huh?" my dad asks, and looks over at my mom and beams with pride. They talk out loud without saying a word.

My dad: *See, you were worried for no reason. She's developmentally right on target.*

My mom: *We should send Dr. Schwartz champagne!*

"Listen, I know your dad spoke to you a little about . . . us . . . him and me, I mean, and I wanted to let you know that sometimes he'll be staying over here," my mom says, laying out the words slowly and carefully, like they are somehow explosive if not handled correctly. "I know it's a little confusing."

"I'm almost seventeen, not five. It's not confusing at all." I take a second slice of pizza. I'm suddenly ravenous. I blame the kissing. "So Dad's moving back home?"

"We're taking it slowly," my mom says. "We're not rushing into anything."

"You do realize you already have a child together, right? No one would call you guys getting back together rushing."

"Your mom would call it rushing," my dad says.

"Your mom's a cautious lady. I respect that," Paula says.

"Your mom's dumb," my grandmother says, and we all look at her, unsure who is talking right now. If it's the dementia, the version of my grandmother who I recently caught dancing with my dead grandfather in the living room, or just my grandma, who in the best of times doesn't mince words. "What? Why are you all looking at me like that? I'm wearing pants, aren't I?"

"Yes, you are, and we appreciate it," I say.

"You don't mess around with love. When you got it, you hold on to it. Simple," my grandmother says.

"Nothing is ever that simple," my mom says, but she looks thoughtful, like she's weighing my grandma's words. She takes a sip of wine, puts the glass back on the counter. My father watches her and for once stays quiet.

He'll wait.

"Maybe it is," I say.

"Not for nothing, but you've been in love for, what? Five seconds?" Paula's tone is teasing, not mean.

"I'm not in love," I say, and the entire room erupts with laughter. I wouldn't be surprised if they broke out into "Noah and Abbi sitting in a tree."

"What? I'm not!"

"Then you're dumb too," my grandmother says.

AFTER THAT

Abbi

The sixteenth anniversary of 9/11 and my birthday fall on a Monday, the most descriptive day of the week.

A beginning.

The ceremony starts at 8:45 a.m., as it does every year, to mark the time when the first plane hit the first tower, to recognize when the world broke into a before and an after. I got up early this morning and blew out my hair and painted my nails a mature pale pink. I'm wearing a recently dry-cleaned dress that my mom picked out and ballet flats and I look both like me and not like me at all. At the last minute, I put on my fox earrings to add something familiar.

This summer I realized that an essential part of growing up is relinquishing all the myths you've previously bought into about yourself. And so now a print of the Baby Hope picture hangs on my bedroom wall. I think of it like something more than bad hotel art, something less than a family artifact. We still have an uneasy relationship, the photo and I, though I feel like we're moving toward a truce. Sometimes my eyes sweep across the picture and I can almost look at it as an impartial observer would. I often discover a new detail I didn't previously notice. The silver bangle on Raj's wrist reflecting light. A corner of blue sky.

Before I leave this morning, though, I take a long look at Baby Hope. I see a one-year-old immortalized in a single, terrible moment, and then decide that's an unfair reduction. I know she's more than that. Baby Hope is a symbol of optimism, a busted frontier myth, the idea of persevering even when all looks lost.

She's also no longer me.

Once upon a time a girl was captured in a photograph.

Those four fairy-tale words finally make sense—*once upon a time*. We can be both fixed in time and outside of it. It can bend us to its will, and sometimes, if we are lucky, we get to bend it back.

Now, though, another question haunts me: What does *happily ever after* look like in a broken world?

Today, while I listen to the names of the dead, I will hold Noah's hand. We will say our prayers in the quiet of our own minds. I will feel overwhelmed by love and grief and gratitude for my own outrageous good fortune. Afterward, we will walk home together, our hands still linked, and eat birthday cake.

I'm 95 percent sure Noah has made me a crown.

And I tell myself that this, all of this, the terrible and the good, could be what *happily ever after* looks like: A Monday. A beginning.

AUTHOR'S NOTE

As much as Abbi and Noah's story and the town of Oakdale feel real to me, this book is a work of fiction. There is no Baby Hope photograph except for the one that I hope now lives within our collective imagination.

I write to make sense out of things—to order my thoughts—and I've long struggled with those moments that cleave our lives, cleave us, into *befores* and *afters*. And there seems to me to be no bigger shared *before* and *after* than September 11, 2001. As Noah says, I often think about "all those people waking up on [that day] not knowing everything was about to change, *everything*, and then I think about all those people waking up this morning who may have to go to sleep in a different world from the one in which they woke."

Though historians (and novelists!) have grappled with and will continue to grapple with the myriad political ramifications of 9/11, I am much more interested in the personal legacies of loss. How they seep in and alter our daily fabric in a million unseen ways almost two decades after the fact, and also the converse: how life goes on. How we continue to fall in love (or fall in love again). Despite the predictions, how we continue to joke and, of course, to laugh.

I would be remiss if I didn't mention that while Oakdale doesn't exist, the community of Middletown, New Jersey, which lost the greatest number of people outside New York City on

September 11, 2001, does. I chose to create a fictional town for a number of reasons, not least of which is because it felt over-reaching and presumptuous for me to co-opt a real community, especially one that's still healing. If you're interested in learning more about Middletown, a good place to start would be Gail Sheehy's nonfiction account, *Middletown, America: One Town's Passage from Trauma to Hope.*

I also want to note that "The Dust Lady" is a real photo-graph, and its subject has a name: Marcy Borders. Sadly, Ms. Borders died in 2015 at the age of forty-two from stomach can-cer, and it's widely believed that her illness stemmed from her exposure to toxic chemicals on 9/11.

As many as four hundred thousand people are believed to be affected by medical conditions connected to September 11, and almost seventy different kinds of cancers have been linked to exposure at Ground Zero; many are aggressive and difficult to treat. Although we rarely see it mentioned in the news, more than a thousand people have died since the attacks, and this number is only expected to rise.

An entire generation has been born since 9/11, and for many of my younger readers, I realize that day may feel remote, something that belongs only to their parents or grandparents or their history class. I hope this book encourages them to con-tinue learning and to close that gap. As Abbi says at one point in our story: "Sometimes it feels like those towers are still falling and will never stop." I think it's everyone's responsibility to con-tinue to bear witness until they do.

ACKNOWLEDGMENTS

First and foremost, a giant shout out-to Jenn Joel, who is one of the smartest and sharpest people I know and who makes me a better writer. Thank you to Beverly Horowitz, for her relentlessness not only in her editorial zeal, but in supporting my work. I'm lucky to have her in my corner.

A forever thank-you to Elaine Koster, who got this whole shebang started.

Giant hugs to Jillian Vandall, who is a rock star publicist and an A+ person.

Huge thanks to all of the wonderful people at Random House Children's Books: Barbara Marcus, John Adamo, Dominique Cimina, Kate Keating, Elizabeth Ward, Kelly McGauley, Hannah Black, Rebecca Gudelis, Cayla Rasi, Adrienne Waintraub, Kristin Schulz, Lisa Nadel, and a million other awesome people I will kick myself for not mentioning as soon as this goes to print. I'm deeply grateful to the international rights team at ICM and Curtis Brown, and in particular to Roxanne Edouard. Thanks also to Nicolas Vivas, the Hatchery, and the Fiction Writers Co-Op.

High fives to the amazing Lola Wusu, Charlotte Huang, Lucy Kaminsky, and the rest of my amazing village. You all know who you are.

And finally, the biggest, most ginormous thank-you to all

the readers who make this writing-books thing possible. I'm so, so grateful for your support.

Love to my dad, to Lena (who is sorely missed), to Josh, to Leia, to my beautiful nephew sweet baby James (welcome to the world, little guy; we already love you), and to the whole Flore clan. Special thank-you to my mom, Elizabeth Buxbaum, who is loved and remembered every single day.

And finally, thank you, Indy, my homespot, for making everything possible, and to Elili and Luca, my heart, for making everything matter. I love you guys to the moon and back and back ad infinitum.

ABOUT THE AUTHOR

Julie Buxbaum is the *New York Times* bestselling author of *Tell Me Three Things,* her debut young adult novel, and of *What to Say Next.* She also wrote the critically acclaimed *The Opposite of Love* and *After You.* Her work has been translated into twenty-five languages. She lives in Los Angeles with her husband and their two children.

Visit her online at juliebuxbaum.com and follow @juliebux on Twitter.

"Fans of Rainbow Rowell are sure to adore."
—*PopSugar*

"You'll eat up this book about a new girl at a prep school." —*Seventeen*

You're right. This place is a war zone, and I could use some help.

Jessie has just started her junior year at an ultra-intimidating LA prep school where she knows no one except for her new stepmonster's pretentious teenage son. Just when she's thinking about hightailing it back to Chicago—to her friends who understand she's still grieving the death of her mother—Jessie gets an email from a person calling themselves Somebody/Nobody (SN for short), offering to help her navigate the wilds of Wood Valley High School.

In a leap of faith—or an act of complete desperation—Jessie begins to rely on SN, and SN quickly becomes her lifeline and closest ally. Jessie can't help wanting to meet SN in person. But are some mysteries better left unsolved?

———

★ "The desire to find out whether Jessie's real-life and virtual crushes are one and the same will keep [readers] turning the pages as quickly as possible."
—*Publishers Weekly*, Starred

Sometimes a new perspective is all we need to make sense of the world.

When an unlikely friendship is sparked between relatively popular Kit Lowell and socially isolated David Drucker, everyone is surprised, most of all Kit and David. Kit appreciates David's blunt honesty—in fact, she finds it bizarrely refreshing. David welcomes Kit's attention and her inquisitive nature. When she asks for his help figuring out the how and why of her dad's tragic car accident, David is all in. But neither of them can predict what they'll find or how it will change them.

———

"An ode to the unexpected relationships that can change our lives." —*Bustle*

"Charming, funny, and deeply affecting all at the same time." —Nicola Yoon,
#1 *New York Times* bestselling author of
Everything, Everything and *The Sun Is Also a Star*

NAMED A BEST YOUNG ADULT NOVEL OF THE YEAR BY *POPSUGAR*